Skywater Publishing Cooperative
Chaska, Minnesota
skywaterpub.com

Library of Congress Cataloging-in-Publication Data
Library of Congress Control Number: 2023939712
ISBN: 978-1-0880-5845-9 (paperback)
ISBN: 978-1-0880-5851-0 (ebook)

Credits
Amanda F. Doering, developmental editor
Connie R. Colwell, copyeditor
Flat Sole Studio, book layout

THE GHOST
OF THE
WICKED CROW

SCOTT R. WELVAERT

TO JEN, JULES, CHRISTA, AND JAKE,
WHO ALWAYS REMIND ME
THERE IS GREAT JOY AND FUN
TO BE HAD IN ANYTHING.

To see a world in a grain of sand and heaven in a wild flower
Hold infinity in the palm of your hand and eternity in an hour.
　　—William Blake

CHAPTER 1

THE ETERNAL STRUGGLE OF PHYS ED

Pull-ups.

Awesome.

Ian Wilder took a deep breath. The steel bar hung above him from the cement wall. A wide stripe of green, black, and white ran around the middle of the gymnasium. Alton High colors. Go Hawks. Nervous, Ian wiped his sweaty palms against his shorts and patted down the rooster tail of brown hair that always crowed its awakening in the morning. Behind him, thirty other juniors waited. In unbearable silence, the smallest sounds took on a life of their own. Sandy Dunham snapped her gum. Janet Tassel texted, her notifications blooping and dinging like a nest of digital birds. Kit Cambridge stifled a snicker. He played football on the JV team.

"While we're young, Wilder," said Mr. Wasserbaum, the phys ed teacher.

Ian shook his head. Better to get it over with. Tear the bandage off quickly. He rubbed his hands together and readied himself. His strategy: jump as high as he could and use his momentum to carry him to his first pull-up. Ever. It was a good plan. No, scratch that.

It was a great plan—even if it hadn't worked in middle school, or freshman year.

Ian leapt up to the bar. In his chronic imagination, he blasted through that pull-up. But he didn't stop at one. He went for a hundred. A thousand. He even got bold and cracked off a few one-armed pull-ups. Sandy's gum fell from her mouth. Kit stared at him in goose-eyed wonder. Even nodded his head and cheered Ian on with a "Yeah, bro!" Janet Tassel looked up from her phone and stopped texting for an entire second.

Pull-ups?

No problem.

In reality, however, it went a bit differently. Sure, Ian jumped to the bar, but once his momentum stopped, his elbows locked in futility. He panicked. Grunted. Shook his body from side to side. There had to be some loophole in the laws of physics he could exploit. He kicked his legs. Twisted his torso. When his shoulders were on the verge of popping from their sockets, he gave it one last try. He rallied whatever strength he had left and pulled. The result: an awkward full-body spasm that left him twitching like a freshly swatted spider.

"Alright, alright," Mr. Wasserbaum said. "Don't hurt yourself, kid." He stepped back and scribbled a note on his clipboard.

Ian let go of the bar. At least he stuck the landing. His hands were red and itchy. He stepped between his classmates to the back of the group. Janet's texting filled the silence. Kit jumped to the bar and rattled off pull-ups with the ease of a champion prize fighter. Ian stopped counting after thirty. The class slogged through the rest of the phys ed assessment: thirty-yard dash, push-ups, sit-ups. The whole enchilada. As luck would have it, Ian excelled at burpees. So that was a positive.

Ian used to hide from embarrassments like this in middle school, but not anymore. After class, he pulled out his journal from his backpack. His mother had given it to him for a birthday present seven years ago, and it was his most prized possession. A nice leather cover that had grown cracked and scratched over the years. A scrolling, embossed Celtic design sprawled over the corners of the cover and at its center sat a large eye, which had creeped him out at first but grew on him. Whenever reality crowded his life, he found refuge in its pages. Since then, he had almost completely filled it and stuffed in additional loose pages with scribbled stories, monster ideas, crappy sketches, and maps. He liked maps. They had order and direction. They quieted the noise around him.

After the rest of his classes, Ian made his way to the bus. He undid the thick rubber bands that held everything in his journal together for dear life and stretched them over his wrists. Without the bands, the poor thing lived on the perpetual edge of flinging open at any moment, scattering its contents about like ashes to the wind. Ian walked and continued sketching a map. He had a knack for navigating while his attention was focused on something else entirely. One summer at Yellowstone, his parents got them lost on a hike. Ian easily led them out while playing handheld video games the whole time. He always knew how and where to go. His only problem: he had no clue where he wanted to go.

Ian stopped next to Penelope Archer's locker. "How'd pull-ups go?" she asked.

Ian wrapped up his journal in the rubber bands. "Can we just go home?"

"That bad, huh?" Penelope loaded her backpack and shut her locker. "Well, when will you ever need to do a pull-up? Don't worry about it."

Together, they rode the bus home through the warm Minnesota September afternoon. Since kindergarten, they had sat up front, and now again they did so to stay away from Pete Stamdahl and his rowdy band of lacrosse minions in the back. Penelope and Ian shared earbuds and playlists. Drowned their days in music and their imaginations. Like Ian, Penelope had her escape—a large sketchpad. In the most recent, she had meticulously rendered portraits and landscapes across its pages. Alien planets with entire canyons and valleys of violet and blood-orange glass. Castles with alabaster towers reaching into sunset clouds. A haunted forest so thick and dank, it blocked out the light and kept an entire eerie world within its darkness.

When the school bus dumped them off in their neighborhood, they walked down Trestle Lane to their adjacent driveways. Penelope walked up hers. And Ian his.

"See you out back in ten?" Penelope asked.

"You bet."

Ian stepped into his backyard, a loop of rope around his shoulder and a can of soda in each hand. Stained wooden plank fences divided the Wilder and Archer lawns. Two 20-year-old oak trees, their branches reaching over forty feet in height, spanned the division between the two yards. A ramshackle treehouse nestled in the crooks of the Wilder tree. At the base of the tree, Penelope sat in the plush grass, plucking the green blades and biting their white tips. Ian handed her a soda. They popped the tops and drank.

"Rope," she said. "What are you thinking? Western? Cactusback Flats. Whiskey Joe Firesky."

Ian burped. "Nope."

Penelope squinted in thought. "A hunt for the yeti atop the Himalayas?"

"Wrong again."

"Pirates?" she asked. "Again? I'm not in the mood for pirates."

"Did you embarrass yourself in front of thirty kids trying to do one pull-up? One, Penelope. I couldn't do one."

"Eat more protein," she said.

"C'mon," Ian said.

Penelope rolled her eyes. "Fine."

"Sweet." Ian backed her to the tree and tied her up with the rope. Each loop around her stirred up the faint whisper of her perfume. Peaches.

As he circled, Penelope said, "Where did we leave off?"

Ian finished and said, "I got the Ruby Spyglass, and you got busted."

"I don't get busted," Penelope said. "I'm the smart one."

Ian stepped back and said, "I can't do a pull-up."

Penelope closed her eyes and shook her head in exasperation. Thinking back to her sketchpads and years of drawings, she focused on a rolling sea and a pirate galleon—The Wicked Crow—tossing about it. Pages and pages of her sketchpad flipped behind her eyes: grizzly pirate crews, ornate figureheads, gleaming cutlasses, and elaborate hats. All of it folded in on itself a thousand times over until reality bled away, replaced by her imagination. Their imagination. Their stories. Their escape.

❁   ❁   ❁

Sea spray smatters her face, mats her hair across her cheek. Through her boots she feels the rough deck of the Wicked Crow and its roll over the sea. Its lamps spit out the sharp tang of burning whale oil. The ropes lashing her to the mainmast dig into her ribs. It hurts to breathe. And even though a warm sun sets in the distance, the chill from her damp clothes wriggles up her spine.

"You're too late, Captain Noface," she yells. "Ian's found the Ruby Spyglass and he's leagues ahead of you. You'll never catch—"

Retching interrupts her. A vomit so knee-buckling and foul, the sour curdled stink of it cuts through the salty bluster.

Bent over the quarterdeck rail, Captain Bradford "Noface" Nolander spews a sickly yellow stream into the curling waves below. Finished, he wipes his mouth and replaces the Venetian mask over his face. Dressed head-to-toe in a mangy, half-burnt, leather long coat, he straightens his haggard tricorn hat and says, "If I am too late, then what say you of this?"

The captain slides his hand inside his coat to remove something, but another fetid gurgle rattles through his belly. He holds his hand to his masked face and bends over the rail again, ejecting more of his breakfast into the sea. Gagging, he spits on the deck and hides his face beneath his mask once again. "Blast the eggs benedict. Such a succulent dish." After a pause he continues, "Where was I again?"

"You wuz about to tell her you had the spyglass, Cap'n," says a greasy deckhand behind him.

Annoyed, the captain's shoulders slouch. He sighs. The crew parts from the poor deckhand like water from the prow. Captain Noface spins around and in one clean stroke of his cutlass, opens the deckhand's throat.

"Those were my lines," the captain says, wiping the blood from his cutlass on the nearest powder monkey before sliding it back into the scabbard.

Penelope swallows. Her throat has gone dry. The wind and spray flatten her long brown hair against her face. Her buccaneer cap with its wine-red plume topples to the deck and rolls to the rail. She shifts her weight and tries to pull her arms free, but it is pointless. Frustrated, her breaths come in short, exasperated huffs. She has to do something. Anything. Helpless, she tries a different approach. "Still haven't found that cure, have you? How much of a face do you have left?"

Noface snaps his head in her direction. With a gloved hand on the hilt of his cutlass, he steps toward her, his boots echoing over the deck. The stench of diseased flesh gets stronger the closer he comes. But the mask is worse. Slick white porcelain with lips turned downward into a frown. The eye sockets rimmed in thick, blood-red paint spatters, as if a raven had clawed away his eyes. Only there they sit in the dark recesses, yellowed and ringed in rot.

"No," he tells her. "Not yet. But I never pass up a good breakfast even if I'm unable to keep it down. Your friend, Ian Wilder, on the other hand, I can keep down. I chained him to the anchor of his own ship and dropped him into the blue. He's a bloated bag of hammerhead bait by now."

Captain Noface takes out a compass and reads its heading. "In one short day, the ghosts of Banshee Bay will have their human flesh, the world will have a new king, and I'll have my face back."

"I think I speak for the world," yells a young, brave voice, "when I say we'd rather have the mask."

Captain Noface spins away from Penelope. A battered schooner crashes through the sea alongside the Wicked Crow. At its bow, Ian Wilder brandishes the Neverblade, a gleaming, silver cutlass, in one hand and a boarding rope in the other. His black leather long coat and pants are stitched with burgundy thread, and his black tricorn hat boasts a band of shark teeth along the edge.

"I should have just slit your throat!" Noface yells.

Ian swings over on the rope and lands on the deck with a thud.

"Shoot him!" Noface yells to his crew.

Flintlock hammers crack, and a volley of shots ring in unison. After the smoke clears, Ian still stands, but most of the captain's crew falls to the decks, riddled with musket shots. The survivors crash to the bulwark as two dozen pirates swing over from Ian's small schooner.

"I didn't come alone this time," Ian says.

Livid, Noface draws his cutlass and swats at Ian, who dodges and parries away from the captain. They duel across the ship. Their swords clatter as Noface presses Ian up the stairs to the quarterdeck. Behind them, the crews engage in a bloody melee. Between the clash and din of sabers, pistols fire in clouds of gunpowder.

"No pirate has bested the Neverblade," Ian says. "It's been passed through history for a thousand years. You're only prolonging the inevitable."

"I only need you to make a mistake," the captain counters, kicking Ian in the stomach.

Ian and the captain duel their way up the stairs to the poop deck. Near the starboard rail, Noface extends himself too far in a fit of howling anger. Ian brings the flat of his blade across the captain's shoulders, toppling him over the rail. On instinct, Ian drops his blade and grabs the dread pirate's hand, holding on with everything he has.

The captain cackles above the hungry waves. "You won't let me fall, Ian," the captain says. Noface reaches for Ian's arm with each sway. "You live by a code. Help me up, and you can take me to the brig. You'll be victorious, as usual." Beaten, Noface reaches upward to Ian with a steady hand of truce.

The captain is right. He can't leave him to die. Ian grabs the captain's extended hand and pulls with everything he has left. When he has the captain almost back over the rail and onto the ship's deck, the hammer to the captain's pistol clicks and the barrel jabs between Ian's ribs.

"And that's your mistake," the captain says to Ian. "You could never do this. Kill a man."

"Rancid, half-cooked pork fat," Ian mutters. "Topped with diarrhea sauce."

Across the mighty ship, the noise of the captain's wheezy grumbling belly cuts through the battling crews, who stop to watch what happens next. An unworldly creak blasts through the captain's gut, bending him over. The sick churning of bile. The tossing of hollandaise sauce, poached eggs, and ham. Slowly it bubbles, froths, and curdles until the captain can no longer stand it. When he turns to relieve himself over the rail, Ian kicks him in the backside and sends him vomiting into the sea.

With the villain dispatched, Ian snaps to Penelope's side and cuts her bonds with a brisk, clean stroke of the Neverblade. She lunges at him, and they tangle into a long-deserved hug. Then, for the briefest of moments, an invisible mooring line draws their lips closer. The remaining crew aboard the Wicked Crow watch on, as their lips almost touch.

CHAPTER 2

WHAT HAPPENS IN THE TREEHOUSE STAYS IN THE TREEHOUSE

"You think you deserve a kiss after that?" Penelope asked, trying to hide an escaping smirk.

Ian opened his eyes, and their fantasy world vanished: the Wicked Crow, the fighting crewmen, the rolling, misting sea, the buccaneer clothes rippling in the salty breezes. In his hand, a small wooden sword he constructed when he was six. Through their battle, they had worked their way up the tree. They stood on the same tree branch, her own more intricately carved wooden sword resting against her shoulder as she bent away from his lips. The leaves above rustled in the cooling afternoon breeze. Dejected, Ian touched the dull wooden edge of his weapon and said, "Not good?"

Penelope smiled and carefully stepped her way past him and into the treehouse. "Your plot was so inconsistent. And saving Noface after you knock him over the rail? It was too easy."

Ian took a deep breath. Reality was such a downer. "I couldn't let him fall," Ian said. "That's not what heroes do."

"But you eventually kicked him in anyway."

"He was going to shoot me!" Ian said.

Penelope sighed. Not like an angsty teen, but like a parent trying to explain real-life lessons to a child. "We're not ten anymore, Ian," she told him. "Sometimes, here, in the real world, heroics don't save anyone. Sometimes nothing goes according to plan and bad stuff happens."

"Next time, I'll make sure to cut everyone to ribbons," Ian said.

"Totally not even the point," Penelope said and escaped into the treehouse. Ian followed and sat down next to her. A bit small for two 16-year-olds, the treehouse still worked for private make-out sessions away from their parents. Penelope picked up a beat-up drawing pad and began sketching their imagined scene into her journal. "Besides, kisses never happen that way, Ian."

"Sure they do. They happen like that all the time," Ian said.

"Just in the movies," Penelope said, her eyebrows furrowed in frustration. "The best kisses come out of nowhere. They steal time. They wrench the entire machinery of existence to a grinding halt."

She had that right. All their "firsts" had been carved into his mind like a woodcut print, their story painstakingly etched into a plank of cedar. When she first slid her hand into his at the mall. When he placed his hand on her thigh as they watched *The Shining* in eighth grade. The playful wrestling during a water balloon fight on the Fourth of July. Her leaning into him during fireworks. The kiss while swimming in Orchard Pond, both of them hot to the touch, but shivering in the cold water. Once, she lay next to him during a movie he still couldn't remember, and it took all of his willpower to hold the popcorn bowl steady as her rousing laughter leapt to him and rippled through his bones.

Her hands flashed over the sketchbook like birds fluttering down the branches of a tree. Wherever they went, they left a portrait of her imagination on the page. New worlds. New landscapes. Dashing elven heroes or cascading celestial panoramas. What she could put on the page could pass for real life far, far away. The tip of her tongue stuck out the corner of her lips in concentration. Her eyes surveyed the sketch marks and the curves. Like a good kiss, she stole life from distant places and put it to the page.

Stealing time.

Grinding the machinery of existence to a halt.

Ian couldn't resist. He leaned in and kissed her, expecting her to push him away in lieu of the drawing, but she didn't. Charcoal pencil in hand, she wrapped her arms around him and kissed him back. Something had changed. A gale rushed through them. A momentum like running down a hill and losing your balance, your control. Adrift in the rank mildew of sleeping bags and blankets in the tree fort, they pawed at each other. Their breath came in soft huffs, warm and salty.

When Penelope lifted his t-shirt over his head, Ian stopped and said, "Are you sure?"

"Yes," Penelope breathed.

"Really?" Ian asked, a big smile across his face as he scrambled out of his shirt. "But what about, you know?"

"I've been on the pill for a year. Now shut up," she answered and lifted her sweatshirt over her head.

There in the treehouse, skin to skin, Ian and Penelope crossed another first from their lists. Like most first drafts, their first attempt at sex started awkwardly, plodded forward full of self-doubt and tentative exploration, and ended far too quickly with not enough action. Penelope lay atop Ian, her face nestled in his neck, her breath hot. "It's supposed to take longer, right?"

Embarrassed, Ian said, "I'm sorry. It's my—"

She pressed a finger to his lips and said, "Shh. Stealing time."

Ian took that as a positive sign.

For a few moments they lay there, chilled in the growing darkness around them. The only warmth in the world existed between their bodies. Penelope lifted her head and looked at Ian closely. "This is not fantasy," she said. "This was clumsy, fumbling, and awkward, but it was real."

While getting dressed, Penelope slipped on her sneakers and said, "Listen. Can I tell you about something?"

Ian stretched his t-shirt over his head and said, "Anything."

"Even weird personal stuff?" she asked. "Crazy stuff?"

Feeling strange, Ian pursed his lips in thought. "Um, sure. What's up?"

"Have you ever thought about your own death?"

Ian squinted at Penelope. "Uh, how so?"

Penelope curled her arms around her knees, eyes on her shoes. "Sometimes, when I'm daydreaming, I see a dark, dark world where everything is rotting and falling apart," she told him. "Vast cities lie in ruins. Forests reach to the sky with dead branches, and the people… they're all dark smudges, inky thumbprints of what people used to be. And they talk in this strange, creepy language. Like if we talked through foghorns."

"Are there great molten pits of fire?" Ian asked. His eyes held a flicker of excitement over the possibilities of exploring another imaginary place. "Wicked, winged harpies?" he asked eagerly.

Penelope's gaze turned on him, first harsh, then crumpling, like that was the worst suggestion in the world. "Seriously, Ian, this is different. The only other time I saw it was when my mom went through, uh, chemo. Her eyes were so dark, sunken. And she had gotten thin and frail. Like her body could have just blown away in the wind."

"I know that was a terrible time," Ian said, lacing up his sneakers. He tried to understand what was happening. How events could go from such a euphoric high to a sodden low. Something seemed off with this Smudge World. With Penelope herself. If there ever was time for him to not be himself and just say something supportive, it was now. "Do you want to…you know…talk about it? I'll listen."

Curtly, she smiled with one corner of her mouth, but the rest of her face didn't follow. She looked through him like he didn't exist, like he couldn't possibly understand what tossed around in her mind. She shook her head and finished stowing her drawings. "Never mind, Ian. It's not a big deal. I can handle it myself."

"Penny!" Mrs. Archer called from the back of her house. Penelope rolled her eyes. She hated when her mother called her that. She shook her head.

Ian had the distinct feeling Penelope hadn't told him everything. "Are you sure?"

She nodded. "I just have to fix it. In my head."

"Penny! Stop playing fairy tales, and come in for dinner."

Penelope sighed in a huff. Ian was losing his moment with her. He scrambled for the right combination of words. They fell from his brain like rainfall, but none stayed long enough or felt right. He had to say something—something good. Think, dammit. But she stuffed her things into her bag, climbed down to the ground, and vanished into her house before he came up with anything.

At dinner, Ian stabbed a chunk of baked salmon adrift in his plate of spinach, red onions, crumbled bacon, and tomatoes. He paused to sniff it before putting it into his mouth.

His father, Harold Wilder, watched Ian's approach and said, "I know, right? I'd burn down an orphanage for a half-pound burger right now." Although his hairline had receded greatly in the last few years, his father tried to stay young. Thanks to his wife's persistence, Harold kept active, as much as an insurance salesman can, and tried to dress sharp, unlike some of the other fathers in the neighborhood.

"Harold," said his mother, Maggie Wilder, "You heard your doctor. More vegetables." She turned to Ian. "And I crumbled twice as much bacon on yours. There should be enough salt and fat to kill a cowboy. So eat." His mother, on the other hand, had aged better. Probably because of all the healthy food she ate (and was always trying to make them eat). She almost always wore yoga pants and a bulky sweatshirt awash in dry streaks of clay or glaze from her pottery workshop in the garage. She taught pottery at the local community center.

Both Wilder men buckled down and ate their salads. Ian's mother was right; his was simply messy with bacon.

His dad paused and said, "So week three in junior year. Any new friends?"

Ian shook his head.

His mother chimed in. "What about activities? Alexandra says Penelope mentioned an art club."

Ian sipped from his glass of water and shook his head in the negative again. The onion had a sinus-clearing bite to it. "I can't even draw stick people, Mom."

Maggie ate and said, "What about a writing club? Your journal is looking exceptionally chock-full these days."

Ian set his glass down quickly, horror crashing across his face. "Those are private stories, Mom! God!"

Maggie waved Ian off. "I just wanted to figure out how you and Penelope escape Taluride Station from the xenozombie horde."

The color drained from Ian's face, only to flare into bright, shiny, embarrassed red.

"Zombies, huh?" Harold said, picking through his salad. "That sounds…neat." He chuckled.

The tomatoes gurgled and bubbled in Ian's belly; raw ones always upset his stomach. A soft squeak ushered from within. To cover the sound, he said, "There's no writing club, Mom."

His mother finished swallowing a hunk of salmon and said, "What about debate club?"

His father's eyes lit up. "Yes! Debate club! I was awesome at debate."

Maggie smiled at him.

Ian shook his head and said, "Yeah, debate club. As if I wasn't already a big enough loser."

Just as exhausted by the conversation as Ian was, Harold said, "I just want you to think about your options. This year and next are the most important in your high school career. You need to start thinking about your future. About college."

Maggie nodded and drank from her wine glass. "Your father's right," she added. "You're growing up too fast." Maggie reached her left hand out to Ian's to give it a nice motherly pat, but he pulled it away.

More than she knew, he thought. He touched his lip, where Penelope's finger had pressed earlier. Stealing time. Their naked bodies pressed to each other for the first time. "I know," he said. "But right now, I just want to be me, okay?"

His parents paused and looked at each other, maybe even remembering themselves saying the same thing at that age. They both offered him reassuring smiles.

"Can I be done? I'm not really hungry anymore."

His mother wiped her mouth with a napkin and said, "Take three more bites of salad. Get some salmon. You need protein."

Ian stuffed three random forkfuls of salad into his mouth at once and scraped the rest into the garbage as his mother and father sipped their wine. "Plate in the dishwasher, not the sink," Maggie called to him.

Ian slid the plate and fork into the dishwasher as he muscled down his wad of salad. Then he ran upstairs to his bedroom, shut the door behind him, and flopped onto his unmade bed. Around him, movie posters, comic book covers, and anime book covers adorned his walls: *Star Wars*, *Dune*, *Lord of the Rings*, *Spider-Man*, *The Walking Dead*, *Watchmen*, *The Ghost in the Machine*, *Flash*, *Akira*. Clothes lay on the floor, and torn pages from spiral notebooks were tacked on a pegboard above his desk, each with the same chicken-scratch writing from his journal. Usually, when he had something on his mind, he'd crack open the journal and just start writing: notes about alien worlds, troubled heroes, and dastardly villains. Instead, he texted Penelope: "Busy?"

No response.

When he rolled over on the bed, a light flashed outside his window. Morse code. He leapt from the bed to his window, where an old flashlight lay on the sill. Their neighborhood had experienced rolling blackouts over the summer, so it came in handy. His dad kept griping about the shoddy infrastructure and how the city needed to upgrade. Ian picked up the flashlight, pointed it at the opposing light, and begin flicking the switch on and off in sequence. After a second, Penelope's light stopped. Ian opened the window and climbed out to the edge of the roof where, if he dangled just right, his feet reached the wooden fence between the yards. Overhead, gray clouds sped across a star-laden sky. Looking down, he saw Penelope's shadow tiptoeing through his yard to the treehouse. Morse code was her idea. She had a strange fascination with the outdated, as if humanity teetered on the brink of the apocalypse and those things would come in handy. Ian dangled to the fence, balancing precariously on the top, before crouching and dropping down to the plush grass of the lawn.

As he climbed the rungs of the treehouse, he wished he had brought gum. His breath was probably horrible. Stupid salmon and onions. Once inside, he said a quick, "Hi."

Penelope sat quietly in pink cotton pajamas and bit her lower lip.

"Are you okay?" he asked. "Is it me? Because I can do better."

"It's not that," she said, reaching out a hand and placing it on his. "Were you serious about what you said earlier? About listening?"

Ian swallowed nervously, sensing the importance of what Penelope was about to say. His saliva grew thick, and he cleared his throat. "Sure," he rasped.

Fidgeting with her charm bracelet, she looked him square in the eye and said, "I see them everywhere, Ian. I think something's wrong with me."

CHAPTER 3

THE SNAPPY COMEBACK IS MIGHTIER THAN THE SWORD

At 6:30 AM, Ian's alarm clock went off. He hated that digital red specter. Swatting at it blindly, he knocked it off the nightstand along with his journal and phone. The whole mess fell in a clatter. Even under his thick journal, that annoying, repetitive, witch-squawking wouldn't stop until he fell out of bed trying to hit the snooze button. Ian sat on his floor and yawned.

He'd gotten like zero sleep. Sure, he went to bed at about 11:30 PM, but after what Penelope told him, the drawings she showed him, how could he sleep? Stuck blearily between asleep and waking, he allowed Penelope's visions to invade his room. As he flopped on his back, an ash-strewn world blossomed on his ceiling, filled with packs of faceless souls walking endless trails. Frail refugees stumbled over hills across trampled meadows of gray grass. Overhead, a pale sun barely shone through an acrid atmosphere of smoke. Along these roughly trod roads great pikes stood, disemboweled bodies staked to each. Entrails slick in rot. Skin sloughing off bones.

Everywhere, the corpses of worldly things sat hunkered under rubble: rusted-out cars, crumbling abandoned buildings, shopping carts bent and awry, streetlights twisted and askew, city streets broken and heaved upward in giant shards.

Ian shook his head to rid himself of the images, trying to forget. He picked up his spilled alarm clock, journal, and phone and arranged them neatly on the nightstand. He sat on his bed and scratched his scalp. The bassinet. Penelope had told him about an old, weathered bassinet she saw. She had reached into it and retrieved a forgotten baby. A girl. The poor thing had no nose. Slits for eyes and a mouth. Penelope held it to her chest. Its arms and legs unmoving, limp, mere lumps of flesh stuffed into skin, cold to the touch.

"I don't know how I know it, Ian," she had told him, her eyes wide and shining with unshed tears, "But that dead thing, that lifeless child was me."

W. T. F.

Shaking his head, Ian walked across the hall to the bathroom. He turned on the shower and slid under the hot water. He didn't know what to think. He thought they had just passed a huge milestone in their relationship. But now this.

Each morning they sat on the bus together. Each morning, he waited for the harp smile—when her lips peeled away from her teeth like a hand across harp strings. Sometimes, he even heard the rising scale of notes in his head. He had never witnessed her flashing that smile to anyone else. Not her parents. Not Kit Cambridge, the resident hottie. Only him. Shampoo suds snaked down his back and over his ribs, racing down his legs as he washed his hair. But it wasn't just her smile, he thought. He couldn't explain it. Whatever it was, it caused their bodies to lurch for each other constantly, and it took all their energy to restrain it, like keeping the opposite ends of two magnets separated.

After drying off, Ian threw on some jeans, socks, and sneakers. He topped it off with a white t-shirt and a blue hoodie. After grabbing his phone, he went downstairs to the kitchen for his breakfast—

one handful of Cinnamon Toast Crunch, one handful of Golden Grahams, and a handful of his dad's bran flakes for a good heart.

"Got all your homework done?" his father asked behind his newspaper, which he still insisted on getting, despite the fact that everyone read the news on their phones now. He was dressed in his usual white button-down shirt, suit pants, and tie.

Ian crunched his cereal and said, "Didn't have any."

Dressed in her dirty gray sweatshirt, yoga pants, and Crocs, his mother sipped coffee. "You still have to read *Lord of the Flies*, remember?" she said. "One month to get it done."

Ian rolled his eyes.

"Enough with the eyes, Ian. It's getting old," his father warned. He had the uncanny knack for detecting Ian's eye rolls without ever seeing them.

Ian scooped the rest of his cereal into his mouth and got up, milk dripping from his chin. "Gotta go." He walked right past his backpack hanging on the railing by the front door.

"Your backpack," his mother chimed, as Ian turned to grab it.

Ian met Penelope on the sidewalk. Her hair was still partially wet from the shower, and the scent of ripe peaches hung in the air next to her. With her heavy backpack slung over one shoulder, she looked nervously at him, then stepped in pace.

Ian offered a short smile. Penelope bit at her lower lip. They walked in silence together. Words backed up against Ian's tongue, waiting to spill out, but they wouldn't come. Visions of sinister volcano mounds belching smoke and eerie white lava stalled him. Leathery flying things hissing overhead, swooping down to pick a cold refugee from the crowd. And the screams. Penelope told him about the night and how the masses huddled together to keep warm, shivering more from fright than from the cold. In that mumbling, weary darkness a scream would strike out of the murmur, shatter their sleep like a hammer against glass. Another one taken.

When they arrived at the bus stop Penelope asked, "Are you okay?"

Ian nodded. Was he okay? Him? "I'm…fine," he said. "But. Are you…well, did you want to talk about it some more?"

Penelope quickly shook her head, a breath escaping from her. "No. No, I'm fine."

The bus squealed to a stop in front of them, and the door opened. "Let's just forget about it, okay?"

Ian nodded. He was more than happy to forget about it. Or at least try to. He climbed on the bus first and immediately looked to the front seats, far away from Pete Stamdahl and his merry band of toadies.

"Oh, it's Indiana Wilder and the Temple of Doomed Virgins!" The toadies laughed and heckled. Bystanders throughout the bus hunkered in their seats, some smiling, but most just laying low, not reacting, hoping to avoid Pete's menacing attention. Heidi Flugalmann was the only one to make eye contact with Ian. She frowned sadly, her freckled cheeks dimpling, not quite a look of sympathy, but at least of solidarity. Pete continued the onslaught as Ian slipped into an empty seat. "Hey, Indiana, where's your bull—"

Penelope stood by Ian's seat, her mouth in a terrible frowny rictus, her eyes narrowed. "Be careful, Cocktail Frank," she said, holding up her pinkie finger to Pete.

Pete froze, and his cheeks flushed. Slowly, he turned around and slumped into his seat.

And like that the smart assery of Pete Stamdahl was silenced. Only after Pete slumped back into his seat did Penelope sit down herself. She yanked the right ear bud from Ian's ear and fit it into hers. "I need something extra today." She swiped Ian's phone and scrolled though his playlist.

Unlike most high-schoolers, Ian only listened to movie soundtracks. Oodles of them. No pop, rap, or country unless they happened to be on the soundtrack. Some of the movies he had watched and loved, while others he had never heard of. But when he heard the samples online, he liked them, so he listened to them.

Penelope stopped on the soundtrack for *Highlander* and clicked on "Princes of the Universe."

With music slammed into their ears, she relaxed, finally releasing the harp smile. "This'll do nicely," she said. But Ian couldn't hear her. With the music, the smile, the warmth of her leg touching his, he felt things tumble back into their proper places like a safecracker breaking into a bank vault. On the 15-minute bus ride, they huddled in their protective bubble of movie themes, Penelope sketching a mountainous landscape in her journal, and Ian busily writing down the worrisome descriptions of the Smudge World.

At school Penelope and Ian filed out of the bus, the entire girth of the Smudge World weighing heavy between them. On the sidewalk, Ian didn't know what to say, so he said, "Have a good day."

Penelope bit her lower lip again, then leaned in and kissed him. Not a peck or a quick smack, but the kind of sloppy, tongue-toggling kiss they only cut loose in the treehouse. When they separated, she said, "I will," and walked into the school. Surprised, Ian stood in a stupor.

When Pete shoved him, he almost toppled over. "Look at that. Dweeb mating season," Pete said. Ian gathered his composure and searched for whatever kryptonite Penelope might have held earlier, but nothing came to mind. Pete strutted off, allowing his much smaller toadies to give Ian an extra push as they walked by. As usual, Ian was a man—no, check that—just a boy of inaction. Heidi Flugalmann exited the bus last. She could only blush at Ian, then scamper to the school entrance.

Ian offloaded at his locker and grabbed his algebra book. He navigated the halls, avoiding eye contact with everyone, before stepping into Ms. Hanson-Feuer's class. He found his seat and prepared for a boring lecture on math he was certain he would never use. While Ms. Hanson-Feuer droned on, Ian escaped into his own world, writing numerous paragraphs about Penelope's visions from the treehouse. When the period ended, Ms. Hanson-Feuer spoke over the din. "Read chapter two and do the introductory worksheet on simplifying radicals."

Ian took the long way to his locker, hoping to avoid Pete. He exchanged his books, slammed his locker shut, and dashed for Ms. White's art class. Math and art were quite the one-two punch in his morning. He found it hard to imagine anyone being worse at art than math, but he managed to do it expertly, even within the confines of artistic subjectivity. He just wanted to get to the ceramics unit. His mom had always gushed about how sensual clay was, so he wanted to impress Penelope with the few tricks his mom had shown him on her wheel at home. Until then, he had to muscle his way through charcoal sketching, watercolor, and oils.

While Ms. White placed a bowl of plastic fruit in front of the class, Ian gazed at the student work hung above the whiteboards and around the perimeter of the room. Tori Feldman had painted a unicorn, complete with silver and pink sparkles. Awesome. Rodd Haley had drawn a beefy, muscle-bound soldier firing an M6D at an unknown assailant. Elizabeth Adler had sketched a very Salvador Dalí-like picture of a faceless girl trapped in a universe of melted windows. In the corner, hung a watercolor of a creepy cave, by Penelope.

Brushed with looping swirls of blacks and grays, the cave entrance opened like a mouth, haunting and hungry. Maybe he was just tired, but he swore he heard an eerie wind blow out of that cave, like breath over an empty glass bottle. The Smudge World.

The painting mesmerized him. Despite Ms. White shaking her head at him numerous times, he couldn't concentrate. Something was wrong. At the end of the period, he dashed out of the classroom. This time, he didn't care who he encountered, he just ran.

"Wilder," Assistant Principal Bowler said near the cafeteria. "Slow down."

Out of breath and sweating, he found Penelope spinning the dial on her locker. "Something's wrong," he said.

Penelope looked at him oddly and said, "Yeah, you're like all sweaty."

"Not that, your painting. The cave in Ms. White's room."

Penelope looked around at the lockers, students dropping off books and picking up others. Doors slammed. Backpack zippers zipped. Gum snapped. Her face grew red. "What do you mean?"

"I'm worried. All those things you told me. Maybe you need to tell someone."

Penelope narrowed her eyes at him. "Like who?"

Ian felt a mistake brewing. He paused, searching for the right words. "I don't know," he said, his voice lowered, almost to a whisper. "Like a, a…"

Her face tightened. "A therapist? Is that what you mean?" Her voice grew louder. Students glanced at them. Footsteps hurried away. The hallway cleared in an ominous, throw-down fashion. Penelope exchanged her books and slammed her locker shut. "Thanks, Ian. But no thanks. I can take care of this on my own."

"I'm not saying you can't. But…" Ian pleaded.

Penelope turned on her heel and walked off to her next class.

CHAPTER 4

THE PERILS OF DORKSWEAT

Ian's stupidity dogged him all day. Between classes he sought Penelope out but never caught her. He had to apologize. Tell her he overreacted. After lunch and his computer lab class, he resigned his effort. After all, she had to ride the bus home.

Or not. Ian sat on the bus alone. Penelope must have called her mom for a ride. Boy, he really messed things up. Without Penelope, Pete had taken residence behind him and continuously, without any steady beat or rhythm, kicked his seat and uttered a litany of names at Ian. Dorksweat was his creative favorite. At some point, the physical and verbal taunting blended into a heavy, woolen blanket of white noise that Ian could ignore. He had texted Penelope, "Sorry," when he got on the bus, but she hadn't responded. He checked his phone every five seconds for a response.

At home, he dropped his bag and ran downstairs. He turned on the television and the video game console and quickly logged in. Maybe he could catch her gaming online. The interface screen showed him that Penelope was "listening to music." He opened up the message screen and fumbled through a quick note to her onscreen: "C'mon, Penelope. I'm sorry."

He waited.

No answer.

Miserable, Ian went upstairs for dinner. Chicken tacos. He built three, smothered in salsa and guacamole. He watched his phone as he ate. No response. His parents ate in silence, aware something was up. When he had one taco left on his plate, his mother finally asked, "Everything alright, sweetheart?"

Ian ignored her, thinking she had meant his father.

"Ian?" she said.

"What?"

"Are you okay, son?" his father asked. "Your mother just asked you a question."

Ian looked at them like they had grown antlers. "What?"

"You seem aloof," his father said.

"Aloof? What does that mean?"

"Is it Penelope?" his mother asked.

"Um, yeah. I said something I probably shouldn't have."

Immediately his father smiled and took up a forkful of black beans. "Been there, done that. The trick is to not say anything."

"You should call her," his mom said.

"I have. I mean I texted her and left her a message online. She won't answer."

"Call her."

"What difference does it make?"

"She doesn't want a text or a message," his mom said. "She wants to hear your voice—hear your apology."

Ian screwed his face into a question mark. "Really?"

His mother nodded.

"Okay," Ian said. "I'll try."

After dropping his plate in the dishwasher, Ian dialed Penelope. The phone rang as he walked to his room. It rang still when got there and closed his door. By the time he fell onto his bed, her voicemail picked up, so he left a message. "Hi, Penelope. I thought maybe you wanted to talk, but I guess not. Give me a call. I'm sorry."

It was maddening. Ian paced about his room, waiting for her to call, text, or telepathically connect with him using some previously unknown mutant power. He bounced a racquet ball off the wall until his mother told him to stop. He paged through his homework and finished that. Finally, he pulled out some graph paper and began mapping. Even though he couldn't draw to save his soul, he was actually quite exceptional at laying out geography, buildings, dungeons, and labyrinthian passageways.

An hour in, the lights flickered and went out. Downstairs, his father hollered at the government. "We just can't let it go to pot. We need to fix this goddamn problem!" Ian grabbed his flashlight and flicked it on. Laying it on his desk, he could still make out his map. A pencil in hand, he marked a secret entrance at the base of a large, lava-spewing volcano, followed by a tunnel, and from there his imagination constructed an intricate subterranean system of caves and bypasses that tore through the crust of a dark planet. After fifteen minutes of darkness, the lights flickered back on. He looked at his phone: 10:30. He rubbed his eyes and backed away from his desk. Outside his window, the Archer house slept, its windows dark.

Curious, he pointed the flashlight at Penelope's window and turned it on and off in succession. Morse code.

No response.

Sullen, Ian opened up his journal. Paging through it, he found a sketch Penelope had added more than a year ago: the two of them dressed in their pirate gear, standing aboard the Wicked Crow. "Details make it more real," she told him once and this sketch was very realistic. The lattice work on the ship rails behind them had miniature birds woven in. Even the helm had a golden crow affixed to it, wings spread, beak in full caw. Ian yawned. 10:55. Screw it. Resolution could wait until tomorrow. He plugged his phone into the charger and crawled into bed.

❊　❊　❊

Lightning wakes Ian. A jagged pain across his cheek opens his eyes. Rain pelts him from every angle. He tries to protect his face, but his arms are pressed tightly against his body. He's wrapped in chain, a stone pillar against his back. Getting his bearings, Ian turns his head to the wind and needle-like rain. Over the outcropping of stone, he can see the Wicked Crow anchored in the bay far below, tossing against a violent sea. Another flash of lightning reveals a broken statue just feet from him—a gorgon—its head once covered with hissing snakes.

Hagshead Peak.

Islas Encantadas.

He recognizes where he is but doesn't remember how he's gotten there or what led to him being chained.

"Wakey, wakey, Captain Wilder." Noface is close. Ian smells the gangrenous breath from his decaying mouth. Another flash of lightning lights up Noface's Venetian mask, the bloody paint around the eyes beaded with rain. Noface reaches out and backhands Ian. Water streams over Ian's eyes, but he can make out Noface standing before an ancient, abandoned Grecian altar. Between lightning flashes, other gorgon statues emerge. Granite serpents hold a huge obsidian bowl at the center of the altar. It has filled with rain, and ribbons of water spill over the side.

"We're going to do this again?" Ian asks. "It'd be far simpler to just gut me with a dagger."

Noface steps toward him and grins. "You just don't get it, do you? It's not just about your death. There's nothing artful in the quick slide of a blade or a ball shot through the head. Any blasted scally can do that. The devil's in the details, my friend. The drips of misery, the tick-tocks of torture, the seasick tossing of emotions, the twist ending, the screaming pain." Noface curls his gnarled finger under Ian's chin, his long, jagged fingernail gouging into Ian's flesh, forcing him to look straight into his eyes. "No, Ian. Any hungry predator kills to eat. I prefer to play with my food."

Ian tosses his head and tugs at his chains. The rain has let up slightly. "Whatever. It doesn't matter, because Penelope will come for me. We always find a way. Together. We created this world. That's why we always win."

Noface bursts into a cackling laughter that doubles him over. "Always win. That's rich." He catches his breath and steps closer, drawing his cutlass. "So I suppose she will magically show up and keep my cutlass from skewering you, right?"

Ian sticks out his chin and says, "Exactly."

Noface points the sword at Ian, who watches the gleaming tip get closer and closer until it presses against his shoulder. She'll be here any minute, he thinks. But the steel slides through his shirt and into his skin. Ian barks out when the blade pierces through fibrous muscle. He nearly passes out when Noface worms the blade under his clavicle and navigates it over his shoulder blade until it punches out through his back. Then, with wide, fiery eyes, Noface withdraws the blade quickly, sending a splatter of blood against Ian's neck. Its warmth oozes down his chest. Where is Penelope? Something is wrong. It never happens like this. "What did you do to her?" Ian asks, voice low.

"That's a great question," Noface says. "You don't recall? I'd be happy to refresh your memory." Noface wipes the bloody cutlass against Ian's shirt to clean the blade. Ian watches as his blood blooms red and then pink against the wet cotton. "You see, she did show up. Just like usual. Heroically consistent. There was the usual exchange of 'You'll never get away with this,' and all that. So when you asked her to release you to fight me together, I thought for sure she would. But she refused."

A dread creeps into Ian. Something deep in his mind sparks familiarity. "She wouldn't have done that. We would have taken you together. We discussed it."

"Ah, well. Perhaps she had a better idea," Noface smirks. Lightning flashes above, illuminating the altar. He turns and paces around the snake bowl, his steps dancing in swordplay moves. "Regardless, we dueled magnificently, steel to steel." Noface mimics their moves, slashing his cutlass through the air against his invisible opponent. "She is rather graceful, I'll give her that. But in the end, the devious always trumps the honorable." Noface ends his soliloquy with the tip of his blade touching the enormous bowl, rivulets of water still streaming from its rim.

Ian pulls manically against the chains. "What did you do?!" he screams.

Noface swirls the tip of the blade on the surface of the water in the bowl. "Are you sure you want to know? I mean, the first time you saw it, you screamed like a child and collapsed in shock."

Ian strains against the chains, pulling them as taut as they can go. Rage seethes through his body, and he grits his teeth.

Noface laughs again, his rheumy eyes flashing in mirth. "You see, now I think you understand my point. It isn't about the quick strike." He sheathes his sword and reaches into the stone bowl with both arms. He raises up Penelope's lifeless body and holds her out for Ian to see. Penelope's head lolls toward Ian, her eyes wide open in terror, her pale face frozen horrifically in a mosaic of fear, panic, and death. The very sight of her knocks Ian's knees out from under him. His entire body goes slack, the chains the only thing holding him upright. The rain beats against his crumpled body, dissolving whatever life remained there. Lightning flashes above him as Noface lays Penelope's body at his feet. Crouching, he whispers into Ian's ear, "It's about the everlasting pain."

❀   ❀   ❀

Ian awoke with a start, inhaling deeply while staring at Kiera Knightly from the *King Arthur* poster taped to his wall. His alarm clock read 6:28 AM. Just a dream. God. He rubbed his face. His neck was clammy. Ian's heart had just returned to normal rhythm when his alarm went off at 6:30, making him almost leap out of his skin. Reflexively, he swatted the alarm clock off.

In the shower, Ian daydreamed as the warm water fell on his head and shoulders. What did his dream about Penelope mean? Was there an unconscious part of him that wished ill things for her, maybe even her death? Did this have anything to do with the sex? He rinsed the soap from his skin, a black seed of guilt falling into fertile soil somewhere within him, and from it sprung a vine that strangled his gut. But that was nonsense. Incorrigible, unbelievable. Of course he didn't want anything bad to happen to her. He wanted to kiss her. Go to college with her. Get married. Have kids. Go on Hawaiian vacations. But by the time he toweled off and got dressed, the thought had bothered him so much that he didn't even wait for his parents to say good morning; he simply blurted out, "If you have a bad dream about someone, does it mean you wish bad things for them?"

His father poked about his oatmeal and said, "No. The human mind is a complex thing, Ian. I wouldn't worry about it too much. You were probably just tired."

His mother sipped her coffee and said, "Your father is right."

Ian spooned cereal into his mouth. He had stayed up late mapping. Maybe he was just tired.

On the way out the door, he took out his phone and plugged in his ear buds. On instinct, he stopped on the sidewalk outside Penelope's house and cycled through his iTunes. Today was a *Top Gun* morning, if he ever needed one. Kenny Loggins riffed into his ear for almost a minute before he realized Penelope hadn't come out. He went on without her, and as the bus stopped to pick him up, he texted her: "U OK?"

He took his seat near the front, and almost immediately, she responded: "Yeah. A bit pukey this morning."

"Bug?"

"No. Food. Mom tried Greek cooking last night. I guess my body hates olives."

Ian could relate. Penelope's mother tried hard, but she was a notoriously bad cook. Once when he'd eaten linguini with shrimp there, he threw up pink seafood curls all night. No wonder Penelope preferred eating at his house. Ian started typing a funny response about the shrimp, when Penelope texted again. "Listen. Sorry, I've been a bitch lately. Girl stuff + some sad stuff. Mom wants me to see her therapist. But I think I have it figured out now. I think I'll be fine."

Ian deleted his message and simply replied: "That's great, P."

"Treehouse after school? I have some ideas about the Royal Navy on the Islas Encantadas. Also, can I eat at your place tonight?"

"You bet."

"C U then."

As quickly as the black vine had grown inside him, it was stamped into the ground. Everything was fine. No evil pirate captains. No gorgon statues. No dead girlfriend. Just simple, boring, plain, wonderful reality. Even the juicy spitball that plunked him in the back of the head didn't bother him. He smiled to Heidi Flugalmann sitting in the seat across the aisle and listened to naval aviator songs.

CHAPTER 5

A TRIP TO THE PRINCIPAL'S OFFICE

In first period algebra, they had a pop quiz. Normally these quizzes freaked Ian out, but he took it with aplomb, knowing that in eight sweet hours, he'd be in the treehouse totally immersed in an imaginary world with his real-life girlfriend. Working through the quiz, he didn't worry about the questions he didn't know. It's just one quiz, he thought. There will be others.

Ms. Boulet was in rare form for fourth period English. First, she dropped her whiteboard marker, and the idiot boys in the front row went nuts when she had to bend over to pick it up. Their bluster drifted away when she started grilling them about Edgar Allan Poe's "The Cask of Amontillado." Ian knew it almost by heart, so he couldn't help but smile at Ms. Boulet's systematic takedown of the front row, each of the boys fumbling for answers and getting them all horribly wrong.

Throughout computer class, the black vine took root again in his gut, wanting to germinate and tangle his insides with doubt. He took out his phone and tapped out a text message but deleted it. He shook his head. It was ridiculous. Having a bad dream about someone does not mean you wish them harm. He repeated his parents' words in his head. Thought about Mrs. Archer's cooking again. But the pesky, negative thoughts were persistent. As he practiced his hotkeys for PowerPoint and Excel, the seed of doubt had grown into a thick hard taproot.

When Vice Principal Bowler showed up at the classroom door, Ms. Gilbretsen stepped out to talk. After a moment in the hall, she stepped back into the classroom. Her face was pale, and she held her hand to her forehead. "Ian," she said, her voice creaking in her throat. "You're excused. Go with the vice principal."

Frowning, Ian collected his books and followed Mr. Bowler through the bare halls. The quietness of the school while classes went on deafened him. "What's going on?" he asked.

The vice principal patted Ian's shoulder. Not the way-to-go-kid pat, the you-have-my-sympathies pat. "Your mother's here," he said. "It's best that you hear it from her."

Something was definitely wrong, and a cyclone of possibilities whirled in his mind, each of them grave. Were his grandparents okay? They seemed healthy, but were getting up there in years. His father had high cholesterol. Maybe he'd had a heart attack. Worse, he thought, maybe he was dead. Ian's knees wobbled, and he felt light-headed at the thought. But even though he tried every other possibility, deep in the soil beneath his skin, the black taproot throbbed, pulsated, telling him he was wrong.

Ahead, the cloudy sky from the entrance windows reflected in the office glass. He ran ahead of Mr. Bowler and yanked open the office door. Feeling breathless and upset, he found his mother sitting in a chair shredding a tissue in her lap. She looked up at him, eyes red and face blotchy. Ian had rarely seen his mother cry. "Mom? What's wrong?" he asked. "Is it dad?"

She only shook her head, the tears welling in her eyes. She began to sob as she clutched Ian's hand. Ian squeezed his mom's hand back, relieved that his dad was okay but still confused, even though the black vine grew in his gut, spooled and strangled his insides. After a moment, Dr. Nelson-Bayer, the principal, stepped forward. She put her hand on Ian's arm and looked at him with sad brown eyes. Though she wasn't in tears like his mother, her pallor told him that she was shaken as well. "It's not your father," she told him. "It's your friend Penelope."

"What?"

"I'm sorry, Ian."

"But she just…she had some bad olives," Ian said.

Dr. Nelson-Bayer shook her head. "I'm so, so sorry."

Ian felt a buzzing in his head, and his vision narrowed. Somewhere behind his eyes that black vine of doubt, of blame writhed up his throat and took hold in his brain. He had done this. He had caused it. His lips moved and words came out, but he knew they were pointless. "That can't be. I talked to her this morning. Texted her. She was going to have dinner at our house tonight. That's impossible."

Mr. Bowler stepped in. "Son, from what we gather from her parents, Penelope had a brain aneurysm. That's when an artery in the brain bursts. Of course, they don't know for sure yet, but…"

Like that's what Ian needed—the facts—a forensic explanation of how it all went down. As if that would make it all better. Ian felt a pair of hands dip into his body, past the black strangle vine, and grab hold of the black root that had grown there. With a few taut tugs, it pulled free, and a sense of relief took over him like a long-infected sliver had been removed. Lightheadedness took him over, and his mind let go. Blissfully, Ian fell deaf to Mr. Bowler's medical explanation. His vision swirled. As he collapsed, his mother grabbed for him, but his body limply fell from her grasp, and both of them ended up exhausted and puddled on the industrial office carpeting.

A hard drive crash. Ian had known it all too well from gaming consoles. The affliction started with symptoms like slow, choppy graphics and garbled sound. Quickly it degenerated to a lack of sound and a ghastly frozen image of whatever the latest zombie-infested first-person shooter had to offer. Rationalization set in next. The console couldn't be dead. The online server had crashed. Too many gigabytes were being used. It just needed to be reset. Powered down. That's it.

But he knew differently. Sure, the hard drive sounded alive. It engaged. It hummed. Even a cool hand to the top of the unit came back warm. But the screen remained black. Despite all the frustrated swearing and rebooting, the console did nothing but flash a red light.

Gone. Fried. Dark.

When Ian stepped out of the principal's office the day Penelope died, only that red warning light blinked in his memory banks. Sure, his body kept him standing, stepping in time with his mother, but his brain had shut down, gone offline, completely crashed.

Ian stayed home from school for the rest of the week. For most of it, he lay on his bed, his eyes transfixed to a different plane of existence—a plane that required a journey far, far too long to ever arrive. When his mother and father checked on him, patted his lifeless hands or warmed his cold cheek, they could see the shudder of an eye, a flinch of a pinky finger. Knowing Ian well, they knew he wasn't really with them but somewhere far away, deep in his imagination. Secretly they worried about where his mind had taken him and hoped his journey would bring him back home to them.

The next Monday, Ian's parents got him ready to go back to school. His father stood watch while Ian attempted to shower, which really meant letting the hot water flow over his head and shoulders. Together, his parents helped him dress, putting his floppy arms into sleeves, guiding his limp legs into pants. Ian allowed his parents to guide his body, but his mind continued to sprint, faster and faster, on its way to some nameless, placeless destination.

Breakfast

Ian sat at the table, eyes straight ahead and his mind on cruise control. Desperate to regain some sense of normalcy, his mom stood at the counter with a carnival of brightly colored cereal boxes on the counter in front of her. "I know it's three separate handfuls, honey," she said. "I just don't know which ones they are."

No response.

"Would you like an egg instead?"

No response.

"Let him be, Maggie," Ian's father said gently. "Maybe if we act as normally as possible, it'll click."

Trying to hide her frustration, his mother reached into three different boxes and placed a bowl of Cocoa Puffs, Froot Loops, and shredded wheat squares in front of Ian. She had no understanding of the intricacies of cereal combinations.

On the Bus to School

Ian sat in the middle, mindlessly filing into a random seat away from his regular seat with Penelope. He stared forward, numb, catatonic, yet strangely focused like a laser.

Autopilot.

All the kids sitting in his vicinity gawked at him. Some whispered about him and Penelope. The times they saw them in the hall holding hands, talking at their lockers. Their nerdy conversations. The brain aneurysm. Heidi Flugalmann saw them all and shot them the stink eye.

Nothing.

In Class

Mr. Spurgeon lectured about the periodic table of elements, how the order of the table was so clean and inspiring. From the blank stares and sleepy eyes all around, no one else felt the same inspiration.

Ian sat transfixed. The autopilot flying to a vacant destination.

From the back of the room Kit Cambridge folded a paper airplane and flung it. It made a quick downward loop and darted into the side of Ian's head.

Still, nothing.

Mandated School Grief Therapy

Ian. Chair. Autopilot.

A weasel-faced man in glasses and a suit sat across from him. Everything about him appeared neat, buttoned-up, and tidy. He held his hands together like he was about to say grace before a meal, but he said, "Now, you are not required to talk, Ian. The school holds these sessions to help students get through a tragedy. So feel free to say anything that's on your mind."

Nothing was on Ian's mind, and he said nothing. His gaze tunneled through the therapist, past the bookcase, the wall, and to no place in particular. Just a grey mash of ether that didn't exist and could never be reached.

"I know you and Penny were very close. Her death was sudden and unexpected."

Nothing.

"It can be therapeutic to talk about it."

Nothing.

"Would you feel better writing it down…your feelings?" The therapist slid a yellow notepad with a pencil across the desk to Ian.

Ian sat motionless. Empty to the Nth power.

"I'm here to listen and to help you get some real closure to these events, Ian."

Nothing.

The therapist sighed. "Like I said, you are not required to talk, but it can be very helpful."

Nothing.

After a few minutes, the therapist pulled out his phone from his vest pocket. He tapped out notes for the session: Ian Wilder displays symptoms of deep emotional shock, catatonia, and obvious depression. Reluctance to speak, react, or emote on any level may indicate a deeper condition than just grief. Recommend continued sessions to determine whether additional treatment is warranted.

The Bus Ride Home

Again, autopilot.

Billy Dawkins and Shep Murray wrestled in the seats behind Ian.

Pete Stamdahl sat behind Ian and said, "For Penny, I'm giving you a one-week bereavement grace period." He made a fist and slammed it into his other palm for emphasis.

Nothing.

Heidi Flugalmann switched seats and sat down next to Ian, picked his hand up, and placed it in hers, then leaned into him.

Dinner

Ian's parents flanked him at the table. No one spoke. His father cut green beans with his knife and fork, producing an ear-twisting squeak of metal silverware on china.

Maggie dabbed her mouth with a napkin and said, "I found a nice suit for you to wear for the funeral, Ian."

Nothing.

Harold sipped his iced tea. Instead of looking at Ian, he looked at his wife. "So I had lunch with a client in Minneapolis. You know, that good deli that stacks those huge sandwiches."

"Not the pastrami, Harold," Maggie said, but her full attention was on Ian.

Harold waved her off. "I got the turkey, don't worry. But anyway, I can't finish the whole thing, because they're huge. So the waiter stops by and says, 'Do you want a box for your leftovers?' And I say, 'No. But I'll wrestle you for them!'"

Maggie's face went blank. She set her wine glass down on the table with a gentle tink.

Ian stared past them both, not registering either of them.

"No," Harold said, "but I'll wrestle you for them. C'mon. It's funny! Right?"

Maggie stared at Harold and sighed.

Bedtime

Ian lay on his bed. Not in it, but on top of it, covers and all, dressed in pajamas he'd never worn before. Pajamas with sailboats. His mother had dressed him for bed.

On autopilot, he stared at the ceiling.

CHAPTER 6

THE UNUSUAL VISITOR

On Tuesday afternoon, at the Van Maur Funeral Home, Maggie and Harold Wilder escorted Ian into the viewing room and sat him down in the first row. Still on autopilot, he registered nothing, not even the casket in front of him. His parents busied themselves at the tag boards propped up on easels and framed photos on linen-covered tables. Maggie trembled at the photos brimming with Penelope from birth to what must have been just a few weeks ago. Maggie herself had been present during the taking of some of these pictures. They had been neighbors with the Archers for most of the kids' lives. Tears streamed down her face as her heart broke all over again.

Harold wrapped his arm around her and said, "Let's be strong for Ian. He needs us now."

Maggie nodded, wiping the tears from her eyes. "I know. It's just hard. They're both so young." She reached out to one of the tag boards and admired the whole creative affair. "When did Alexandra have time for this?"

Harold patted her shoulder and said, "Her sisters." Maggie nodded absently.

Together, they walked through a panorama of Penelope's life built of old photos, birthday cards, ribbon, and stuffed animals. The photos tracked Penelope from infancy to grade school. Toothless smiles from when she lost her front teeth. The skinned knees from learning to ride a bike. Trick-or-treating as Peter Pan. Birthdays with overly elaborate bakery cakes. Helping her mother through her cancer and chemo. First day of high school.

Ian showed up in a lot of the pictures. Building the treehouse. Penelope and Ian playing aliens from outer space. Penelope and Ian playing knight and princess. Penelope and Ian building snow forts, in the treehouse, chasing each other through backyards, eating birthday cake, watching movies and smiling with broad, toothy, popcorn-speckled grins. In the more recent photos of the two, only Penelope looked at the camera. Ian's gaze was always on her.

Maggie left the room sobbing.

Harold went after her.

In the foyer, visitors milled about.

Ian sat in a chair at the front of the parlor. The casket sat before him. On autopilot, Ian stared forward, past her casket, past the wall, and past the town of Alton, Minnesota, beyond, forever searching for that nameless world where Penelope now lived, happy and robust amidst rolling prairies of bent grass and warm winds. Ian sat alone in his silence. He didn't notice the "Employees Only" door to his right creak open and a head emerge from behind it.

"Pssst!"

When Ian didn't react, it happened again.

"Pssst!"

A third time.

"Pssst! Ian!"

Annoyed, Ian looked to the sound, and there she was—Penelope—peeking from behind the door. Her hair appeared a bit darker, more blackish than her usual chestnut brown, but he would never forget that face: the slender nose with little bean-like nostrils, lips full like truffle chocolates, and green eyes the color of Brazilian tree frogs on biology textbook covers.

"Come here," Penelope whispered, curling her finger towards the door.

Ian rose quickly from the chair. "Penelope? Is that you?" Ian hadn't spoken in more than four days. The words sounded a lot louder than he wanted.

Penelope winced and slid back behind the door, closing it.

His voice carried into the annex, and his ever-watchful mother noticed his movement and rushed to her son. Penelope's mother, Alexandra, followed. Ian stood by the "Employees Only" door, pointing at it like a golden retriever who'd found a quail.

"What is it, sweetheart?" his mother asked.

"Penelope," Ian stuttered. "She didn't die. She was just here!"

Nervously, his mother escorted him away from the door, trying to calm her son with gentle shushing noises.

"I'm sure of it!" Ian said, his mouth turned up in one corner. "She was just here."

Lifting a shaky hand, Alexandra turned the knob and opened the door to a hallway leading to offices and bathrooms in the back.

Curious, Ian peered in as well. Nothing. "She was just there, Mom. I saw her!"

Maggie exhaled, tears returning to her eyes. She reached out to touch his face. "Ian, honey. I'm so sorry, but Penelope is…"

Ian pulled away from his mother and Alexandra, backing unknowingly to the front of the parlor. Each time they reached their hands to him, he stepped back further. "No. You don't get it! I saw her. Right behind that door!" He backed up, closer and closer to the casket. Alexandra gently gripped his arm and turned him to face the casket. Penelope lay in a flower print sundress and enough makeup to gain entrance to clown college.

Ian gaped. This couldn't be her. Penelope never looked like that, so waxy and lifeless, her hands crossed primly, artificially at her sternum. And the make-up. She looked like a life-size doll manufactured out of plastic. Penelope looked like the girl behind the door. It wasn't possible. But before he could rectify anything in his mind, he noticed the charm bracelet wrapped around her wrist, the turquoise bead the color of the ocean turned to the top. He'd given the bracelet to her for her 15th birthday, and the turquoise bead symbolized their getaway island. Warm lapping waves on white sand beaches. The red warning lights fired up in his brain again, threatening to wash it all away, back to a state of nothingness. Only one thought kept it at bay: Who was behind the door?

Ian grew agitated, confused. A vein in his temple throbbed like a worm under his skin. He looked to the door and back to the casket in panic. His mom tried to settle him, but his agitation grew to embarrassment. All around him mourning faces placated him:

Look at the poor, sad, crazy boy.

Silly thing. He thinks she's still alive.

He has to let her go.

He's definitely going to need therapy now.

His face grew hot and his forehead sweat. He had to do something, so he ran out of the funeral home and around the corner of the building. He slumped down to the cement, breath heaving and trying his best not to cry. What the hell was wrong with him?

"You were just going to cry, weren't you?" Penelope asked. "Over me."

Ian wiped his eyes and looked up. Penelope stood in front of him, with more shadow in her hair, black boots, ripped jeans, a white t-shirt, and a faded, worn-out black denim jacket. "What's going on?" Ian asked her. "I saw you. In there! In the casket!"

Penelope smirked and sat next to him. "Are you positive?" she asked. "Because I'm pretty sure I'm right here."

"I've cracked, haven't I?" Ian said. "That's the only explanation. That's the only reason you're in there, in that casket, and out here talking to me. No other explanation." He shook his head, unable to reconcile the two versions of Penelope.

"You're probably right, then," she said, nodding in agreement. Still, she leaned closer to him.

Ian looked into Penelope's green eyes. "Are you going to be in my head forever, then? Or is there some unfinished mystery that you need me to help you solve so you can pass on?"

Penelope stifled a laugh. "Nothing like that," she said. A jagged little smile split from her lips. A harpless, yet lusty and inviting grin. "I just need something from you."

"Ian!" yelled his mother from the front of the funeral home, searching for him. Before long, she turned the corner and saw him. "There you are! Come with me. We'll just go straight home."

When Ian turned back to Penelope, she had vanished again. But he figured only he could see his own hallucinations. He stood up and said, "No, Mom. I'm fine. I can go to the funeral."

She combed his hair with her fingers and looked at him with worried eyes. "Are you sure? I can take you home if it's too much." Ian nodded and headed for the entrance.

Ian sat between his parents, his father's arm around his shoulder. He listened to the pastor speak about death and remembrance, how everyone must make the journey and all that. He found it boring and overly sentimental. Penelope would have scoffed and rolled her eyes. When the time came for people to speak, only a few people stood: her mother and father, her aunt, and an older cousin. None of them were able to capture Penelope—only who they thought she was. If he could have gotten out of his own head for just a second, he would have seen that they were all suffering deeply and likely still in shock. Much like him. But at the time, it infuriated him. This was Penelope. She had stories. Dreams. A vibrant imagination and a way of bringing her worlds to life. She had an enormous life beyond the one her family knew about. Someone should say more. He should be speaking. He knew her best. But the thought of standing in front of all these people made him want to puke. But he had to. If it had been him in that casket, Penelope would have. It was the least he could do.

So when it felt like no one else would speak, as much as it scared him, Ian stood up and went to the podium, careful not to look at the body lying there. "Hi," he said. "I'm Ian. Um. Penelope and I... well, we were friends. Ah, more than that, really." His face grew hot, remembering the treehouse. "We're...kind of...nerds." The crowd murmured. A lone chuckle sounded in the back. It reminded him of a cartoon laugh-track. "See...we played a lot. Pirates. Space zombies. Superheroes. She designed this elven dress for her princess character in Fharendale. It was beautiful. With tiny ivy leaves and gold thread. She never actually made it, but, ah, the drawings...well, they were really good. I was never really good at drawing, but Penelope..." His mouth got dry and he wiped his forehead. "The point...I guess there isn't really a point, but...she was my girlfriend. My only friend, really. We spent our lives adventuring in imaginary worlds. Saving people. Saving each other." He licked his lips and swallowed. "I just wish I could have saved her in this one."

His knees shook. His thighs wobbled. He needed to sit down. But before he could move, his eyes caught Penelope in the foyer, his own personal hallucination, and that new, sly, infectious smile. With one look at her, relaxation set in. A calm snaked through his legs.

She mouthed the words "I need you."

A grin lit up his face. Being crazy would be fun, he thought. He might as well get something out of the tragedy. His hallucination vanished, just like she had before.

By the time they arrived home, Ian had resigned himself to being insane. It made him happy. Through dinner, Penelope stayed close: through the dining room window, just outside the back door to the garage, jumping up and down into view through the kitchen window above the sink.

Each time, she mouthed, "I need you."

Pleasantly ignorant, Ian ate his entire dinner. Either his appetite was back, or he was simply relieved that he hadn't lost her, not really. His parents exchanged cautious smiles, encouraged by Ian's return.

At bedtime, he crawled under his covers and let his mother tuck him in, burrito style, like she did when he was young. Weary, he wondered if he'd had any real sleep in the last five days. His mother sat on his bed next to him. She looked tired, as well. "Quite a…big day today, huh?" She said 'big' like it was a replacement for a word she couldn't quite find.

"Yeah," Ian said. "I feel much better."

"Really? Are you sure?" His mother felt his forehead. "It's just that everything was so sudden. And when you thought you saw her, I…"

"I'm fine, Mom." Ian cut her off.

She sighed. One of those relieving utterances that suggested she'd just taken off a pair of uncomfortable shoes. She pulled something wrapped in pink tissue paper from her pocket. "Alexandra asked me to give you this," she said, handing him the small package. "Penelope worked very hard on it. Alexandra said you'd know the deeper meaning."

Ian unfolded the tissue and lifted up a necklace made from a slender leather lashing and numerous engraved wooden beads. Some had been stained a variety of colors, while others were just marked with unique, hand-etched symbols. A circle with a line through it. Saturn. The launch planet to Taluride Station. Another with an s-shaped swoosh with feet. A dragon. Labyrinth, the pet dragon on Fharendale.

He shuffled through the beads until he saw the lone turquoise one. Just the feel of it in his fingertips eased his mind. He thought about the white sand beaches, the arching palm trees, and the water stretching out for miles.

"Cool," he said.

"What do the beads mean?" his mother asked.

"Just our stories," he said. "This aquamarine one, that's for her mermaid story. The gray, our interstellar voyage to Baven-Khan." His fingers fumbled to a black bead, slightly larger than the rest. He remembered his last conversations with Penelope, and he quickly skipped past it and back to the turquoise one.

Maggie smiled. "That's wonderful," she said. "Now get some sleep. You need it."

After his mother left, Ian sat up and tied the necklace around his neck, then nestled back into the covers. But before he could fall asleep, his bedroom window squeaked open and Penelope stepped in. "It's about time. I thought she'd never leave."

Ian sat up in his bed. "You're using the window. Why would a hallucination need to use the window?"

Penelope cinched her mouth up and shook her head. "I don't know. For the realism?"

Ian nodded in agreement. "Of course. To be a better replica of the real Penelope, you have to act as if you physically exist, even though you're just a figment of my imagination."

"Yeah," Penelope said. "Listen. Like I said before, I need something from you before I can pass on to the next, uh, realm or whatever."

"Okay," Ian said. "But do you have to go? You just got here."

Penelope crawled onto his bed and inched closer to his face. "Oh, I'll come back to visit."

"Promise?"

Penelope inched closer, until he could feel her breath against his cheek. Ian's heart raced. His thoughts bent back to their last rendezvous in the treehouse. "Promise," she whispered.

He couldn't believe a hallucination could get him this excited. For a hallucination, she sure felt like the real Penelope.

"I really, really need you," she said. Her lips brushed his ear and cheek. Ian remembered what she told him about great kisses stealing time, and this was another moment to steal. He pulled her tight to him, not caring if he fell deeper into crazy. He would never let her go. He kissed her until his lips buckled under hers into a confused affair.

Penelope answered him with her tongue, more aggressive than usual. It felt like she was crawling into his mouth, but he didn't care. He'd devour her whole if he could. He closed his eyes and kissed back with everything he had. His blood coursed faster, harder, careening through his veins like a bullet train, until it spent itself at the base of his brain. Somewhere in the deep recesses of his mind an iridescent soap bubble flitted on a breeze, rising gently into a sun-drowned day, until at its peak, it shimmered and popped, and Penelope was gone.

CHAPTER 7

A New Substitute Teacher Named Steve

Ah, morning.

He felt like he had stepped out of a time machine and into a new world. The principal's office. The news of Penelope. Marching through the days on autopilot like some lovesick zombie. The visitation and funeral. His hissy fit. All of it was in the past. Penelope had returned. His own private Penelope.

Ian sprang from his bed and took a deep breath.

He felt good.

No. Scratch that.

He felt awesome.

He stretched his neck from side to side and jogged in place for a few steps. A late September breeze drifted from his open window. The day seemed bright, and his stomach quaked in hunger. He grabbed his jeans and a red t-shirt and dressed himself by the window. He made sure to look out to see the love of his life—the hallucination of his dead girlfriend, Penelope Archer.

But she wasn't there.

She said she'd be back, he told himself. He shrugged his shoulders. He was happy to dive head-long into crazy if it meant he could be with Penelope. It no longer felt weird to have a romantic relationship with a hallucination. In fact, it comforted him that maybe he hadn't lost her at all.

Downstairs in the kitchen, his mother and father went about their breakfast routines as the dervish that was Ian walked in and grabbed his three boxes of cereal.

"You certainly are chipper this morning," his mother said. "Are you alright, Ian?"

Ian thought about it and said, "Yeah, Mom. I think I'm alright." He set his cereal boxes back down and said, "You know what, Ma. Make me an omelet…with the yolk. I don't have high cholesterol. And could you throw some bacon and cheese in it?"

Ian sat down across from his father, who had lowered his paper and looked at him quizzically.

Behind them, his mother looked dumbfounded. "I hadn't planned for bacon this morning. I guess I could fry some up…if we have any."

On the bus ride to school, Ian watched out his window, confident that he'd see Penelope leaning against a tree, smiling at him, or running along the sidewalk to keep up with the bus. But each time he glanced out she was nowhere to be found. It seemed odd, given how much she had wanted to see him, but he thought nothing of it and continued on, indulging in the soundtrack to *Excalibur*.

Throughout each of his classes, Ian gazed out the window, hoping to see her, but she never showed. He checked for her in the stairwells and the janitor's closet. Knowing she had preferred to visit him when he was alone, he loitered in the hallways between class periods, trying to make himself the last student to arrive in each classroom. Nothing. For as eager as she had been the day before, she had since disappeared.

Ian stepped into Mr. Spurgeon's environmental science class, but Mr. Spurgeon was gone. Instead, a skinny, funny-looking man with glasses stood at the front of the class writing his name on the whiteboard.

As Jeremy O'Connell walked to his seat, he asked, "Who are you?"

The teacher turned around and gestured to his name clearly written on the whiteboard. "Will LeGrand. I'm Mr. Spurgeon's substitute teacher for the day. He had some bad Arby's last night and can't make it in today."

As the rest of the class filed in, Jeremy sat down and said, "Your voice sounds funny."

"Why, thank you," Mr. LeGrand said. "I didn't get enough of that in high school."

But Jeremy had a point. The substitute had a nasal, high-pitched voice, bordering on whiny. Though, with those buggy eyes, snaggled teeth, and pale complexion, perhaps his voice was the least of the man's worries, Ian thought.

"You're weird," Zakk Falin said.

"From the kid who greased his shorts in front of his whole middle school four years ago," Mr. LeGrand said. The class laughed. Mr. LeGrand raised his hands to calm the crowd. "Alright, alright. Settle down. Let's just take our seats. Maybe learn a little about science?"

Everyone settled into their seats, and Ian took his place back by the window, where he glanced out to see if Penelope was waiting for him.

Nothing.

With a lonely sigh, Ian turned and faced the front of the class. Mr. LeGrand wasn't much better than Mr. Spurgeon. His lecture was equally, if not more, boring than Mr. Spurgeon's. The hour droned on, and Ian caught himself bobbing asleep a few times.

When class ended, Ian packed up his things and lined up behind his classmates who filed out to leave the room. But before he could follow them out, Mr. LeGrand stepped across Ian's path and closed the classroom door, wedging the doorstop underneath it.

"Okay, let's not beat around the bush here, pal," Mr. LeGrand said, arms crossed over his skinny chest. "Have you seen her?"

"Seen who?" asked Ian incredulously. LeGrand couldn't mean his hallucinations of Penelope. She only appeared to him. Right?

Mr. LeGrand stepped closer to Ian and poked a finger at him. "Don't play games with me, man. This is an unprecedented breach, buddy, and it'll be my ass if we don't find her!"

Ian had the sudden urge not to be crazy anymore. "What are you talking about, sir?"

"The girl, Einstein. The girl that tracked you down yesterday. You know exactly what I'm talking about! So drop the funny business!"

The gears in Ian's mind didn't connect. Like a blown transmission in a car ground to a startling halt. Somehow and for whatever reason, Mr. LeGrand knew about his hallucinations. But how? Was he under surveillance? Had he been watching him? Was he a mind-reader?

"No, I am not a mind-reader," Mr. LeGrand said. "And that's not because I just read your mind. Generally, that's the first thing interactants ask when I approach them. Telepathy isn't possible in this reality. In others, yes. Just not this particular one."

Whoa.

Ian felt gravity multiply on itself threefold. He thought the Earth may have lurched to a stop and cracked open like an egg. What was going on? Who was this guy and what the hell had happened?

Mr. LeGrand reached into his tweed suit coat and pulled out a deck of notecards. "Here," he said, handing the cards to Ian. "This will be easier. Just read them."

Perplexed, Ian looked at the first card. It displayed crisp text in a brilliantly clear, almost otherworldly blue font. He read the words carefully, then, confused, looked up at Mr. LeGrand.

"You have to read it out loud," Mr. LeGrand said. "Reading out loud stimulates the cognitive and auditory portions of your brain… makes it more tangible…real."

Ian looked back to the top card and read: "Interactant Orientation. Number one. Yes, this is real. This is happening, and it is normal to be confused." Ian looked up at Mr. LeGrand, who spun his index finger in a circular pattern, gesturing for him to continue.

Ian moved the first card to the back of the deck and continued to read each one: "Number two. You ARE NOT crazy. We cannot stress this enough. This is a very delicate situation that is absolutely, 100% true. Number three. Don't talk about this with anyone. Knowing your feeble grasp on number two, you can imagine what the people around you might think if you actually mentioned any of this to them. So let's keep this between you and me. Number four. Welcome to enlightenment and your journey into understanding the never-ending confines of the Infiniuum."

Before flipping the card, Ian looked to the teacher again. "What the heck is an Infiniuum?"

Mr. LeGrand sighed. "Just read the damn cards."

Ian flipped to the next card and read: "Infiniuum you ask? What is it and how does it affect me? Infiniuum is short for the infinite continuum, or as you would understand it: the ever-growing, expanding universe and/or consciousness that is multi-planar dimensional existence." Next card: "Imagine it this way. The universe is infinite. That means for every decision you have made here, there's another reality with another you who made a different decision, and so on and so on. An infinite universe comprised of multiple realities with every possible outcome. The raw data of the imagination and existence itself."

Ian looked up from the card, squinted his eyes, and said, "What?"

Defeated, Mr. LeGrand sighed and said, "The multiverse, man. Jeez."

Ian shook his head and looked at the next card. "So why are you here in this moment right now? Good question. Chances are you have committed an act that has disrupted the stability of the Infiniuum, or you have had your continuum disrupted by someone who committed these types of acts. Either way, we apologize for what is about to happen and encourage you to strictly follow the instructions of your assigned feron."

Brain. Blender. Liquefy.

Ian had no idea what was happening. Infiniuums, continuums, ferons? What. The. Hell? He didn't like being crazy anymore. He must be stark raving mad for sure. Whatever had happened earlier had to be pure fantasy, because this was full-blown, running-maniacally-down-the-hall-covered-in-peanut-butter-ripping-your-hair-out insane. That was the only plausible explanation. He imagined the therapist at school would have fun with this. The numerous sessions with the weasel-faced man looking and acting all smug as Ian grappled with his insanity.

And his parents.

Surely his mom would have an emotional breakdown and his father, well, he'd probably just nod his way through it and tell his mother, "He's turning into a man, Maggie. He'll learn to take care of himself."

No, he wouldn't!

His hands shook. Images of his imaginary arch-nemesis Captain Noface bubbled through his head, puking up his elegant pirate meals and laughing at Ian behind his gory Venetian mask.

"Remember number two, kid," Mr. LeGrand said.

Ian shook his head and made a fist with his free hand to stop it from trembling. He had to get out of there. Ian threw the notecards at Mr. LeGrand and yanked at the classroom door to no avail.

Behind him, Mr. LeGrand stooped over and picked up all the notecards that had fluttered to the floor. "Just great. You know I really put a lot of time into these cards. You have to harvest the ripest kiklack larvae to get this shade of blue."

Ian ran to one of the windows facing the soccer fields behind the school.

Locked. They all were. And, let's face it, he wasn't brave enough to throw his body at it.

Mr. LeGrand approached Ian, holding the cards in his hand. "You're just making it harder, Ian. Trust me. I've seen thousands of your kind before, and organisms like you all act the same. You think your reality is always the real one, the important one, when in fact it is just an infinitesimal speck compared to the immensity of the Infiniuum. It's understandable to feel denial or fear. It's natural. But you freaking out like this isn't going to help."

Ian traversed the perimeter of the whole room looking for any possible way to get out or even a closet to hide in, to get away from this insane hallucination. But there was nothing. Like a caged beast, his eyes darted from side to side, expecting a net or some tranq gun outfitted with a suppressor to drop him in his tracks. The vein over his temple throbbed again, and the ice-cold spike of a headache racked his forehead. He stopped his frantic movements. "Who are you?"

Mr. LeGrand smiled, for what Ian thought was the first time since he met the strange man, and said, "I'm your assigned feron. Just like the cards said."

"What is a feron?"

Mr. LeGrand sighed audibly, the kind Ian heard from his parents quite frequently throughout his childhood. It was the sound of having to explain the same thing over and over again because kids just don't listen. "Listen, pal. I'm just here to help."

"But this is all a hallucination," Ian said, leaning against the wall. "My girlfriend died, and I've cracked. You're not real. I'll bet you're not even Mr. LeGrand. I'm probably not even conscious right now. I'm probably still in my bed staring at the ceiling." Ian held out his forearm and repeatedly pinched it, wincing in pain.

"That's great!" Mr. LeGrand said. "Now you're getting it. And if it makes you feel better, you can call me, uh, Steve, if that's easier. You wouldn't be able to hear, understand, or even comprehend my real name anyway."

"What do you mean 'that's great?' It's not great. It's crazy."

Steve finally sat down in a chair across from Ian and said, "Comprehending the existence of multiple, parallel, and even conflicting dimensions of reality, man. That's what's great. It's sinking in."

"Sinking in," Ian said, shaking his head. "Fantastic." He stood up and walked to the door.

Steve smiled and stood. "Excellent. Now we can get started. We've got to find Penelope—" A thunderous crash stopped Steve's words cold as Ian slammed the metal coat-stand into the frosted glass of the classroom door. Tiny diamonds of shattered glass flew everywhere, and an alarm erupted from the intercoms in the ceiling.

Steve bolted to the door and kicked the doorstop away beneath it. He pulled Ian away. "No, kid," he said. "You don't want to do this."

Ian wriggled free of his grasp and said, "Don't worry, Steve. This isn't happening here. It's happening in a different reality." He sprinted to the windows, smashing the coat-stand into three of the seven windows before the school security guard stormed in, grabbed him, and forced him to the floor. Ian kicked and punched, screamed and cried.

"Stop," the security guard said. "Just stop it."

Ian worked himself into such a lather, his lungs seemed to not work. His body too. His breathing intensified, and his heart raced off rhythm. The burly guard pressed his body against Ian, firmly keeping him at bay. Ian's muscles locked in spasm, and his mind slipped like a needle on one of his dad's vintage records. Darkness crowded the edges of his vision, like he was falling slowly down a well.

Steve could only shake his head and get out of the guard's way. Mr. Caulderon, the assigned grief counselor and therapist, raced into the room. Winded from running the school halls, he looked down at Ian and said, "Poor kid. I just knew he had some pent-up feelings about Penny's death."

Steve scowled at the therapist and said, "Her name was Penelope. She hated being called Penny."" Without waiting for a response, Steve left the classroom, the tiny crumbles of glass crunching under his feet.

CHAPTER 8

Exploring the Infiniuum in a Closet

Ian lay on his bed, facing the window to the backyard. His flashlight sat on the windowsill, lifeless. If only he could shine it up to the stars and click out Morse code until his fingers cramped up. Beg for time to be reversed. Or be given just another day or two with her. Or maybe switch spots. He'd kill just to have one more conversation with her. But what would he say? It had to be "I love you." That's what she'd want to hear, right? That he'd do anything to get her back. No matter what.

His parents stood at the foot of his bed. His father rubbed his head. His lips moved like he was biting the inside of his cheek. His mother's eyes were red and glassy. She held a balled-up tissue in one hand.

"We're just glad no one was hurt," Maggie said.

His father stayed silent. The shadows in Ian's dimly lit room hugged the grooves and furrows over his face.

"But the school," his mother said, trailing off. "We're going to have you work with Dr. Caulderon for a while. To make sure you're getting the type of help you need to get through this."

"For now," his father finally spoke. "Try to get some rest."

They left his room and slowly closed the door with a click. Ian didn't move at all. He knew what happened. What he did. How his parents sat silent in the car on the ride home. His dad looking into the rear-view mirror every thirty seconds to check on him. His mom stifling her sobs, but her shoulders heaving gave it all away. What he did had a toll. That much he now knew. As much as he wanted to believe his parents were strong, grown adults, they too had moments of frailty. A frailty he had cracked.

A loud crunching sound came from behind him.

Startled, he quickly rolled over in bed, and there stood Steve, the weirdo substitute teacher from earlier, decked in Ian's own clothes: a black *Firefly* t-shirt, flannel pajama bottoms, and a pair of flip-flops Ian hadn't seen in years. He ate from an old bag of Doritos.

Ian bolted out of bed. "How did you get in here?"

"The closet," Steve said.

Ian grabbed the Doritos from him and sniffed the bag. They smelled rancid and stale. "Where'd you find these? They smell horrible."

"Also the closet," Steve said.

"And these clothes," Ian said. "Let me guess."

Steve stole the Doritos back. "The closet."

"How can you stand those rotten chips?" Ian asked, turning his face away from the stink. "I think I threw those in there five years ago."

Steve shrugged his shoulders. "It's carbon. It'll do."

"So are you a hallucination too?" Ian asked. "Part of my brain made to torment me?"

Steve sat at Ian's desk and paged through his overstuffed journal. "I wish," he said. "Had you listened to me earlier, man, we could have avoided your little schism back there. As crazy as it may sound to you, I'm actually here to help you."

Ian reflected on what happened earlier: his reaction to Steve, the trashing of his classroom, the struggle against the guard. He evaluated the outcomes. What if it was all real? Steve. The Infiniuum. He seemed pretty damn desperate to find Penelope. But if Ian was needed so badly that a feron was sent here to get his help, then maybe it was really important. Like epically important.

On the other hand, if it all was a hallucination, a fabrication within his own mind, created solely to help him cope with Penelope's death, then the worst thing that could happen is that he'd live his lifetime on this Earth as a lunatic, spiraling further and further inside his own fabricated world and becoming a shell of his former self. How could he tell? What proof was there either way?

"There isn't any proof," Steve said. "You're just going to have to trust me." During Ian's internal musings, Steve had stood up and admired Ian's *Star Wars* poster affixed to the wall.

"For someone who claims not to be a mind-reader, you do it a lot."

"You looked like you were deep in thought. No doubt grappling with the existential nature of it all," he said. "You do it often, don't you?" Steve asked. "Drift off. Daydream. Lost in your own mind."

Ian shook his head and crossed his arms over his chest. "Sure. I suppose. Penelope and I, we were kind of nerds. Liked to fantasize about things."

"Yeah," Steve said. "All watchers do."

"Watchers?"

"Organisms in tune with the Infiniuum," Steve said. "Like I said before, the universe, as you know it, is infinitely expansive, and watchers can see into the tapestry of multi-dimensionality. Hell, every great idea your people have ever had has come from a watcher seeing something in an alternate reality. Airplanes, cell phones, string theory, Apple. Whatever the hell CrossFit is."

"A watcher?" Ian asked.

"Right," Steve said. "Imagination is simply access to multi-dimensionality, access to all possibilities. Like Google. The Infiniuum is just the all-streaming content of the universe. Watchers possess an innate ability to tap into those dimensional energies and see the possibilities they connect with most. Pirates. Space zombies. Superheroes. A remote desert island shared with the love of your life."

Ian reached up with a hand to his necklace and felt his way across the beads and their etched symbols. A small triangle wearing an upturned bracket. A longhorn skull. Cactusback Flats. Another sporting an upright fork with three spires. A trident. The Atlantis City logo. He felt his way past others until he found the turquoise bead.

Steve patted Ian's shoulder and slumped back into Ian's desk chair. "That's why I need you," he said. "I'm tracking a real nasty malig."

"Malig?"

"Maligs and ferons were cut from the same cloth," Steve said. "We ferons, we're the good guys. We investigate within certain ethical boundaries. We don't just invade a watcher's mind and use it as a cosmic springboard throughout the Infiniuum, then throw them away like rubber gloves after a proctology exam. We ask nicely. Like I'm trying to do now. Well, this malig, she caught Penelope bridging the Infiniuum and killed her. Now she's jumping into Penelope's alternate existences. Looking for something."

Ian cocked his head drunkenly to the side and said, "For what?"

Steve rubbed the skin at his temples and said, "I don't know. That's why I'm here. Whatever Penelope did is big. It's set things in motion and has everyone's undies in a twist, pal. Problem is, the malig, she doesn't know either, but if they follow their very predictable nature, she had to find someone who knows how and where to retrace Penelope's steps. Like you. After killing Penelope here in this reality, she needed the next mind for her cosmic springboard. She needed someone who knew Penelope and her imagination so well she could regain access to it. Like GPS. So she assumed Penelope's identity and found you."

Ian brought his hand to his forehead. "The kiss."

"Yeah," Steve said. "She needed another watcher to get access to Penelope's alternate existences."

"I feel so stupid."

Steve shook his head and said, "There was no way you could have known. But that's why I need you. If Penelope hid anything in her alternate realities, any plans or clues as to what she did, or if she had contact with her alternates, that could really get us out of this jam."

"Alternates?"

Steve nodded. "The other versions of herself scattered throughout the Infiniuum. The malig will hunt down the alternate Penelopes to try to uncover the plan."

"Wait," Ian said and looked at Steve with wide eyes. "There are other Penelopes?"

Steve rolled his eyes. "What part of infinite alternate realities did you not get? Do I need to pull out a Schrödinger lecture for you?" Steve stood up and gripped Ian's shoulders and stared him down. "I need someone who has been to those worlds before, someone who knows the terrain, knows what Penelope may have done."

Ian thought for a moment. "So Penelope was a watcher too? Like me?"

Steve stepped to the bedroom window, where the moonlight had just started to peek out from a passing cloud. "A traveler, to be exact. In every dimension, there are many watchers, but very few, if any, travelers."

Ian looked up, confused. "Traveler? Like going to those places."

"In a way," Steve said. "Listen, that's not important right now. What's important is finding that malig and finding out what Penelope did to raise every single alarm in the damn Infiniuum."

"How do we do that? We don't know where she went."

Steve sat back down. "And that's why I have you. We have now come full circle."

"I don't know where she went or how to get there."

"Don't worry about getting there," Steve said. "Maligs and ferons have similar gifts as travelers. I can bring you. But I need a navigator."

"This is crazy." Ian's eyes grew wide.

Steve huffed out a laugh. "If you think this is crazy," he said, "you're going to have trouble with this. Steve held up his bare hand; the prints on the ends of his thumb and fingers glowed a bright neon blue and formed nodule-like pads. "What's the point of seeing the improbable and creating the impossible if you never leave your room?"

Ian stared transfixed on Steve's glowing hand. "What the hell is that?"

Steve looked at his hand. "It's a construct, kid," Steve said. "What I am about to show you is more limbic…messy, so I've masked it to represent something more familiar to you in order to ease the transition, so to speak."

Steve webbed the fingers of both hands together and pushed, cracking his knuckles in unison. "Now try to keep up." Steve's hands fluttered as he seemed to unwrap an invisible package. Then, grabbing at its seams, he yanked outward with both hands and the entire bedroom shuddered. Ian squinted his eyes and rubbed them repeatedly as his vision seemed to have doubled. No. Check that. Quadrupled. His head jabbed in pain, like a railroad spike hammered into the center of his skull.

"What you are seeing here is the true Infiniuum," Steve said. "At first it's painful to even comprehend, and that would explain your headache. But as you get used to it, you can see the effect your mind has on it."

Ian opened one eye and saw multiple versions of himself bloom outward like the petals of a flower. In the versions near to him, he stood in the same bedroom, only each layer had a minor detail switched.

On his wall a Kiera Knightley *King Arthur* poster swapped out for a Daft Punk poster or a vintage Atari 2600 poster, a watercolor painting of a bison, a map of the United States with red pins scattered across it. As Ian turned around his room, he saw the infinite loops of other realities blossom, of other Ians and their bookcases. Pulp novels and manga replaced with books of poetry, C++ coding manuals, pottery technique books, fusion cookbooks, banjo songbooks. Even his desk showed numerous alternatives. His messy writing desk covered with his stories changed to be covered with empty liquor bottles and beer cans, then neat and tidy astronomical charts and a fancy computer, stock-trading charts and graphs and business plans.

"Any possibility is possible?" Ian asked. As the thought registered, the hundreds of alternate realities bloomed differently, a kaleidoscope of variations of a different room. A grass hut with a view of a blue ocean and white sand beach, palm trees. He turned his head to reveal Penelope lying in bed. Even the salty brine and the scent of sweet coconut navigated their way to his nose. But with every variation came the jagged spike at the core of his head, his poor brain trying to adapt to the possibilities. Ian closed his eyes to the madness and said, "Is it always like this?"

"Yes," Steve said. "As a watcher, you have the ability to see the many layers of the Infiniuum, but your mind has always built constructs around it to protect you. That's why you only see one, maybe two layers at a time. As you can imagine, the Infiniuum unleashed on an unwitting mind would cause a person to descend into madness. Your mind simply tells you that it's your imagination, déjà vu, a fantasy, or a dream."

Keeping his eyes closed, Ian said, "Really, dreams?"

"Think about it, Einstein. When are you the most relaxed, the most vulnerable, and the most open to accepting things? When you are sleeping. The Chinese and Japanese figured it out millennia ago."

"So dreams are real?"

"They are for someone in a different dimension, yes," Steve said. "That's why they feel so real to you."

"I suppose," Ian said. Around them, the multiple variations of Ian's reality shuddered and blossomed anew, each one containing a different version of his fantasies: Penelope the champion rider of Cactusback Flats; Penelope as the hero, Deathpriest, of Atlantis City; Penelope the elven archer of Fharendale; Penelope the first mate on the Islas Encantadas; and on and on.

"What are you doing?" Steve asked as Ian's Infiniuum spun out of control, projecting a myriad of different worlds. In a huff, Steve used his blue hands to collapse the Infiniuum back into Ian's present reality of his bedroom. "Easy, man," Steve said. "Howard Hughes tried to outsmart the Infiniuum and look how that turned out for him. You can open your eyes now."

Ian opened his eyes, and the alternates were gone, only his bedroom back home remained. He touched his face, neck, and chest for any changes. He was all there. "So how does it work?" Ian asked. "Navigating?"

"The existence of the Infiniuum is based on the choices available to you. Imagine your life as a jagged, branching lightning bolt of choices. Take a left turn on Elm Street versus a right. Kiss the next-door neighbor girl or the boy. Skip class, or take an AP class. Every choice leads to a different outcome that compounds your future choices a multitude of times over. Imagine that lightning bolt breaking off into a trillion branches of choices over your lifespan. The number of branches is astronomical. It's a blinding, convoluted patchwork of lightning bolts, man. And that's just you. If you factor in all the people and the environment around you, it opens even more possibilities. But in all that mish-mosh of potential outcomes, your life—this one right now—only traces one path through that network. All those unused branches represent different possibilities in the universe. Possibilities that exist, but that you can't perceive because you didn't explore them. The Infiniuum is the chaos of them all existing together. Most sentient beings don't perceive, feel, or see them. But, with a little practice, we can."

"I don't know about this."

"Don't think about it too much," Steve said, walking over to Ian's closet door. "Remember, Penelope needs you, man. Or at least her alternates do." He held up a neon blue padded finger and traced a vertical blue line around the frame of the door. Then he dramatically flung the door open, revealing the blackness of the cosmos through the closet-shaped rectangle in Ian's reality. Quickly, Steve stepped in and disappeared.

Ian sat on the corner of his bed, reluctant to move toward the darkened shape, a sudden fear striking him about black holes sucking matter into suffocating oblivion. These hallucinations were the very reason he took that coat rack to the school windows. But he stood up and shuffled closer. Steve's head appeared from the void and said, "You couldn't possibly move any slower."

Ian gingerly stepped into the abyss and entered the cockpit of a starship. Somehow, the cabin looked familiar. A dashboard of seemingly useless levers and red buttons sprawled out before him, contained in a fabricated console that was obviously plastic trying its hardest to masquerade as steel. Even the lights adorning the navicomputer on the side walls appeared more 1970s than anything resembling the future. Even the hexagonally segmented windowpanes of the cockpit stumped him, so he guessed. "Is this the Aluminum Falcon?" Ian muttered, gently biting the tip of his index finger.

"What?!" Steve jumped into one of the two swiveling captain's chairs and said, "Millennium Falcon! It's a classic, man. It's a whole institution here. Fanboys made it such a big deal, a whole sector of the Infiniuum exploded in golden bikinis, corny dialogue, and light sabers."

"So we're flying there? To the place where this Penelope is?"

"No," Steve said. "Again, this is just a construct. It makes your mind think we're actually sitting in a starship with gravity and physics and all that. Organisms tied to physical realms, like yourself, tend to freak out when they're floating ambiently in the great abyss. They always think they're falling into infinity. I need to use your mind to find her. You have a deeper connection to your Penelope than I do.

So I need you to, uh, navigate." Steve swung around in his chair and adjusted the controls at his leisure, none of them doing anything functional at all.

Ian reached out and felt the navicomputer wall. It felt like hard-grade plastic. He jumped on the floor, and it felt stable, real.

"Amazing what the mind will believe when given the right cues," Steve added. "Sit down. The ship is yours. Time to learn to ride the lightning."

Ian sat down and flipped levers and buttons on the console. Just like he suspected, they didn't do a damn thing. Until a panel opened in front of him and a mechanical arm extended what looked like a cardboard cup with a red straw. He could smell an overpowering artificial fruity sweetness. Ian peered inside. "An Icee?" Ian asked. Hesitation spread across his face like a sweeping forest fire.

"Sure," Steve said. "Try it."

CHAPTER 9

THE SWEET CHERRY RUSH OF AN ICEE

Ian wrapped his lips around the straw and took a pull of the cherry Icee. The moment it hit his tongue, he fell into euphoria. The coolness of the ice. The sweetness of the syrup. Holy fructose nirvana. But as he swallowed the sweet treat, he felt a gravity within the drink tugging back at him. Before long, it grew in strength, pulling his insides toward the straw. Panic drowned him, and he broke the seal, pushing himself away from the sinister Icee. "That thing is going to kill me."

"No, it's not," Steve said. "Trust me. You don't want to see or understand this process. It's best you just close your eyes and enjoy it, kid." Steve spun Ian's chair closer to the drink held by the mechanical arm.

Ian exhaled. This was stupid. He had trusted Steve up to this point, so what purpose did it serve to disbelieve him now? He moved closer to the Icee and its foreboding red straw. He thought of Penelope instead. If the roles were reversed, he was sure she would suck that Icee down in order to save his life (or at least the residual alternates of himself). He wrapped his lips around the straw again.

This time, when the gravity settled in, he didn't resist it, even though it felt like it was turning him inside out and sucking his whole body back through the straw. A severe pressure drew in around his brain like a dying star, its gravity falling in upon itself, packing his body tighter and denser. When the pressure became so unbearable that he thought he would pop, he did. He couldn't explain it or comprehend it, but his physical body seemed to gently loosen itself and dissolve, atom by atom into the Infiniuum. He existed only as a small point of consciousness tugged towards a jagged blue ribbon of light, a dandelion seed on an unseen, unfelt wind, only to enter the torrent of a full-on rushing garden hose.

Upon entering the ribbon, the Infinium rushed in all its chaos like a television snapping through channels at break-neck speed. Each branch of choice showed him a different version of what his life may have been. Him playing little league baseball instead of watching movies. Him shoplifting and being arrested. Him growing up in an orphanage instead of with his parents. Him falling in love with the boy next door. Snippets of alternate lives interweaving and blossoming out to an infinity of stranger worlds. Him living with his parents on a Mars colony. A different life as a pickpocket in Victorian London. Another life as an insect-like fairy in a colorful forest. He recognized nothing. A splitting headache lunged through his head, though he couldn't exactly pinpoint if he even had a head anymore and, if he did, where it was. The shuddering frames of existence drew into a blur, where he could no longer differentiate between them. Ian felt tired and cross-eyed. Everything moved so fast, they appeared to flicker slowly, the infinity of choices blending into a larger mosaic. When he tried to focus, tried to keep his eyes open, he saw Penelope tied to the mast of the Wicked Crow. And when he trembled to realization, he broke contact and fell backwards, away from the pull of the Icee and onto the floor of the faux Millennium Falcon.

Steve leaned over him and gently slapped his cheeks. "You okay, man?"

Ian's eyes wobbled in their sockets, rolling white in palsy. He tried fixating on Steve's face. His headache faded as the happiness of seeing Penelope again filled his mind. "That was amazing!" Ian yelled.

"Pretty cool, isn't it?" Steve extended his hand and helped Ian back to his feet.

Ian coughed, producing faint gray smoke from his mouth. "That's…that's…"

"Kind of indescribable, huh?"

Ian stared past Steve, through him, like every destination he had ever wanted to travel to had been encompassed in one voyage. Numbly, Ian said, "Yeah."

Steve patted him on the head and cheeks, then checked his pulse. "No after-effects. No adverse reactions," Steve said. "I'll have to say your first attempt was a success. I mean, you didn't die. Your physical form took it rather well."

Ian batted away Steve's hands and said, "My head aches a bit, but I'm fine. I saw her, Steve. I saw Penelope."

"That's great, kid," Steve said. "We'll try again later."

"No way," Ian said, drifting over to the Icee. "I'm going back in." Ian leaned forward and was about to drink, but Steve slapped the control panel, causing the mechanical arm to retreat into the bowels of the console, taking the Icee with it.

"Easy, kid," he said. "You'll get back in there, trust me. But we have to be careful. I've lost too many interactants wanting to push the envelope. Take it slow and steady."

Ian folded his arms over his chest. "Slow and steady? You tell me someone may be hunting her down throughout the Infiniuum, and I'm supposed to take it easy?"

"Listen," Steve said, "I know you want to go back in, and you will, but rushing in and risking oblivion won't save her. Learn to navigate it, learn its turns and takes. Its nooks and crannies. If we're going to stop this, you'll need to be fluent in the Infiniuum and ride its gleaming edge to control it instead of letting it consume you. Take your time and do it right, Ian. For Penelope. I mean, for her alternate existences."

Ian slumped in his chair. Steve was probably right. As much as he wanted to get in there and save her, he also didn't know what he was doing. He thought about riding the lightning of infinite existences and how it made him want to let go of his own being and join it. He imagined letting go of everything he had known: his mother, his father, especially the weaselly-looking therapist. It was indeed a fine edge, and he had to keep his wits about him, or everything would be lost. "You're right," he told Steve.

Steve finally smiled at him. "Good. Then we're on the same page. We'll have another go at it soon."

Ian's parents insisted he join them for grocery shopping. They made him push the cart around the supermarket as they oohed and aahed over fragrant peaches, the unique softness of the bakery's pretzel rolls, or the incredible deals on Greek yogurt. On the way home, Ian sat in the backseat of his father's Yukon, wishing he was back in the faux Millennium Falcon with its mysterious Icee of the cosmos.

"We have a surprise in store for dinner," his mother said from the passenger seat. Her left arm extended over the console cubby between the front seats, holding his father's right hand.

"Okay," he said.

His parents had never held hands while driving before. His dad always drove with both hands on the wheel, had always insisted on it for safety and control of the vehicle. He often alternated a drum beat between his thumbs to some silent song playing in his head, usually "Free Falling" by Tom Petty. And his mom, she always fidgeted with the radio, the other settings on the console, or her phone. Ian looked closer at their hands. This wasn't a tender, loving grip. Their skin pulled a ghastly white at the knuckles, like they were clinging to each other.

"Is everything alright?" Ian asked.

"Fine," they both answered simultaneously.

But they were lying. They used the same tone when he probed them about his Christmas presents. Or when he caught them once on the living room couch giggling and pawing at each other. Yet something like a cottony, fibrous fog hung in the air around them, almost asphyxiating him. He had to cut through it and come up for air. "What day is it, Mom?"

She clenched Harold's hand harder and said, "It's Saturday, honey."

"Cool," Ian said. "It's the weekend."

Harold chuffed out a laugh and said, "Yeah, the weekend."

When they got home, Ian ran up to his room and collapsed on his bed. He hated the fact that he had worried his parents so much. But also, the malig was on his mind too, stalking the different worlds Penelope had ventured off to when she did something to upset the balance of the Infiniuum. His journal sat where he'd left it on the nightstand. He picked it up and felt its weight. A disheveled and plump thing, the book was almost rounded on the top and bottom covers from the additional pages of sketches and graph-paper maps folded and stuffed between pages.

Ian sat down on his bed, carefully removing the rubber bands and opening the book. The first thing to fall out was a folded piece of yellowed graph paper. Unfolding it, a rudimentary map appeared, hand-drawn in pencil with a flourishing banner at the top that said Cactusback Flats. In the center an old-time Western town had been penciled-in, showing each small building from Sully's general store to Flashing Sally's saloon to a post office.

Spreading out from the small town were other landmarks like 10 Humps Cemetery, showing the small gravel-strewn graves of the dead; Last Chance Mine complete with a skull-and-crossbones warning sign; and even Firesky Ranch, the home of the heartless cattle baron, Whiskey Joe Firesky. Ian perused the map carefully, running his thumb over Penelope's additions and laughing over the furious erasure of Lover's Lagoon, a wonderful pond with cattails bobbing in the gentle breeze.

He folded up the map and tucked it back into the journal. Then he carefully paged through different sections: the Islas Encantadas, festooned with blood-thirsty pirates and even Captain Noface himself; Taluride Station, the interstellar nexus of scum and villainy in the universe. He smiled at Fharendale, the lordly lands of King Nazeroth at constant battle with his arch-enemy Moliande, the wizard, and his pet dragon, Labyrinth. And then there was Schwarzwald, the eerie, monster-filled lands of the Blut Konigin, and even Atlantis City, home to the masked wonders Shadowstrike and the Deathpriest and their ongoing exploits against Redcrowne and his Brotherhood of Chaos. He had become so lost in all their crafted worlds, he hadn't even realized how many hours had passed.

"Dinner's ready, kiddo," sung his dad a floor below.

"Double cheese, double pepperoni," Ian muttered to himself. "Your favorite."

Seconds later, his mom chimed in below, unable to hold back the surprise. "We got double cheese and double pepperoni. Your favorite."

Downstairs, he ate three slices and drank a soda. His father nibbled at his tiny slice, then smiled broadly like he actually enjoyed his smaller portions, and then topped it off with an antacid and a salad. His mother never ate pizza, but she dove in and had a slice too. While he ate, his parents passed along platitudes about being glad that the worst was behind them. Ian nodded in the right places as he thought about his journal and all the great places he and Penelope had seen. What could she have possibly done to cause so much trouble?

Midway through his salad, Harold stopped, folded his hands above his plate and said, "Destruction of school property is a felony."

Ian broke out of his thoughts. "What does that mean?"

Maggie dabbed her mouth with her napkin and said, "Oh, Harold. Daniel said he could get it dismissed. At least down to a misdemeanor."

Ian poked around his slice of pizza and kept his eye on his plate, afraid to look his parents in the eyes. "Who's Daniel?"

Harold started in on his salad again. "Our lawyer, Ian."

Eager to keep Ian at ease, Maggie reached across and patted him on the shoulder. "Don't worry about it, Ian. Let us take care of that. You focus on getting back on track in school." She smiled, but Ian could tell it was more for show. His dad batted around a few leaves of Romaine lettuce on his plate, sighed, and put on the same smile his mother had. "Your mother's right. Let us worry about that."

For the remainder of dinner, Ian couldn't help BUT worry about it now. A felony? His thoughts rewound to the moment he bashed out the school windows, the glass sprinkling on the tile floor like spilled jewels. His frantic fighting with the guard. The screaming. The crying. What was he thinking? He remembered Steve's notecards. The rules. He should have just listened and none of this would have happened.

After dinner, he cleared the plates and started to go back upstairs, but his mother caught him. "Ah, ah, ah!" she said, pointing around to the dishwasher. He loaded the dishwasher and started it, then dashed back up to his room.

Once there, he planted himself on his bed and opened the journal again. He needed to clear his head of the mess he'd made. He continued paging through and looking at all the drawings and stories he and Penelope had created. The Deathfist landing a right cross to Redcrowne's jaw. The sleepover they had on Taluride Station during the xenozombie breakout. Even an almost disastrous battle with the dragon Labyrinth that left Ian with a wounded leg and being nursed by Penelope. He took his work to his desk and opened the journal to one of the few remaining pages and began writing.

CHAPTER 10

FRUITILICIOUS PANCAKES

Ian woke in the morning with a start. His journal lay scattered across his bed, rolled into his sheets and comforter. He wrapped his hand around the almost-empty soda can on the nightstand and downed the last dregs. His mouth was dry, and his head hurt. He really needed another soda, something cold and sweet to start the day. Something fruity.

An Icee.

A thought jerked through his mind like a hooked trout. The journal. The worlds. An Icee. He had an idea, and Steve was the only one he could share it with. Ian leapt out of bed and flung open his closet. "Steve!"

The closet was empty. Well, empty of Steve, but full of dirty clothes.

Icee. The Pump and Munch. That's where he could get one! He smelled his armpits. No BO—good to go. He blew his breath against his hand to smell and recoiled. Strong enough to kill a dragon. He grabbed a plastic canister of gum from the nightstand drawer and shook a few pieces in his mouth. He threw on a flannel shirt over his tee while chewing, bound up his journal, and dashed out of the room. He took the steps in rapid succession, making it sound like a giraffe falling down the stairs.

As he sprinted through the kitchen, his mother said, "I thought we could have pancakes this morning." She watched as he flew past the kitchen, out the front door, and to the driveway. "They're your favorite," she called.

Ian hopped on his black Schwinn and took off like the Flash himself. Pedaling through the streets of Alton, Ian mused on how he and Steve needed a better communication line, like a bat phone or something. The Pump and Munch was four miles away. He had it— the idea. They could start looking in all the worlds he and Penelope fantasized about. If what they were seeing were real worlds across the Infiniuum, then the chances were that she went to those places first. They could start there!

When he arrived at the gas station, numerous people bustled about, filling their tanks and grabbing their snacks. Ian dropped his bike near a picnic table off to the side, where the employees took their smoke breaks. He dashed to the doors and pushed his way in. Just past the beef jerky shelf and next to the donuts sat the Icee machine. Bingo. He walked to the checkout counter, where a beefy guy with acne and a sparse beard manned the register in his yellow Pump and Munch polo shirt.

Ian looked at him and asked, "Steve?"

"Sorry, bro," the man said, pointing to his nametag that read Seth.

Damn. He stepped through the aisles and found a skinny woman squatting down and restocking the candy bars.

"Uh," Ian said. "Are you Steve?"

She turned her head to him and said, "Do I look like a Steve?"

"No," he said.

Ian bumped his way through the gas station, asking every customer if they were Steve. All except one said no, but that one guy clearly wasn't *his* Steve, just *a* Steve.

In a panic, he walked into the employee back room next to the restrooms and called out Steve's name. He got no answer. But when he turned around, Seth stood behind him and said, "Listen, kid. You can't be back here. Employees only. You have to buy something, or I'm going to have to ask you to leave. You're upsetting the customers."

Ian's face grew red. He had done it again. Something crazy. What the hell was wrong with him?

Instead of answering Seth, Ian chose to run away. He burst through the door and bumped past all the customers on the way out. He even forgot his bike, but that was the last thing he was worried about. Running down the sidewalk home, he tried to tally it all in his mind. Perhaps he was wrong. Maybe there was no Steve, no Infiniuum, and no epic important mission to save the alternate existences of his dead girlfriend.

Even when he said it in his mind, it sounded crazy. Maybe these delusions were all just part of his grief or some mysterious illness.

He pumped his arms and legs as fast as he could down the street. Endorphins surged through his veins. Air rifled into his nose and mouth as he breathed. His lungs grew salty and exhausted.

He stopped at a nearby boulevard tree close to his neighborhood, catching his breath, when his mother's Dodge Caravan screeched to a halt before him, her pottery supplies shifting noisily in the back cargo area. "Ian Ralph Waldo Emerson Wilder!" his mom shouted through the open window.

Ian groaned, still gasping for breath. Great. All three middle names. That was never good. He approached the vehicle, sheepishly.

"I understand you are going through something I can never fully understand, but running out like that? You had me worried sick!" his mother yelled from the driver's side.

"I know. I'm sorry," Ian called. "I don't know what's wrong with me." He thought about the school windows. Steve's notecards. The lawyer named Daniel. He needed to keep his cool. Deep breaths. Calm. Once he had collected himself, he asked, "You still have those pancakes?"

His mom didn't answer, but the distinct clack of the car's power locks opening was all he needed. Head down, he climbed into the passenger seat and buckled his seatbelt. Only after a moment did Ian realize that his mom hadn't put the car in gear to drive. She sat, tears dribbling down her face, her shoulders gently heaving.

He'd made his mom cry. The penultimate of sonly sins.

Sure, he had embarrassed her before, spray painting the Palecki girls down the block came to mind, and he had, on more than one occasion, made his mother angry. And he knew he'd disappointed his mom, made her sad, maybe even to the point of shedding tears. But not once had he ever witnessed a breakdown like this before. It made his gut ache in a way he'd never felt before. What a terrible son he was. He briefly imagined a world where mothers never cried because their sons and daughters did everything right and made them proud. Too bad his mother would never be able to visit that place.

"I'm sorry, Mom. I am better," he told her. "I'm fine, really."

After a deep, shuddery breath and a quick wipe of her eyes, she silently put the Dodge Caravan in gear and began the drive home. "Yes," she said. "There are still pancakes."

"Good," Ian said, patting his stomach, trying his best to fake his hunger. "I'm starving."

"Dr. Caulderon said you can go back to school tomorrow," Ian's mom said as she turned on their street. "But, due to the windows and police, you'll have mandatory weekly sessions with him after school. To start with, at least. Then we'll see what Daniel can do for you."

Ian thought about Dr. Caulderon. He couldn't wait to express his feelings about Penelope's death with that crackpot. But it could have been a lot worse, he figured. "Whatever it takes to get better, Mom." Ian tried his best to forge the most authentic smile he could muster.

Ian sat at the kitchen table while his mom poured pancake batter on the griddle. She too used her best show smile. When finished, she brought him a huge stack of cakes with a carousel of syrups. Like ten of them. "I know you like combinations of flavors, so I got a bunch of different kinds."

Ian lifted one of the syrup bottles from the cradle and read the label. "Chokecherry." He set it down and picked up another. "Loganberry." Another. "Orange Marmalade." Another. "Gooseberry. I didn't even know that was a berry."

"It's very popular in Sweden," his mother added.

Amid his fascination with the syrups, a baleful desperation unfolded on his mother's face. He had the distinct feeling her emotions hinged on his actions or reactions to these crazy syrups. He tried to imagine the pain she felt at that moment, knowing her son, her only child, teetered on the wobbly edge of madness. Steve's words came to mind: how he said all realities, every millisecond of them, were vast combinations of decisions and choices that branched off each other to infinity. How it was impossibly hard to ride the bolt of lightning and predict where and when a new vein would branch off. At that moment, with his mom's emotions balanced like a house of cards, he predicted where this reality would branch off.

Ian picked up two random syrups and drizzled them over his pancakes. Then he set those down and grabbed two others and repeated the process. Then again, until a real smile broke out on his mother's face. She began laughing. Just a chuckle at first, but then so hard he thought he heard a snort. Smiling at her reaction, he cut into his vibrant pancakes and wolfed down the first bite. "Very berr-ery," he said.

Still chuckling, his mother sat down next to him and squeezed his hand. "I suppose I went a bit overboard with the syrups."

"Naw," Ian said. "Sometimes you have to push the envelope."

She grabbed a fork and cut a piece for herself and swallowed it. Covering her mouth, she said, "God. That's nasty. You don't have to eat them if you don't want."

"I do," he said. And despite the garbled sweetness, he ate the whole stack. As he put his plate in the sink, he remembered: his bike. "Aw, crap. I left my bike...at the gas station."

"Your dad can take you to get it when he gets back from coffee with Daniel."

"So what exactly happened today?" Ian's father asked him, his eyes focused on the road. They were on their way to pick up Ian's bike at the gas station. "Your mom got all panicky again, but I figured you just had to clear your head. What's up?"

Ian sat in the passenger seat, his fruitilicious pancakes tossing in his stomach like a flock of drunken moths. "I kind of had a panic attack, I think."

"I see," his father said. "And this panic attack had something to do with the Pump and Munch?"

"I thought an Icee would take the edge off."

"And do you feel better now?"

Ian thought about the rules on Steve's notecards, his mother's emotional reaction, and the pancake confetti churning in his belly. "Yes. Loads better."

"Good," his father said. He paused a few strategic moments. "Who is Steve? Your mom said she heard you call for a Steve before you burst out of the house. Is he a classmate of yours? A friend?"

Ian felt an overwhelming desire to blurt out the truth, that Steve was either A) An interdimensional mentor come to guide him on a mission of infinite, universal importance, or B) A complete construct of his addled mind bent on helping him cope with Penelope's death. But neither answer would help him deal with his parents. "He's a classmate," Ian lied. "I don't even know why I mentioned him. We were friends in the third grade, but then drifted apart."

"Interesting," his father said, pulling into the gas station parking lot. "Perhaps you should reconnect with this Steve. Maybe he could be a friend to you now." His dad gave him a quick glance.

"Okay," Ian said. If his dad only knew.

Ian's father parked the Yukon in front of the gas station next to the car wash exit. "Go get your bike. We need to get home and rake the yard."

Ian forced a smile and got out of the truck. His bike lay on the other side of the gas station, closer to the bike path. On his way to the back of the building, he thought about the day. He found it increasingly difficult to hold together this reality, let alone attempt to travel to another. He wondered if this is what it meant to get older, keeping everyone at arm's length and lying to them to save their sanity. Because if this was what adulthood was like, it sucked.

Behind the gas station, he found his bike stashed where he'd left it by the smoker's table. Ian stood it up and was about to hop on it when Steve burst through the back door, wearing a yellow Pump and Munch polo shirt and khakis. "You're finally up."

Steve's name tag read 'Greg.'

"What are you trying to do to me?" Ian asked.

Steve faked an innocent look. "What?"

"Do you possess these people's bodies?" Ian asked. "Or are you some kind of shape-shifting freak?"

"Shape-shifting freak? Really? Ouch," Steve said. "I'm a polymorphic organism. I can blend. At a genetic level."

"Who is Greg then?" Ian asked.

"He's a Pump and Munch facility auditor. To them, I look like Greg, but to you, I look like my same beautiful self. I just have to borrow their clothes," Steve said, his brows knitted together in a frown. "You humans will believe anything. You really need to open yourself to these types of possibilities if you're ever going to help me figure out what Penelope was up to, pal. The shit you're going to see in the Infiniuum will peel your eyelids back, man."

Ian rolled his eyes. "Fine. But can we keep the crazy from the sane?"

"The what?"

"We need a schedule. To help me keep everything straight," Ian said, pointing to his head. "In here."

"Fine," Steve replied. "We'll do our work at night, or at least when your world is asleep. Just know, though, that this is so pointless.

The reality stitch manifold between alternate realities makes space-time irrelevant. But you'd have no idea about that would you?"

"Probably not. But it will help me," Ian said, folding his arms across his chest. "And if I remember correctly, you came looking for my help, right?"

Steve sighed. "Yes."

"Good. Then let's try again tonight."

CHAPTER 11

WELCOME TO THE ISLAS ENCANTADAS

After raking the lawn with his father and faking his way through dinner, Ian lay on his bed and waited until he heard his parents snoring far down the hall. The stoic red numbers of his alarm clock read 11:17 PM. Around him lay the contents of his journal: drafted character studies; stories written out in long-hand, the handwriting so fast and furious it was barely legible; and the landscapes sketched in charcoal and colored pencils. Penelope was the artist of the two; Ian couldn't even manage stick people. So he tried his best with words. He held up a drawing Penelope had rendered of Moliande, the wizard, who looked like a scarecrow marionette wrapped in brown and purple robes. His pet dragon curled around him, its wings unfurled and jets of black fire blazing out of its nostrils.

It made more sense now. When she wasn't scribbling out landscapes, buildings, and flora, Penelope painted the people, creatures, and settings she saw in her head. If what Steve had said was true, and she was a traveler, she didn't just look into the windows of their other worlds, she was able to bridge that gap and venture into them.

Ian remembered seeing Penelope at her funeral and how jarring it had been. He had a hard time seeing just one smidgeon of an alternate reality. He couldn't imagine the mental strain that came with trying to keep multiple levels separated, or even stepping into them. The pressure of processing that type of vision and differentiating it from her existence, her own reality, had to be tremendous. No wonder she had been such an emotional rollercoaster. Had her whole life been what his last few days had been like? Ian shuddered to think about it. He was already yearning to go back to being an ignorant teenager only worried about his next burrito fix.

He picked up a new drawing, one showing the two of them riding Appaloosas through the Broken Maw Valley outside of Cactusback Flats. If Penelope could bridge realities, perhaps that was why she couldn't escape the Smudge World? Did she find that soulless place by accident? And if so, did she try to go there? What else could she do? A shiver tickled down the ladder of his ribs like an electric eel. Did she manifest the Smudge World into being simply through her imagination? Was that even possible? He couldn't think about it anymore. He didn't want to. Penelope never could have done that, and if she had, she hadn't realized what she was doing.

A neon blue line traced itself vertically down the separation between his two closet doors. Finally, Ian thought, getting up and popping the tab to a fresh can of soda.

At his closet, he slid open one of the doors to reveal Steve leaning back in the co-pilot's chair to the faux Millennium Falcon, this time, wearing Ian's robe and eating Cheez-Its. Steve eyed the can of soda and said, "That crap'll rot your guts out."

Ian backed into the cockpit and slid the door shut, erasing his reality behind it. "Says the guy eating cheese crackers."

Steve waved his hand up and down his body and said, "Construct, kid. My polymorphism makes things easier for you to comprehend. You wouldn't want to see what I normally eat. Remember amoebas in biology? Well, imagine it a million times larger and with more pus-like cytoplasm."

Ian made a face before slumping down into his chair with a harrumph and a sigh.

"What's eating you, man?"

"What can a traveler do?" Ian asked. "You dodged it before. Now I want to know. What the hell was going on with Penelope?"

Steve stopped mid-munch and set the box of crackers aside, his face reluctant. "I didn't want you to worry, kid. You have a lot to learn and absorb. Some things are best left for later."

"I'm not going with you until you tell me."

"Um…you're already with me," Steve replied.

Ian got up and walked to the faux entrance of the ship as if to leave. He turned around, arms crossed over his chest, waiting expectantly.

Steve expelled an air of exhaustion from his mouth. "Fine. Your friend was a glitch."

"What?"

"Travelers. They're anomalies, glitches in the Infiniuum. In the natural order of things, sensitivity to the Infiniuum is scattered, diluted amongst organisms in variant, but low degrees. But occasionally an anomaly occurs with a concentrated sensitivity."

"What the hell does that mean?"

"Over time, the anomaly figures out this sensitivity. Mildly at first. But most often, organisms with concentrated sensitivity don't know how to respond. Most can't comprehend and simply fall into insanity. This time, well, Penelope learned much sooner and faster than usual. Normally, these anomalies don't do much. They step into one, maybe two worlds, and then they paint pictures of melting clocks or work out the equations for noncooperative equilibria after chatting up chicks in a bar. But Penelope, she did more than that."

"It sounds like she knew what she was doing," Ian said.

Steve rubbed his whiskered chin. "Yes. Amazingly so. I mean, we were monitoring her, but then things went crazy, man. Across thousands of realities. This wasn't typical anomaly stuff. This was like full-on malig- and feron-level ability. By the time we could triangulate where she was going next…" Steve paused.

"The malig found her first," Ian said.

Steve shook his head and patted Ian's shoulder. "I'm real sorry, kid. We really tried to get to her first."

Ian thought about Penelope and his theory that perhaps she traveled to the Smudge World, or even created it, but he kept it to himself. From how she described it to him, he didn't want to believe she'd go there, let alone create something like that. It was impossible. No. She'd go somewhere else. "I forgot to tell you something at the gas station," Ian said. "I think I might have figured it out."

"You have, huh?"

Ian took a swig of soda and twirled himself around in the chair. "Finding this…" he paused in thought, trying to remember whatever it was they were after.

"Malig," Steve finished.

"Right. This malig is like looking for a needle in haystack, right? Shouldn't we be focusing on the realities Penelope and I spent the most time in? I mean, sure we looked in on hundreds of worlds, but we really only hung around a handful of the cool ones, you know. Wouldn't those worlds hold more of her energy or something? A greater fingerprint of her?"

Steve grabbed his box of crackers off the dashboard and leaned back in the chair. "I see what you're cooking, man."

"Then why don't we go there?"

Steve leaned towards Ian, his face serious. "I've seen those worlds, kid. Okay, I haven't seen yours specifically, but others. They're not exactly as tame as you think. They're dangerous. Extremely. And as urgent as this is, we can't rush into it. You're not ready."

Ian felt a flame of anger ignite in his neck. "Not ready? I've spent more time there than you."

Steve shook his head. "Drop the hero routine, pal. That's not what I meant. The worlds you two played pretend in were just that.

Pretend. A look into a real world in a reality far, far away. You never actually stepped into them."

Ian looked confused, befuddled.

"Yeah, I know it looked and felt real. Your friend Penelope was really good at painting the pictures, that's for sure," Steve said. "But you were never actually in those worlds, interacting with the organisms and environment. Yes, a version of you actually does reside there, but that person isn't you exactly. They're just an alternate. Like a clone only with a different personality, life, feelings, memories, etc. You'd find upon a real visit that these worlds you so easily played in are actually life-threatening and very, very frightening."

Ian waved it off.

Upset, Steve said, "No, no. Don't wave it off. If we go to any one of those worlds, Ian, and you aren't prepared for what it truly is, you can kiss this little party goodbye."

"What do you mean?!"

"If you drop us into a different reality," Steve said. "And there are zombies and they eat you, you're dead. Game over, man."

Ian took another drink of soda and shrugged his shoulders. "So don't tussle with Whiskey Joe Firesky."

"Especially him," Steve said.

"Fine," Ian said, returning to his chair. He kicked his feet up on the console and tossed his now-empty soda can behind them. "We start small."

Steve watched Ian's actions with disdain. He pushed Ian's feet off the console. "Does your mother approve of this behavior?"

Ian ran his hands up and down the multi-buttoned console, pushing buttons and toggling levers, proving nothing worked and it was all just a fake anyway. "Construct, remember?" Ian said in a sing-song way, mimicking Steve's high voice.

Steve ignored him. "Start small," he said, rubbing the sparse whiskers on his chin. "Like on the outskirts and work our way in."

Ian spread his arms out in approval. "Exactly. How much trouble could that be?"

Steve squinted his left eye, gauging whether it was the right move. "Famous last words, buddy." Steve gave Ian a searching look, then said, "Fine. Outskirts only. We're just getting our feet wet, okay?"

Ian pumped his fist in victory.

"Don't get too excited," Steve said. "This is just a way to get you to respect the true nature of the Infiniuum and its inhabitants."

Ian rubbed his hands together and said, "Alright, let's blow this joint."

"Really? That's the best you can do?" Steve slumped in his chair and flipped the lever that activated the Icee mechanism. Ian leaned forward and sucked in the cold fructose rush that gave him access to the Infiniuum. Soon his gravity reversed and sucked him through the straw and into the streaming cosmic torrents.

This time, Ian knew where he wanted to go: The Islas Encantadas. In his transitive state, he couldn't feel his body. No arms. No legs. Just a consciousness adrift in the circuitry of the universe. Automatically, his memories and emotions guided him, snapping off choices and turns in a frenetic flutter. Speeding through the Infiniuum, he thought about Penelope and Captain Noface and the Neverblade. Scenes of their adventures spun through his mind: the flash of cutlasses, the quest for the spyglass, and the ghosts of Banshee Bay. And even though he didn't know how it could be possible, he tasted the briefest moment of briny air against the back of his throat and the curdled eddies of seafoam collecting in tide pools.

At that point of sensual clarity, he felt the rush of the ground coming up fast to meet him. With what he could only imagine as a flash of lightning and the crash of thunder, Ian hit the ground hard with a thump. Pain chewed through his shoulder as he rolled across long, green grasses coated in dew. After the shroud of ozone lifted, Ian lay on his belly and took a deep breath. A cool, damp wind blew overhead, and the wet, grass-matted soil pressed against his face. His nose sensed a rogue fire nearby burning driftwood.

Steve and Ian stood up and rotated in place. The night was clear. A wide, full moon hung in the darkened sky. Ian paused at it. Almost double the size of the moon back home, it cast more light across the island, and the bay reflected its face for miles. They stood atop a large bluff on one of the isles. The dark splotches of other islands lay scattered throughout the ocean around them. Below the bluff, a town dimly lit by whale-oil lamps wavered in the night.

Steve broke his dreamy silence. "Good call, kid. You brought us down at night."

"Of course," Ian said, unsure of exactly what he had done. "Totally the perfect spot." Ian looked to the night skies of the Islas Encantadas. Above, in the reddish murk of a far-off nebula, a star steadily twinkled millions of light years away. Ian couldn't place his knowing of it, but he felt an incredible and sudden distance within himself—like a part of him was left behind and longed to connect back up with him.

Seeing Ian struggling against the twinkling light, Steve said, "The first time is always toughest. Interactants feel a heavy detachment from their reality. Like death or an impending dread of never seeing your family or your old life again."

Ian stood up slowly and rubbed his head. "It feels like fishing line is tied to the small of my back and extends all the way home," he said. "It tugs at me with every movement."

Steve wrapped his arm around Ian's shoulder. "Tetherline syndrome. Under circumstances of isolation, the mind builds a tether to keep the individual grounded. It's a simple mental construct that occasionally exhibits very physical feelings." Ian moved away from Steve's arm and reached a hand to the small of his back. "It's psychosomatic, kid," Steve said. "You'll get used to it. More importantly, we should find some clothes to try to blend in."

Blend in? Ian hadn't realized it since they landed, but Steve still wore his old robe and Ian his hoodie and jeans. "So everywhere we go, we have to lift a disguise?" Ian asked. "Can't you just draw a line into a reality with pirate clothes and grab some for us?"

"Is this a joke to you?" Steve asked. "This isn't some genie's lamp or magic bag that holds every wish and answer. Do you know how much energy it takes to stitch the seams of realities like this? I'm frickin' exhausted. Travelers don't just bebop in and out willy-nilly. Ferons and maligs, our physiology is eternally linked to the dimensional energies binding the Infiniuum together. There are no technological gizmos or magic spells that help us do all this. We're part of the living, pulsating plasma of everything. When you take, you must equally give."

"Sorry," Ian said.

Steve shook his head and mumbled. "Like I would be wasting my time here, if I could just open a seam and—oh-look-at-that, the answer to everything."

"I suppose that makes sense," Ian said. "Sorry."

"I think we should start there," Steve said and pointed to the flickering lamps of port just below the bluff. "We'll stay out of the town. Maybe find a home on the outskirts to swipe some clothes from. Let's go."

They found a worn path in the grasses down the hill. Ahead of them, lightning bugs zigged and zagged over the path. In the bay at the base of the hill, a large brigantine swayed on its mooring in the bay, the moonlight making its canvas mainsails blue. Three longboats oared into the harbor, their lamps swinging to the haul of each wave. Halfway down the hill, a wayward goat traipsed up to them, its bell clanking a low, hollow rattle. With each step, Ian grew more confident. Honestly, he wasn't sure what Steve was worried about. This world seemed just as he and Penelope had experienced it. It wasn't frightening and deadly. He watched the very ordinary goat as it approached them. It was just a silly goat. Make way for the terrifying goat, he laughed to himself.

Just outside of the town a quiet cottage stood among a small grove of orange trees in the moonlight. They crept to the back window and peered inside. Embers crackled in the hearth, and gentle snoring droned from the bedroom. They ducked down and Steve said, "Go in there and swipe some clothes."

"Why me?" Ian asked.

"Why not?" Steve said. "You got us here. You know the terrain better than I do, right?"

Ian huffed, then opened the back door and snuck inside. He passed through a one-room kitchen and dining room and stepped into one of the bedrooms. But a child lay sleeping in the bed, so he quietly slipped into the room adjacent to it and found a man and wife snoring in bed. He slid a drawer from the dresser along the wall to find it stocked with pants and shirts. But after he had his arms full, he heard voices out in front of the cottage and smelled the tang of whale oil lamps burning. So, Ian did the first thing that came to mind: he ran.

When Ian burst out the back door to the sound of yelling and musket fire, he slammed straight into Steve, carrying an armful of freshly picked oranges. Both of them fell to the ground amidst a flurry of spilled clothes and oranges. They scrambled to get up. The torches and voices within the cottage stormed their way.

Ian got to his knees and scampered to collect the clothes.

Steve did the same with the oranges.

"What are you doing?!" Ian asked.

"I was starving," Steve said.

An odd metal, knuckle-cracking sound came from behind them. When they lifted their heads, pistolas, and muskets pointed at them from all directions as a troupe of pirates stood before them.

"Aye," said a voice from the pirates. "We was robbin' that cottage!"

CHAPTER 12

ON THE DECKS OF
THE LEAPING LIZARD

Steve immediately held up his arms and nodded at Ian to do the same.

"What the hell, Steve?" Ian said. "Do something!"

"What would you have me do?" Steve asked.

"Unleash your Infiniuum powers!"

Steve shook his head. "You still don't get it, do you?"

The scallywags dressed in filthy pantaloons, faded linen shirts, salt-encrusted bandannas, and weathered hats of all kinds. The largest of them sported a wide, fat belly that stretched the boundaries of his blue and white striped shirt underneath his tattered long coat. He stepped forward and said, "Enough of this scatter-talk, you two. Empty your purses!"

"We don't have purses," Ian blurted. The guns frightened him. Their muzzles like dark eyes staring him down. He had the sudden urge to pee. His heartbeat slogged in his chest, and his muscles buckled and quaked. He needed the Ian from his fantasies right now, the cutlass-slashing, swinging-from-a-rope hero Ian—the one who could jump into a fray at any moment. He did the only thing he could think of: he reached for his wallet. An old pirate stepped forth and knocked it out of his hand.

"Gold," the fat one said. "Give us your gold."

The old pirate, skinny with a round eye patch and a purple bandanna fit loosely to his head, picked up Ian's wallet and picked through it, pulling out old movie stubs, receipts, an iTunes gift card, and a couple of ones. "Nothin' here," the old one said. "Just kill 'em."

"Aye!" the crew exclaimed.

Ian and Steve looked at each other. The knot in Ian's throat made it hard for him to swallow, to breathe. Around them, the cagey eyes of the misfit pirates darted from sun-dried, dirty faces. Even their wild beards and greased mustaches looked alive. The fat pirate paused. "No, we'll bring 'em aboard the Leaping Lizard and let Cap'n Longbottoms decide. He might want a couple lubbers to ease our workload, aye?"

"Or a ransom," the old pirate offered. "The skinny one looks to come from money."

"A ransom it is," the fat pirate announced. "Glad I thought of it."

"Aye!" the pirates chanted in unison, except for the old pirate who gave the fat one the stink eye for stealing his idea.

With cold irons clamped to their wrists and ankles, Steve and Ian were pushed down the path and goaded by a dozen rum-soaked voices. Before long, they reached the outskirts of the small town of Port Paveo. As much as Ian feared being captive to this rag-tag group, his curiosity got the best of him, and he was eager to see the pirate town. But much to his surprise, it was largely quiet. No rapscallion pirate songs sung to the clanking of rum bottles and no shoot-outs. No rioting good times or laughter. When they did pass the tavern, a faint tinkling of a piano murmured out of the door. A shout ushered forth with a cadence of low laughter. Nothing about the town seemed very piratey at all to Ian. The bakery sat quiet and dark. Same with the blacksmith and the stables. Even the garrison looked oddly dark and asleep. At the edge of town, a palatial home complete with a bell tower loomed from a stand of palm trees. What a bust.

Moments later, they arrived at the docks. Six different ships rocked in port. A beaten-up frigate had a beautiful mermaid for a figurehead. It looked so real, he thought it watched them as they passed. Another had an eagle with its wings outstretched. Another, a shooting star. The very last ship had a giraffe's neck carved into its bow. The crew dragged them aboard that ship and threw them onto the freshly scrubbed deck.

Steve and Ian kept their eyes to the floor as they knelt and waited to hear the death-knell footsteps of a captain's polished leather boots. But they heard no booted footfalls on the wooden deck. Instead, a pair of bare feet padded their way into view. When they looked up, a dark-skinned man over seven feet tall stood before them, wearing only an old scimitar and a loincloth across his hips. From their vantage point, two-thirds of the man's height seemed to be his legs.

"I told you to cut a few purses," he said, his voice elegant and educated. "Not bring more mouths to feed."

With a wave of the captain's hand, a great winged creature swooped down and landed in the rigging behind him. Ian ducked in fright, recovering once the raptor settled in next to the captain. Longbottoms turned to stroke the smooth pink head of the condor. It darted its head at Ian and let out an awful shriek.

"We figured you could work 'em, above and below decks. Ease our burden, my lord?" said the fat pirate.

"Or ransom them for a small fortune," the old one piped in, proudly making his voice heard.

The captain rubbed the neck of the bird, then folded his arms across his chest. "And which of you gives up your rations and rum for these dregs?" The lot of them grumbled, but no one stepped forward. "And ransom? The skinny one looks like a manservant and the other one," the captain paused, looking over Ian, his t-shirt, hoodie, jeans, and sneakers far too strange for the captain. "I know not which land he comes from, but I assure you his attire does not suggest a station worth ransom. Slit their throats and let Abigail here feast on their eyes." In a fury, the condor shrieked, flapping her wings in a fervor and taking to the air.

The pirates brought Steve and Ian to the bulwark, their rusty daggers held fast to their prisoners' throats. Only the captain stopped them from completing the deed. "Wait!" he called out. With his large hand, he reached out and grabbed Ian's chin, jerking it upwards to examine his face more closely. "You look…familiar," he said, then poked at Ian's arms and belly. "A bit bony and thin, but I know those eyes."

The captain turned Ian around and showed him off to his men. "The last time I saw this one he sailed the Outlander through the Rackham Straits, bore the Neverblade, and threw Captain Noface off Hagshead Peak." The crew stepped back, gasping and spitting to the deck. The captain himself spat at the feet of Ian, then continued. "But that was a long time ago. Since then, I heard he is no more than a paper skeleton in the private brig of Noface, a wraith of his former self, chained and stricken to serve him until the end of time."

"Gentlemen," the captain asked, "How in this god-forsaken, water-logged world did you manage to capture Captain Ian Wilder?"

Of all the sloops, brigantines, and galleys afloat in the port, Ian figured the Leaping Lizard was the ship in most need of a good cleaning. Locked below deck in the brig with Steve, Ian rubbed his nose every three seconds from the rank mold and mildew stink. Besides that, when the crew hauled them in, his calf snagged a rusted metal burr on the door. He hoped his tetanus shots were up to date. He was also pretty sure he saw maggots crawling over a salted beef shank in the barrels on the other side of the deck. He definitely wasn't ordering the hamburger from the menu. "So you can't get us out of here on principle?" Ian asked Steve.

Steve slumped against the bars of the brig, his arms threaded through the spaces between them. He leaned his face against the cool metal. "I cannot," Steve said, his voice drowning in physical exhaustion and the weariness of having to explain something repeatedly to a teenager. "Base organisms have issues grasping and even perceiving the quantum mechanics of the Infiniuum. Ferons are bound not to openly display this to base life forms for fear of upsetting the natural balance of their existence." Steve crouched on the greasy wood of the brig floor and wiped his face with the robe. "And also, I'm going to pass out. You can't stitch realities without energy, kid. And I'm all tapped out. Why couldn't I keep the oranges?"

Ian shivered. "Fine, whatever. Just wait until the guard falls asleep and get us out of here."

"I can't."

"What do you mean? If no one's looking, you're not affecting their existence, right?"

Steve looked up at Ian from his brooding place. "I mean I can, it just wouldn't change anything." Ian's face was pure confusion. "Once you've stitched the realities, we can only travel back to the exact coordinates we left, including time. It's a continuum protection protocol." Ian wasn't getting it. "We can't just pop in and out. It disturbs the stability of each reality. Eventually destroys it."

"So when we're here we have to get out of our own situations."

"Yes," Steve said, slumping against the bars. "I was trying to tell you this earlier. Ferons use interactants by permission to create the stitch. Maligs do it by force. I can bring us home, but when we come back, we come back here," Steve said, pointing to the ground for emphasis, "to this point and time in the reality. So we need to figure a way out ourselves."

Ian froze at Steve's answer. Had he thought Steve existed as his own personal genie? Even though he had come to trust Steve like a funny-looking older brother, there was obviously much more he needed to understand about his feron counterpart and his limitations in the Infiniuum. It made sense. Steve was locked up with him. If he had anything up his sleeve, he would have used it by now. Ian's shoulders slouched. It had been almost 24 hours without a scratch of food or water, and he would have killed for a soda or some leftover pizza. Ian shook his head. 'Think!' he demanded of himself. But he couldn't. He longed for the quick wits and daring demeanor that the Ian of this fantasy world had; it would come in handy.

"And on that note, I'm guessing you're a cornucopia of escape ideas," Steve muttered.

"I don't think well under pressure," Ian said. "I'm not like the characters I play."

"Great," Steve said, rolling his eyes. "Unhelpful and whiny."

"I just need some time to think!"

Steve turned his head slowly to Ian. "Well, luckily for you you're going to have a lot of that on your hands, kid."

"You're not helping!" Ian huffed.

Clambering footsteps cascaded on the decking above them and down the stairs onto their level.

Holding a lit oil lamp, the wide, fat-bellied pirate who had held them up approached. "You boys need to eat with the cap'n," he said. "He needs a wee talk with you." While the rotund man fiddled with the key in the brig door, Steve and Ian backed away. The pirate's breath reeked of sour liquor and rot.

Ian took the moment to nudge Steve. "See. Food."

"You sure are a miracle worker, kid," Steve mumbled.

Brandishing his pistola, the fat pirate swung open the rusted door with a high-pitched groan from its hinges. Ian and Steve shuffled out ahead and let the pirate close the brig. Together they struggled their way up the steps and above deck to the captain's cabin. At the door, the fat pirate with the striped shirt smoothed out his stained long coat, knocked on the door and said as gentlemanly as could be, "Your guests have arrived, my captain."

A faded voice from within said, "Enter."

The fat pirate opened the door and ushered the prisoners into the cabin, where he unlocked their wrist manacles and released them into the cabin. Captain Longbottoms waved away the pirate saying, "Dunlop, leave us. I'm sure you have other duties that need attending."

"Aye, Captain." The pirate turned on his heel and left, closing the door behind him.

Dumbfounded, Steve and Ian stared at the large table before them. Decked out in piratey opulence, the meal had three meat courses: a roasted piglet, a turkey with crispy brown skin, and a sea turtle, blackened and toasted in its shell. Among the other courses, Ian eyed up a covered basket of what was likely bread, a bowl of caramelized yams, a silver dish of golden-roasted potatoes, a crock of glistening peas and carrots, a pile of charred Brussels sprouts, and at the end of the table, a large, steaming, fresh-from-somewhere apple pie. The heavenly smells of roasted meat, fresh-baked bread, buttery vegetables, and sweet cinnamon and cloves made Ian woozy with joy.

"Come, sit." The captain gestured to the table. "You must be hungry, and I'd be a poor captain to let my prisoners starve to death—"

Without hesitating, Ian and Steve tore into the food—Ian dashing for those caramelized yams first and Steve, oddly, going straight for the blackened turtle. Neither of them waited to sit. They immediately dolloped their plates full and began shoveling in their feast as they took their seats.

"—before I had the chance to kill them myself," the captain finished. With a wide smile, he swirled his pewter goblet of wine.

Steve and Ian stopped mid-chew and looked at the captain for a moment. Steve shrugged, and they both continued eating. If it was their last meal, so be it. As they devoured every morsel on their plates and went back in for more, Captain Longbottoms, still dressed in just his simple loincloth, sipped his wine and picked at his food. "Tell me about him."

Steve and Ian paused in their gluttony and exchanged glances, looking each other up and then down. Both looked at the captain with quizzical looks.

"Noface!" he said. "His weaknesses! His ship! His crew! His fleet! Give me every little detail I can use to end his reign of terror."

Ian popped a yam into his mouth, chewed, and swallowed uncomfortably. "Uh, he likes to monologue."

Longbottoms crumpled his brow. "Monologue?"

Ian sopped up caramelized yam sauce with a tuft of buttered bread. "Yeah. Monologuing. You know, when he knows he has the upper hand, he likes to relish the moment by talking nonstop about what he plans to do with you and how painful it will be."

The captain ruminated on the info. "I have never heard this of him before."

Ian nodded. He felt more confident as he scooped a large piece of pie onto his plate. "He also likes planning overly complicated death sequences and then doesn't bother to watch them play out. I think deep down he's kind of squeamish. He once tied me to an anchor and dumped me in the ocean rather than slit my throat."

The captain stood up suddenly and slammed his palm on the table. "He slit my first mate's throat! My brother! And he did none of this monologuing while doing it!"

Ian dropped his spoon in surprise and looked at the angry captain, suddenly aware that his assessment of Noface was no longer trusted. He had to think! Think, dammit! Think! But the only thing that came to mind was Noface's bouts of seasickness. "Due to a cursed disease, he gets seasick quite a bit?" Ian offered, more question than statement.

Captain Longbottoms looked Ian square in the eyes. His dark face bore two scars. One ran horizontally under his left eye and across the bridge of his nose. The second, much smaller, cut vertically down the cleft of his chin. Ian couldn't tell if the captain was going to spit at him or chew his face off.

Suddenly, the captain broke into laughter. "Seasick?" he asked. "The most feared pirate in all the seas gets seasick?" His laugh degenerated to a raspy cackle. "Seasick. You have a humor about you, boy, but still, if you have no worth to me, I need to kill you. My Abigail is hungry."

Ian fumbled for ideas, words, anything. He scanned the room for escape points. He examined the table for a knife or any other sharp object, but there were none. Just the dull, round spoons they were given to eat with. Ian briefly imagined a duel playing out between him and Longbottoms—the captain with his scimitar and Ian, a spoon. It would have been knee-slappingly comical if it had been happening to someone else.

Steve cleared his throat and said one word: "Penelope."

CHAPTER 13

A PIRATE'S GAMBIT

The captain squinted at them. Ian shot a hard elbow into Steve's side. "Penelope?" the captain muttered. "What is a Penelope, and why is it of any importance to me?"

"Penelope's not a thing. She's a young woman," Steve said, simply. "And you need her."

The captain got up and paced about the cabin, his head barely clearing the cabin's ceiling. At every turn on his heel, he looked at Ian, planning, plotting. "And why would I need her? I have him." Longbottoms gestured to Ian. "Captain Ian Wilder defeated Noface on numerous occasions. As long as I have him, I can defeat Noface."

"Once upon a time, yes," Steve said. Gaining confidence, he ripped off a hunk of bread and put it in his mouth. Ian watched him, wondering himself where Steve was going with this. "But not anymore."

The captain's wine goblet paused at his lips as realization flashed through his dark eyes.

Steve smiled and said, "See, now you're getting it. Captain Ian Wilder over here isn't the same kid…er…man, he once was. His strength was always with the blade. The brains of the operation, though, that was Penelope."

Under the table, Ian knocked his knee against Steve's.

The captain resumed pacing. "I was wrong to question your worth, my friend," he said, nodding at Steve.

"That's what I've been saying. Can you tell the kid?" Steve joked. This time, Ian elbowed him hard in the side. "Would you stop that?" he exclaimed, turning to Ian.

The captain immediately snapped his fingers and said, "Yes. You must find this Penelope and bring her to me."

Steve gave Ian a thumbs up. They stood to leave, but the captain grabbed Ian by the shoulder and pointed at Steve. "Just you. Wilder is far too valuable to leave the ship."

"I need him," Steve said.

"No, you don't," the captain said.

"Yes," Steve said, "I do. I've never seen the girl. I've never been here. I wouldn't have the first clue where to start." He pointed at Ian and continued. "He does."

The captain let go of Ian and clapped his broad hand on Steve's shoulder. "Then he goes, and I hold you as collateral."

Steve raised his hands to gesture at Ian. "Look at him. Does he look like he could find his own ass in a windstorm?"

The captain frowned and studied Ian. Ian tried his best to look stupid.

"Believe me, Penelope was the brains," Steve said. "He was the brawn. Together they were invincible. Apart…well, he's terrible. I mean, look at those ridiculous shoes." Steve gestured to Ian again. "So you see, it's either both of us or neither of us, Captain. What's the plan? Two dead nobodies or Noface on a platter?"

Ian tried to swallow but couldn't. The captain's grip on Steve's shoulder tightened with the ultimatum. He waited for the captain's scimitar to rake against Steve's throat, spilling his blood down the front of his linen shirt. But instead, the captain nodded and slipped out a sly, breathy laugh. "You have a forked tongue about you." The captain relinquished his grip on Steve and opened the cabin door. "Gargle and Boils! My chambers. NOW!" he bellowed.

The captain turned to them and said, "You shall have escorts." In a thundering mass of footfalls, two well-muscled, wind-burnt scallywags stepped into the chamber. One had open, oozy boils peppered all over his face and neck and the other a gaping mouth with only a few fragments of teeth left.

The captain patted each of his men on the back, towering over them. "We set sail in three days. If you haven't returned with this woman in that time, these gentlemen will put a ball in the back of your heads. That is the arrangement."

Steve nodded. Ian followed suit.

"See you in three days," said the captain. "Or sooner."

On the quarterdeck, Gargle and Boils armored up with a cutlass and two pistolas each. Gargle helped himself to an extra musket, while Boils added a dagger to his belt. Ian eyed the weapons rack and wondered if he could grab a cutlass and fight his way out like the other Ian. He reached for the hilt of a cutlass, but his hand shook so terribly in fear he pulled it back. Who was he kidding? He could never do this. What was he thinking?

Their escorts waved Steve and Ian down the gangplank. Along the shore and into town, the two buccaneers led the way as Steve and Ian fell back and whispered to each other. "I can't believe you sold out Penelope like that," Ian hissed.

Steve whispered back, "We're off the ship, aren't we? Now we only have two of them to deal with. I was hoping he he'd stick us with the weak, dumb ones." Frustrated, Ian knew Steve was right.

Nothing about this world was how Ian and Penelope envisioned it. Sure, it looked, smelled, and seemed like the world where they had their adventures, but it felt like it had gone bad somehow. He thought back to science class, when he had to swab the toilet lid for a petri dish. The idea was to monitor bacteria growth. That first day nothing appeared, and it all looked normal. Then he forgot it at the bottom of his locker for over a month. By the time he found it—

or smelled it, actually—a whole different world of yellow pus-like colonies and green fuzzy villages had sprung up. It had almost made him puke. That was this world—totally unexpected.

"Any idea yet where this particular Penelope would be?" Steve asked.

Ian shook himself out of his thoughts and shrugged. "No."

"Well, you may want to work faster, because the whole reason we're here is to figure out what your Penelope did and try to prevent the untimely demise of her alternate here. And that malig won't wait for you to make your move before she makes hers."

Ian rubbed his head and said, "I know! I know."

At that point, they realized they had walked through Port Paveo and slowly edged a bend in a rutted road outside of town. Gargle and Boils had stopped. "Hey, wait a minute! We're supposed to be followin' you!" Boils called.

Steve shrugged his shoulders. "Not the sharpest knives on the tree, huh?" He waved at the two buccaneers to follow him. "Come on, Bargle and Goils," Steve said. "Penelope is this way." Steve led them to the path up the hill outside of town, back to where they first arrived. "Now just follow me exactly and everything will be all right," Steve whispered to Ian.

The foursome made it to the top of the hill where the sea breeze had grown to more gusty levels. Steve grabbed Ian's shoulders and positioned him to his right. Ian gave Steve a questioning look but complied. Then Steve held up his hand, pointing to the sky. "Hey, look up there. Is that a dirigible?" While their escorts cast their gazes skyward, the pads on Steve's fingertips glowed bright blue. Quickly, he cut a line through reality and pushed Ian though it and followed him.

Ian fell to the floor of the faux Millennium Falcon.

Outside the ship's windows, Ian could see the Islas Encantadas and before them, the two buccaneers standing in the grass, looking upward, dumbly, at absolutely nothing. Everything stopped outside, like a video game on pause. Clouds ceased to roll. A gull froze mid-dive. Even each grass blade bent in unison to some windless wind. Steve sat down in his seat and asked Ian to sit as well.

"Did you just stop time?" Ian asked.

"No," Steve said. "It's the stitch. Think of the Infiniuum as warp-speed internet access, kid."

Ian sat down in the other seat. "Do you need me to do the Icee thing?"

Steve smiled. "Nope. Because of your help I now have the waypoint mapped." He pulled back on the fake plastic controls, and they rose above the ground and through the atmosphere. When Steve engaged the drives, Ian felt reality melt before him, blending into multiple layers of other realities, until his eyes could take no more of the gooey mess. "Close your eyes, Ian," Steve said. "Your processor is tired. Rest. I'll take it from here."

With heavy eyelids, Ian felt himself falling backward as his eyes closed.

Ian opened his eyes and lurched upright in his bed. His bed at home. In his room. He tossed about in the covers for a moment as he gathered his bearings. He spotted his rubber-banded journal on the other pillow and the empty soda cans on his bedside table. The clock flashed 6:01 AM back to him in bright red digits. "Aw," he said, "I could have had another half hour."

Yawning and feeling like he had gotten very little sleep, Ian fought his way into a Chilly Willy t-shirt and basketball shorts and padded barefoot down to the kitchen. There, his mother and father sat at the table, Mom with a glass of orange juice and a toasted English muffin, while his father worked at a bowl of plain oatmeal and held the sports section up in front of him. "Good morning, sweetheart," his mother chimed.

"Good morning, son," said his dad. "You're up early for a Monday."

No kidding, Ian thought, but chose to say, "Early bird gets the worm, right?" He set to fixing his cereal for the morning: one handful of Cinnamon Toast Crunch, one handful of Golden Grahams, and a handful of his dad's bran flakes. As he poured milk over the combination, he remembered the pirate feast. He still felt full. But he sat down at the table with his parents and shoveled the cereal down.

Looking down, Ian's mother noticed a thin, but swollen pink scratch on his calf. "Oh dear, Ian," she said, leaning over to get a closer look. "That's one nasty scratch. It's infected," she said. "I'll get the Neosporin."

Ian touched his mom's arm as she rose. "Mom, it's fine. I'll take care of it, OK?" Ian smiled at her reassuringly.

She slowly sat down. "There's some Neosporin in the bathroom cabinet. Didn't you get a tetanus shot last summer? After that sprinkler thing?" She bit into her English muffin.

His father folded the paper in half. "He did. Right after the sprinkler thing."

"I'll take care of it, Mom. Thanks."

His father cocked his head and interlocked the fingers of his hands. "It's your first day back to school since the, uh, incident."

Right. The tizzy. Ian had forgotten all about it. "Don't worry, Dad. I won't freak out again."

"Did you shower yet?" his mother asked. "You smell like farm animals and candied yams."

Ian lifted his arm and sniffed. He did reek.

Ian showered and gingerly rubbed the Neosporin on his cut before dressing himself. When he got on the bus, everyone stopped talking and looked at him. He should have expected it after his ransacking of the classroom. Their thoughts flashed across their faces in their awkward expressions, brandished like rusty cutlasses and loaded pistolas. He found a seat up front, away from everyone, took out his phone, and jammed in his ear buds. He needed something strange and weird today. Cycling through the movie soundtracks on his phone, he settled on *Beetlejuice*.

Throughout the ride and walk from the bus to the school, Ian thought about Penelope. Not the dead one, but the live one back on the Islas Encantadas. He thought about all the places they had frequented: Hagshead Peak, Coralton, Hammersquall, Davestown, and Fort Shackle. The list was endless. But he fixated on how different the real Islas Encantadas was from their fantasies. Had Penelope changed too? Ian walked to his locker, opened it mindlessly, and got his things for first period.

He was about to shut his locker when Pete Stamdahl slammed it shut for him. Ian looked at Pete blankly for a second, said, "Thanks," and stepped into the hall.

Annoyed by Ian's reaction, Pete stepped in front of him. "Where do you think you're going, nutso?"

"Art," Ian said.

"No, you're not," Pete said. "You shouldn't even be here. First you go all zombie and then you tear up Spurgeon's classroom. You're a freak. Another headline waiting to happen."

Ian sighed. The other students had stopped what they were doing to watch the confrontation play out. Ian felt their eyes on him. Pete usually made everyone nervous, but Ian could tell by the nodding heads and murmurs that this time, quite a few people agreed with his assessment. Before, Ian was just lame, a nerd, someone who could easily be ignored. Now, Pete was right. He was a freak, and the whole school knew it.

"Things have been...weird lately," Ian said softly, his head down. "I'm working on it."

Pete scrunched his face and pulled his head back. "Right. It looks like it. Your bereavement grace period is over." Pete paused. "It's too bad. I liked Penny. She may have been a dork, but she was cute."

Ian wanted to be angry, but he couldn't muster it. He could actually relate to Pete for those three whole seconds. "Yeah, she was."

Pete took a quick scan of the hallway and doubled Ian over with a punch to the gut. Ian curled to the floor, dropping his algebra books. He wanted to throw up, but held it in.

Pete muttered, "psycho," to him, before walking off.

Pete and his toadies silently followed Ian to art class. When Ms. White stood outside the art room, they scattered.

Ms. White stepped out of her classroom and asked, "Trouble this morning, Ian?"

Ian looked down. "Not really," he said, darting into the room.

In class, he ignored the lesson completely. It took almost twenty minutes to wind down from Pete's latest round. Throughout art class, he started to realize a school bully was nothing compared to what he faced on the Islas Encantadas. He thought about pirate Penelope. How she could survive in a world of constant thievery and chaos. He didn't think she would be easy to find. He thought maybe each alternate Penelope across the Infiniuum had felt the tremor of her death and gone into hiding, like prairie dogs down a hole. Maybe this Penelope had gone underground. Off the grid. If he wanted to figure out what had really happened to Penelope, he would have to think like her.

Tired already, he stared at the art projects hanging at the front of the room. He came to the place where Penelope's cave painting was supposed to be, but it was gone. His feet grew cold. Where did it go? Frantic, he scanned the room but found nothing. It felt like Penelope's death all over again. Like this reality was erasing all traces of her one by one.

Before he could dwell on it anymore, the class bell rang, and he bolted upright to gather his books. But when he turned on his heel, his foot slid away from him on a loose piece of paper on the floor. He nearly fell but dropped his books instead to catch himself against the desk. After a second book dumping of the day, Ian reached for the stray piece of paper on the floor and turned it over in his hand.

Penelope's eerie cave painting.

The whirling maw of darkness. The moaning breeze blown over rum bottles in the sand. Vultures circling the sky overhead.

Ms. White rushed to him. "Oh my gosh, Ian. Are you okay?"

Transfixed on the cave, he peered past the paper, past the school, the town, the state, and into the Infiniuum. Back to the isles and Captain Longbottoms, Gargle, and Boils.

"Oh, look at that." Ms. White said looking at the painting. "The tack must have come loose on this." She looked from the painting to Ian. "She was your best friend. Would you like to keep this?"

Ian didn't say a word, he just nodded.

CHAPTER 14

THERAPY WITH DR. CAULDERON

"Ian," Dr. Caulderon greeted him at the door. "Glad you could make it. Come in. Have a seat."

Ian stepped into the office marked "Ms. Regina Sutter, School Psychologist" and looked around. A docking station and speakers sat next to a closed laptop on the desk. A crystal statuette of a great blue heron sat on the bookshelf behind the desk. That looked to be new; Ms. Sutter was not the crystal figurine type. It looked like Caulderon was moving in. Beside a foam container of lunch leftovers sat his key ring, with a Porsche crest fob.

Ian sat in the cracked faux leather chair. How many fractured psyches had this guy fixed to run around in a Porsche? "So you filling in for Ms. Sutter while she's out with her new baby?" Ian questioned.

Caulderon ran his hands down the front of his suit before sitting behind the desk. "Yes. Well, I got my start at this school, so when they called, I couldn't help but give a little back." He let out a sigh and gestured at Ian. "So how are you feeling?"

Ian thought about it. He felt fine. But not here. Here he felt odd. Like he was being watched. Ian looked around for cameras or recording devices but couldn't find any, unless one was hidden in that crystal heron.

"What are you looking for?" Caulderon asked.

"Cameras, recorders," Ian said. "I just figured you wanted to document my insanity, maybe write a paper about it or something."

The doctor smiled, an I-have-no-idea-what-you're-talking-about look on his face, but when his lips parted, he said, "We're friends, Ian. No need to record anything. I want our interactions to be organic."

Ian suppressed the desire to continue his inspection of the room. Instead, he said, "How long are you here?"

Again, the false smile. Ian stared at the doctor's teeth. They were marvelously white, almost too white. "A few of us are in rotation," he said. "I'm really here just for you. Your parents and the school felt it important." He laced his fingers together and held them under his chin. "Your mother told me about your trip to the Pump and Munch. What brought you there, Ian?"

Ian thought about it. Obviously, he couldn't say anything about Steve, the Infiniuum, or the alternate Penelopes, so he told the same lie he had told his parents. "I…I just needed an Icee," he said. At least his story would be consistent.

"Ah, yes. The adventures of high school metabolism." Dr. Caulderon paused as he thought, then continued. "Nonetheless, alarming to your mother. She also said you and Penelope shared a lot of creativity activity."

Ian squirmed in his seat. He didn't like this stranger knowing everything about him. His diary came to mind. All the drawings and stories he and Penelope created. "Penelope and I liked to hike," Ian admitted, leaving out all the mock swordplay, gunfights, and magic against imaginary beasties and mercenaries.

The doctor seemed pleased with Ian sharing his feelings. "Long walks with a good friend, a girlfriend from what I hear, are very hard to beat," he said. For a moment, Ian felt maybe the doctor did have at least one small, sincere bone in his body. "You and Penny shared many things," he continued. "You confided in each other.

Did you ever tell each other about depressed feelings or moments of isolation?"

Ian's feet got antsy. His legs bounced in agitation to the questions. Depressed feelings. Isolation. Penelope's descriptions of the Smudge World came to mind, but he couldn't reveal that, couldn't betray her trust like that. So Ian shook his head.

"What about troubling thoughts, fights with parents, or struggles fitting in?"

Ian shook his head again.

"What about lapses of darkness? Were there any times you thought the world was just a dark blot, an inky smudge that you couldn't escape?"

Ian's feet stopped bouncing and instead dug against the floor, ready to spring him from the chair and into a run. The Smudge World! How could Caulderon know about that? Ian's eyes fluttered and a shivery tingle ran down the right-side of his body. A dizziness hit him. The same symptoms he had experienced when Steve first told him the truth of the Infiniuum. There was no way Caulderon could have been a feron. But was he a malig? The malig that killed Penelope? Steve said they were both cut from the same cloth. How could he know? Ian took a breath, the first in what seemed like twenty minutes.

"Are you okay?" Dr. Caulderon asked. "You look agitated. Distressed. Anxious."

Ian gripped the chair, his knuckles turning white. He willed his body to stay put, even though he wanted to run. "Of course I'm distressed!" Ian said loudly. He hadn't intended to raise his voice, but he couldn't take the condescending tone of this guy. "Of course I'm pissed off. My girlfriend died of a sudden brain hemorrhage. I don't even know what the hell that is. All I know is that the one person in this world who really understood me is gone. Penelope and me...we could have whole conversations without talking. We were in love."

Caulderon no longer smiled. He cocked his head and listened to Ian, either fully interested in what he had to say or faking it incredibly well. After a moment, he leaned back in his chair and opened the desk drawer. He removed a clump of papers containing drawings, paintings, and sketches. "Your girlfriend was a very talented artist," the doctor said, paging through the artwork. Ian was familiar with the images: Cactusback Flats, Taluride Station, Fharendale, Atlantis City, and even the Islas Encantadas.

"Such a terrible shame," the doctor continued. "Real potential here." He flipped through another stack. A forest burned to black, hands reaching from the ground. A cast iron sun strewn in an ashen sky, rolling prairies of trampled, trodden gray meadow grass, a ribbon of pale, diminutive people in ragged black clothes marching into infinity. A city avenue torn asunder with crumbling buildings and rebar jutting out of the ruin, a solitary pale child impaled on a rebar spike. An abandoned bassinet with a dead, nose-less infant wrapped in black cloth, the child's existence smudged in ink onto the paper by Penelope's thumbs.

"Interesting drawing," the doctor said. "Were you worried about your friend's mental state?"

But Ian wasn't listening. His eyes devoured the Smudge World artwork, the stark monochromatic tones and destitute expressions. So that's how the doctor knew about the Smudge World. Ian reached for one of the drawings, the dying child. It was exactly as she had explained it to him—a smudge of existence. Ian took in every smear and swipe of the drawing, noticing Penelope's fingerprints embedded in the black dust.

And even though they were just fingerprints, they represented a piece of her. He leaned forward and gathered more of the drawings, each one a precious memory he never wanted to lose again. With every pencil stroke or brush stroke, he recreated her hand, her arm movement, her body as she sketched. From pirates to cowboys to space zombies, he gathered them all up in a haphazard pile against his chest, until he came to a new sketch intermingled with the others.

The cave.

A slightly different version of the one in art class, it still possessed a gaping maw of an entrance, whorled to near pitch blackness by her thick pencil. His eyes fixated on that opening. It drew him in, reached out to him. This version had variations: palm trees, a frothing gray seashore, and run-down rope bridge leading to its entrance. The more he looked at it, the more the briny sea breeze batted against his cheek and the faint, sweet smell of ripening coconuts curled to his nose. "Can I have these?" Ian asked, clutching the pile of artwork to his chest.

The doctor paused to assess Ian's request. "I'd have to get her parents' permission first."

Ian placed the artwork on the desk, stood up, and turned around to leave. But Caulderon cleared his throat and pointed at the clock. "We still have forty-two minutes of the session."

Ian looked at the clock and rolled his eyes. Defeated, he sat back down in the chair.

Dr. Caulderon leaned forward. "Let's talk about the classroom and Mr. LeGrand. You displayed considerable anger, and I'd like to explore the roots of those emotions."

Ian blew out an exasperated breath. Maybe if he expelled all the air from his lungs and didn't breathe again, it would make the session go by quicker.

It didn't.

On the activity bus home, Ian quickly slumped into a front seat as far away from Pete's exclusive back seat as he could. Great. Sessions with a shrink and catching the late bus with Pete. Fabulous.

When he walked in the house that evening, his mother stood at the sink in the kitchen, washing her hands. Her clothes bore the dry and wet smears of clay from her studio. "How'd the session go?" she asked.

Ian rolled his eyes. More awesomeness. He had just talked to Dr. Caulderon for an hour, and he did not want to rehash it. "Fine." He wanted to change the subject. "How was your...ah...day?"

His mother dried her hands on a towel. "Had a couple classes at the community center. Spent the afternoon on a tea set for an online customer order." She asked, "What did you talk about with Dr. Caulderon?"

"Just some stuff," Ian said. "I should get started on homework." He took a step out of the kitchen.

"Sit, Ian." She motioned him to the couch in the living room across from the kitchen. "I want to hear details."

"I should really get started. I'm behind on so much—"

"You will sit down right here and tell me about it," she called, gesturing to the couch in the living room.

Ian shook his head and sat next to her. For twenty minutes, he told her about the session, although he kept the eerie cave drawing to himself. Amazingly, it worked. His mom clammed up and listened. When Ian's father came home, they ate dinner, and he found himself recanting his day once again to his father, albeit a more streamlined version.

But even though they talked and ate together, the atmosphere between Ian and his parents felt distant. To him, it was as if everyone in his life balanced on a plank of wood suspended perpendicular over a taut length of piano wire. His mom and dad stood on one end and Steve and Penelope on the other end. Ian stood in the middle of the plank, and everyone's balance depended on his actions. A step too close in either direction would topple the whole act. After dinner, he scraped his plate and asked, "Can we see a movie this weekend?" Both of his parents glanced up at him. "I mean, together," Ian said.

His father smiled and reached his hand out to his mother. "That would be fun," his dad said. "I heard that new action flick is really good."

His mother extracted her hand from her husband's and stood up with her dinner plate. "I could go for a night out too."

"Then it's a date," Ian said, flashing the surest, most happy smile he could muster.

In the family room downstairs, he fired up the video game console and logged in. After the welcome screens booted, his friend notifications flashed on screen. He only had one gaming friend: Penelope. And her avatar blankly stared back at him as 'offline.' A part of him willed the avatar to change, to show him that he had an incoming message from her, but he knew that was impossible.

He needed to take his mind off her, but it was hard. He missed her. This new world without her fit him like an oversized shirt. He needed a release. *Call of Duty* would do. Once into the game, he noticed how slow his hands were at the controls. It had been a while. He joined a match on a European map and picked off a few guys before running into a busted-up shop full of mannequins.

Only, when his video game avatar fully entered the room, it wasn't the mannequin shop but the faux Millennium Falcon. And sitting in his usual chair was Steve. "How did the session go with der doktor?" Steve asked through the television.

"Oh, God. Not you, too," Ian muttered.

"Hey, it's your mental health, not mine, pal." Steve said. "Got a plan for finding Penelope before Longbottoms finds us?"

"No," Ian replied, "But I have this." He opened his backpack and pulled out Penelope's detailed drawing of the ominous cave from Ms. White's art classroom. He held it in front of his chest for Steve to see from the television. "I saw another version of this in my meeting with Dr. Caulderon. It had other details. Palm trees, a smaller island, and a rope bridge."

Onscreen, Steve stepped closer to the picture, making his face appear bulbous. "It's very mesmerizing," he said. "But how does this drawing help us find Penelope?"

Ian turned the drawing around and looked at it again, hoping the answer would show up in the carbon swirls and strokes. "I don't know," Ian said.

Steve turned his back to Ian and paced about the interior of the faux Millennium Falcon onscreen. "Great," he said. "We'll just walk around the whole damn archipelago, knocking on doors and asking for a girl named Penelope." Steve turned to face Ian again, leaning on the control deck. "I should have trusted my instincts. It was too soon. Why I let you convince me otherwise is beyond me."

"Give me a break, huh? I'm trying," Ian retorted. "And we can't just sit around feeling pissy about it."

Steve shook his head. "Right."

Ian stood up and paced. "Listen, I just think if we find this cave, we'll find more answers, that's all."

"Ian?" his father's voice interrupted. "Who are you talking to?"

Ian turned to see his father holding a half-painted model of the Stealth Bomber. Ian's first instinct was to stuff Penelope's sketch under a couch cushion. Stammering, he said, "I was just quoting a line from the movie." Ian pointed to the television. But no movie played, only a *Call of Duty* match in which Ian's character lay dead on the floor of the mannequin store.

"That's a video game, son," his dad said, his brow furrowed.

Ian put on his best sheepish grin and said, "Right, I meant to say video game. I was talking to another player in the game."

His father's skepticism waned, but only slightly. "Okay," he said. "Your mom said you had a lot of homework. I think you'd better go do that."

"Right," Ian said, shutting off the console and television. He grabbed his backpack and said goodnight to his dad.

Walking up the basement steps, Ian felt his father's eyes bore into his back. He hadn't even heard his dad come downstairs. He needed to be more careful. He had to do better.

CHAPTER 15

A First Hangover

Ian fiddled with his dirty linen shirt and brown cotton trousers while Steve knocked on the thick wooden door of the next cottage. "I just don't know why we couldn't have found something more cool-looking," Ian said. "Like black leather or something."

"Look around. Where you going to find that here?" Steve said, shaking his head and waiting for the homeowner to open the door. "Be happy with what we found, kid. Besides, black leather in this heat and humidity? You'd burst like a grape."

The door swung open, revealing a haggard woman in a dirty green dress. Sweat rolled down her brow, and her apron looked to have dried blood splattered all over it. Inside the small cottage, two kids fought noisily over a wooden soldier until it broke, then both began firing, "You did it!" back and forth at each other.

"Pardon our intrusion," Steve said, rolling out a yellowed spool of paper to reveal a crude sketch of Penelope's portrait. "But would you happen to know the whereabouts of one Penelope Archer?"

The woman looked at the portrait, spat on Steve's authentic buckle-topped shoes, and slammed the door. "Guess that's a no," Ian said.

Steve didn't even bother with a smart-aleck remark. They'd been at it all day, going door-to-door with their pirate friends Gargle and Boils at their backs, who were ready to place shots in their skulls at a moment's notice. Ian's body ached. He had thoroughly sweated through his shirt and pantaloons to the point where he was mighty chafed. Ian wondered if Steve could sweat or chafe if he was, in fact, an oversized amoeba.

"I don't understand how you can do this," Steve said. "You sweat to keep cool. Yet, in this environment the sweat not only doesn't work, but chafes all the parts that rub against each other. Seems like a lot of bad evolution if you ask me."

"Ye bloody bellyachers," Gargle said, kicking at Steve's backside.

"The cap'n wants that lass of yours," Boils shouted into Ian's ear. He brought his pistol to Ian's temple and continued. "By my count ye have two more days to find her. We could just as well shoot ye now, I figures, but the cap'n's got moral fiber, see. He honors his deals, even when they're rotten." The muscle-bound deck ape pushed Ian up the slight hill toward the next cottage.

Ian recovered and climbed the hill with shaky legs. Steve moved slowly too, his legs bowed to reduce the chafing. He found a log next to the cottage and sat down on it. Pointing to Ian, he said, "I'm selling your clothes for a bath tonight. You take this one. I'm taking a break."

Gargle yanked Steve up as quickly as he sat down. "Ye'll take a break when I say so."

Ian grabbed the scrolled paper from Steve. Above them, a large black bird circled in the sky. Squinting at it, Steve nudged Ian and said, "Look. The bird."

Ian peered up, shielding his eyes with his hand. Abigail, Longbottoms' condor soared in the updrafts above them. "He sent the bird too?" Ian clutched the paper and walked to the next cottage, a squat thing with white-washed sides and a tall chimney puffing gray smoke. After a quick knock, the door opened to reveal a barrel-chested, hairy brute of a man, dressed in brown smithing leathers. His face was sunburnt and streaked with charcoal. A half-eaten meal and a homely wife waited at the table inside. "Sorry, for interrupting," Ian said, unscrolling the parchment. "Would you happen to know the whereabouts of this girl?"

The man wiped the soup from his lips with the back of a hand. "Neva saw her in my life." As the man swung the door closed, Ian stuck his foot in to stop it. The buckle on his shoe prevented the door from crushing his foot. The man swung it open again and said, "I oughtta pummel you red, you little bonebag."

Nervously, Ian unfolded a piece of paper from his pocket and showed the man. "Please, sir. Maybe you know where we can find this?" The man grabbed the sketch of the cave with the roped bridge by the sea, looked at it, and handed it back. "That's Drop-Dead Island. There's only one way onto it, and if you don't know the bridge code, you drop dead."

Ian moved his foot from the door. "Really? This place actually exists here?" A smile sparked across Ian's face. He had a hunch about the picture but couldn't imagine they landed on the one reality Penelope once visited. He knew he and Penelope were close, but perhaps their connection spanned beyond the physical. Ian looked back at the man standing in the doorway and asked, "Do you know how to get there?"

"No," the man said, slamming the door in his face.

Behind him, Gargle bent over in raucous laughter. "It'll take him ten years to find her at this rate!" Boils said. Gargle waved his pistola at Ian and said, "I might just have to put a ball in the back o' your head, mate."

Ian and Steve turned together and walked down the hill dejected. For the rest of the afternoon, they questioned another two dozen huts, houses, and inns. No one knew Penelope. Ian wondered if they were too late and this alternate Penelope had already met her doom.

But as they travelled up the coast, more and more people knew about the island and the freakish cave. Of course, none of them had been there, but they had heard of the place. A sheep farmer said, "That thar is Drop-Dead Island. Resting place of Cap'n Topper. My grandpappy said his headless ghost haunts the cavern and the shores around it." A bar wench pulled Ian into a dark corner and said, "My lover went in search of Cap'n Lopper's treasure. He came back madder than cattle, his tongue cut out. He threw himself off the bluffs less than a year ago." The master tailor of Gullspray told them that he had made a one-armed frock for a man claiming to have fought the ghost of Captain Sopper in the mouth of the cavern. "Barely made it back alive," the man said. "Crazy with fever too. Can't really say how much of the story is true."

Each story they heard shared similarities, but the details were different. Ian couldn't put together a straight story out of the mess. The only thing they knew for a fact was that no one dared go to Drop-Dead Island and if they did, they didn't come back whole.

At an inn called the Poisoned Apple, Gargle and Boils burst through the doors and announced, "We're gonna need two rooms, two meals, and a stall in your stables!" Boils slammed down a fistful of gold on the counter and grabbed a nearby bottle of rum. Tossing back a mouthful, he briskly wiped his beard when he was finished.

For the waning hours before nightfall, Gargle, Steve, and Ian watched Boils drink himself into a stupor. He shared a huge meal of lamb shank and potatoes with Gargle, and they allowed Ian and Steve to eat the crumbs and lick their plates. Then Boils, drunk as a badger, led them to the stables. Pointing to the fly-infested dung heaps, he told Steve and Ian, "Your accommodations, milords." He almost fell into the muck himself, bent over in laughter.

"Get off to that room, ye miserable louse." Gargle pushed Boils toward the door. "I'll keep a wary eye on these two." He grabbed a nearby stool and propped himself up against the door to block any escape.

Steve and Ian cozied up in the rank straw of the stables. "Best get some rest, kid," Steve murmured. "We'll think of a back-up plan tomorrow."

Nestled in, Ian covered his nose against the ripe manure and moldy straw. He didn't want to think about a back-up plan tomorrow. He had a back-up plan now—the cave. The more he thought about it, the more it made sense. It existed here. Penelope drew it back home. There had to be a connection. Even if it was simply the grave of the Penelope of this reality, he'd find it, and they'd move on to another world. It was better than wandering aimlessly through coastal villages hoping to run into her.

Besides, he hadn't come all this way to be pushed around by second-rate powder monkeys and then be shot in the head. His stomach twisted in hunger, and his throat had shriveled from thirst. He'd had it up to his eyeballs with everything. So when Gargle nodded off to sleep, Ian pushed at Steve to wake him up, but he wouldn't budge from sleep. Frustrated, Ian snuck out of the stables alone. He'd have to come back and get Steve if he found anything.

Ian's first stop was a nearby tavern called the Busted Hump. Once there, he drank the leftover dregs of ale and rum sitting on tables, ate the remaining scraps of bread and cheese he found on finished plates, and questioned everyone sober enough to speak. By the time he finished, his stomach had stopped growling, but his eyes grew tired. But he needed to press on.

When he turned up no leads, he moved on to the next tavern up the coast. When that one turned up nothing, he moved on. After three stops, with his belly full of scraps and sloshing brew, he was riding the fast track to his first hangover, and no one would venture with him to find the cavern. Two hours before sunrise, he stumbled upon a waking fisherman, who as part of his new pact with the lord and savior Jesus Christ, offered to take him there. "But only to the foot of the bridge," he had said, making the sign of the cross. "For the devil hisself has made a home in that black pit and I darest not tread a sober foot in that den."

By the time they made it back to Steve and the pirates, day had broken. Ian and the fisherman snuck into the stable, and Ian kicked Steve gently, who rubbed the sleep out of his eyes.

"Get the two morons. Jacob here has a fresh horse and a wagon, and he's taking us to Drop-Dead Island," Ian ordered. "He said it's about a day's travel from here. If we start now, we should reach it by nightfall. We'll need flint, steel, and some oil lamps. Oh, and food and water." With that, Ian climbed into Jacob's wagon, propped himself up in the back corner, and quickly fell asleep.

After his nap, Ian awoke to the brightest, bluest sky he had ever seen, with a few wind-swept clouds bustling across its seam. The brightness and weather, although beautiful, did not remove the terrible thumping in his head or his cottonmouth.

Steve handed Ian a piece of bread and a flask of water. "Here, eat and drink," he said. "How much did you drink last night? And where did you go?"

Ian quenched his thirst and picked at the bread. The water helped, but his headache remained. What he really wanted was an ice-cold soda.

"You should have woken me," Steve said.

"I tried, but you wouldn't get up."

Steve nodded. "Heavy sleeper." He paused to sniff himself. "I don't think I'm ever going to get the smell of horse ass out of my clothes. And why are we going to the cavern? Is Penelope there?"

Ian swallowed more bread. "I don't know, but she drew that picture, Steve. And it exists here. There has to be a connection."

Steve took the flask back and drank from it. "Sounds logical," he said. "But in my experience, more often than not, it's simply an irrational grasping of straws."

Ian feared he would say something like that. Still, it was all they had.

Their escorts rode at the front of the wagon. Gargle dozed uncomfortably, his lower lip covered his upper, hiding the blackened maw of his jagged smile. Boils shook his head in a dazed stupor, mouthing a silent monologue.

Ian nudged Steve. "If she's here, what do we do?" Ian whispered.

Steve shrugged. "I don't know what we can do. Hide her. Protect her."

Ian rolled his eyes. "Not Penelope, the malig."

Steve flinched and then caught on. "Oh, right," he said. He dug his hand into the pocket of his pantaloons and dredged out something in his closed hand. "I have this." Steve opened his hand to reveal a small hole in his palm the size of a bottle cap, but beyond the hole was the indigo mash of the cosmos. Ian had the urge to utter something ridiculous, but he remembered that he was supposed to leave the quantum mechanics to Steve. "I was expecting a weapon of some kind."

Steve closed his hand. "You humans," he said. "It's always violence with you. I have to release her."

Ian scrunched up his face in question. "What?"

"Release her," Steve hissed.

"What is she in prison?"

"In a way," Steve said. "Maligs abuse the Infiniuum. Steal its power for their own purposes. Ferons prefer it to be scattered. Released to the natural ebb and flow of nature."

Ian frowned. "That's it? No explosion or melting? She killed Penelope. I think she deserves more than that."

"Melting?" Steve made a tsk-ing noise with his lips. "You don't get it. You and me, although we hail from different places, we're made from the same stuff, the same energy. Stars, planets, moons, air, water, life forms, we're all the same matter, just in a different state of transition. At the end of our lives, we'll all be released in some fashion, scattered to the cosmos. When you see that, realize that we're all connected, then death, grief, sadness—it ceases to exist and only life remains, only the Infiniuum. This malig will realize it too and understand the error of her ways."

Ian picked at a rogue piece of straw from between the wooden slats of the wagon and looked at it. He tried to apply Steve's idea, analyzing the structure of the straw, its energy, and how it would eventually decompose and merge with everything else and become the building blocks of more life. But he just couldn't grasp it yet. "Like reincarnation?" he asked.

Steve smiled, like a teacher who felt lucky that at least some of his lesson was sinking in. "Not exactly," he said. Then he stopped talking and looked over Ian's shoulder to the right of the rutted path, where a worn driftwood plank read, "Beware!" in dark brown ink.

Ian followed Steve's stare to the sign behind him. "Is that blood?" Ian asked.

Gargle and Boils woke from their dazes to peer over the edge of the wagon. Ian told them the tales he had heard about the ghost of Captain Topper, Lopper, or Sopper, and even though he intended on scaring them away, Boils said, "There be only one sea ghost that scares the bed sheets outta me and that's the death-breath hisself, Cap'n Noface."

Gargle agreed, "Aye."

Jacob the fisherman worked the reins to his horse and laughed at the two pirates. "Captain Bradford Nolander was a blow-hard and a luck-suck."

The two pirates bent their ears to the old man. "Oi, what do you know about it?" Boils asked.

"A mangy, ol' fisherman. Who the hell are you?" Gargle chimed in.

Jacob watched the road. "An old fisherman who served in the King's Navy with a swabbie named Nolander, that's who. And back then he was but a whiny, sniveling deckhand who'd just as soon drown you than admit he was wrong."

Steve perked up and asked, "Did he have a face back then?"

Jacob nodded. "Aye. And an ugly, pock-marked thing it was."

Ian smiled, eager to enlighten them on Noface's backstory. "It's a cool story. See, Nolander rose through the ranks quickly," Ian offered. "Too quickly for his own good. When Commodore Tiberious put him on protection detail for the King's sanctum during the Blood Coast War, Nolander thought he could murder the King's guards and make off with his finest treasure."

Boils nodded and said, "The Wicked Crow. Was the King's Screaming Eagle 'til Nolander cursed it."

Ian held up a finger. "Close, but not really. The King's finest treasure was the Cask of Eve." The pirates squinted in ignorance or disapproval; Ian couldn't tell which, but really didn't care. "The Cask of Eve, the golden sarcophagus that housed the skull of Eve. Made by God from the rib of Adam. Eater of the fruit of knowledge." Ian said loftily, anticipating the pirates' admiration, but getting nothing but blank looks. He sighed. "The cask supposedly contained the knowledge of God," Ian said. "Knowledge Nolander wanted so he could be King."

Gargle and Boils nodded. "Then it worked," Gargle said. "Cause he's king now." Boils nodded in agreement. Jacob too. Ian frowned, looking around at his companions. His breath came rapid, and the fine hairs on the back of his neck sat up. "What do you mean he's king? He can't be king!"

CHAPTER 16

A WALK THROUGH THE CEMETERY

Jacob turned to Ian and said, "Sorry, mate. Tis' the truth."

Ian's hands shook. His breath became wheezy and short. He felt dizziness circling his head. Steve grabbed his arm, "Ian? Buddy? What's wrong?"

"Everything," Ian said. "Noface, Penelope, me. Everything is backwards. Nothing is what it should be. It doesn't feel right."

Steve put on a sympathetic face and patted Ian's shoulder. "I told you this wasn't going to be easy, kid. You and your friend just captured glimpses, mere frames of this world in your pretend games. Sure, you got enough to paint a romantic picture, but here, this reality abides by its own rules. In your imagination, you always win, but these people aren't just characters in your play, Ian. They have minds of their own. Feelings. Lives. This world you and Penelope saw is a feral, violent, real creation. And eventually every world, every reality, even yours back home, has an absorption point, where it dies and decays, only to become the seeds of something new. That's just life, pal."

Ian sniffled and said, "I want to go home."

Steve nodded. "Sure. We'll take a break." Steve looked around the wagon and waited for a moment when everyone looked away. Then the world slowed to an unseen crawl. With a few swashes of his glowing hands, they were back in the faux Millennium Falcon. Steve eased the controls and they again rose high from the islands and arched through the atmosphere. Ian slumped in his chair, the Infiniuum melting all around him as they voyaged home.

Ian's mind tumbled end over end. He closed his eyes, let the Infiniuum penetrate him, slip between his cell walls and wash over his mitochondria. And even though he thought maybe he understood what Steve had talked about earlier, a fermented sickness welled inside him. His stomach churned and gurgled just like Noface's belly aboard his version of the Wicked Crow. The tighter he pressed his eyes shut, the easier it would be to forget it, he thought. Still, a story spun out of the fog and dust of his mind.

He dangles over the deck rail of the Wicked Crow. The frothing sea rears up at him. His feet bear black leather boots, and his body, a burnt leather long coat. Confused at the attire, he raises his free hand to his face and finds a porcelain mask. Underneath the mask, diseased flesh hangs over his skull and jaw. Hot breath rises underneath the mask and settles rancid on his brow and cheeks.

This is not right.

In a panic, he looks upward, where Ian Wilder awaits, holding onto his hand and keeping him from the sea.

How can this be?

He is Ian, not Captain Noface.

He knows this story. He wrote it. He knows how it ends. Only this time, he plays the role of the villain. Below, the sea churns, an abysmal, watery grave waiting to devour him. Above, Ian struggles to hold on. He knows the words by heart, so he plays the role of

Noface. "You won't let me fall, Ian," he tells himself. "I know you. You live by a code."

And like before, Ian makes the hero's choice. When the young man hefts him to the rail, he reaches for his pistol, Noface's pistol, and cocks the hammer back. He doesn't know why he continues. He could stow the gun and give up, change the story, but he doesn't. The story demands its finish. A darkness like black oil bubbles into his blood and clouds his mind. Like the Infiniuum, his cells bathe in it, drink it like an addictive wine. His lips move of their own accord, telling Ian, "You couldn't do this, Ian—kill a man."

Past the boy's shoulder, Penelope stands shackled to the mast, watching it all unfold and mouthing the words they had written for this scene.

In the breathless silence, he waits for Ian to speak, to say the words that would ultimately befoul Noface and send him retching into the ocean. In those seconds, he deserves his watery grave and even prepares for the inevitable splash and the suffocation of salt water. He even closes his eyes in anticipation.

But Ian says nothing.

Unable to control his hand, Noface's hand, he raises the pistol to Ian's face. He takes a step forward. The muscles in his legs react instinctively and boldly with each step. Even his rotted lips curve upwards in an evil smile. The pistol rings, and the ball buries itself under Ian's chin. The boy staggers and falls backward against the mast. Blood bursts from his neck like a freshwater spring. Ian clutches at his throat, his hands slick with red, trying and failing to hold it all in.

Penelope wrenches her body viciously against her bonds, her animal screams degenerate into exasperated gulps of air before unleashing the screams again. When Ian's foot ceases its spasmodic twitching, she stops thrashing at the ropes and slips into a hoarse, dry-throated sob. Beneath Noface's mask, dressed in his enemy's skin, he stows his pistol in his belt and walks across the deck. His footsteps clamor louder, more menacing than he has ever heard them before. With sickly eyes, he watches the color drain from Ian's face.

Penelope's guttural cries play like the most beautiful music he's ever heard. Below his feet, the sea bucks and rocks. His legs adjust to the motion, and he no longer feels sick to his stomach.

He feels steady, clear-minded, and full.

❊   ❊   ❊

"I'm so sorry," Ian told his mom in the hallway.

Wearing her robe and a pair of elbow-length yellow rubber gloves, Maggie Wilder carried a bucket of steaming water ripe with carpet cleaner. "That's okay, sweetheart," she said at the entryway to his bedroom. "You just got a little sick."

"I don't know," Ian said. "It looks like a lot of sick."

He hoped the remark would make her smile. And it did. But as quickly as it appeared, it slipped away. And with it, Ian saw for the briefest of moments, his mother as she truly was: her hunched shoulders, dull eyes with puffy dark circles, her hair dry and unkempt. Then with a quick blink, she regained her façade and said, "Just get in the shower and get cleaned up. I'll handle this. You can repay me by loading the dishwasher tonight."

"Yeah," Ian said, trying to shake the exhaustion he just saw draped over his mother. "Deal."

He closed the bathroom door and turned on the shower. Under the warm massage of the water, he tried to forget his last foray into the Infiniuum. He let the water spray into his mouth, where he sloshed it around and spit the acrid contents onto the shower floor.

In his bedroom, his mom had scrubbed out the pool of vomit from the carpet, leaving a discolored mark that smelled like cleaner. He quickly dressed in ripped jeans, his green Alton High hoodie, and sneakers. Downstairs, his mom ate her English muffin in her bathrobe. His father munched a bit of whole wheat toast. The morning paper, neatly folded into a tight rectangle, lay next to his glass of orange juice. Ian toasted a bagel and spread cream cheese on it. From the corner of his eye, he noticed his father watching him. It looked like he had words backed up against his teeth just waiting to gush forth.

"How are you feeling, son?"

Ian scrunched his face, then sat down to join them. Nothing good ever came from that opening salvo. His parents' eyes held an exacting look. Each blink seemed to slice at him like a scalpel, intent on opening him up and peering inside. "I feel fine, dad," Ian said, biting into his bagel. "How are you two feeling? You look...weird."

"We're just worried about you, sweetheart," his mother said following a sip of coffee.

Ian wiped cream cheese from his lip. "I'm fine, Mom." His anger built like it had with Steve. He quickly tried to calm himself. Anger would not do in this situation.

"It's just...with the vomit and talking to yourself at all hours of the day," his father said. "I don't know if you've noticed, but we're kind of freaking out about this."

"And you think I'm not?" Ian said, the anger rushing back. He thought back to the incident in the basement. Had they heard other conversations too? Were they spying on him? "I told you, I'm fine. You just...you need to leave me alone. It's like you said, Dad, I need to process things on my own time."

A smile tried to emerge from his father's face, but he stamped it down. "Okay. But maybe we should lay off the video games for a while."

Ian finished his bagel. "Fine, Dad. Whatever."

Ian rode the bus to school totally cut off from the world. He shoved his ear buds so far into his ears it would take a needle-nose pliers to get them out. Ironically, his favorite soundtrack to blow off steam was his dad's favorite movie, *Rocky IV*. Ian had sat through the film at least three times with his father, but he didn't know what the big deal was. The soundtrack, however, was dead-on and contained enough 80s synthesizer and heavy beats for him to feel like he was swinging haymakers and ducking uppercuts.

The music almost made him forget about Pete Stamdahl, who had moved to the seat behind Ian mid-ride and continuously kicked Ian through the seat. Just muscle through it, he told himself, mouthing the words to "No Easy Way Out."

It will get better.

At least that's what his mom always said.

When the bus emptied in front of the school, Ian hung a left and decided to enter through the industrial arts door to avoid Pete. It was bad enough trying to save a different Penelope from pirates, but he also had to contend with his parents, who probably thought he needed a 24-7 residency at that Oakhaven place Caulderon ran. He didn't have time for Pete too. His continued harassment could wait. He had much larger fish to fry.

As the tunes spiraled into his ears, he thought about the Islas Encantadas. Steve was right; it was nothing like he and Penelope had envisioned. The more he thought about Noface's rise to the throne, the more it started to make sense. Captain Longbottoms said as much when asking for his weaknesses. Longbottoms even knew about his alternate self, Captain Ian Wilder, captured and kept in a cage on Noface's ship, never to be seen again. An unusual ribbon of black dread crept through him. Could his alternate be dead? And if Noface had captured or killed his counterpart, had he done the same with Penelope?

When Ian finally cleared his mind, he noticed he had walked past the industrial arts entrance, past the school entirely, and up the hill, a half a mile from school. A panic set in, but it disappeared a lot faster than he thought it would. Ian shrugged and continued to walk. He didn't know what to do in either world; in this one, his parents would unravel further once they got the phone call from the principal, and in the Islas Encantadas, he didn't have the smarts to even find Penelope, let alone the bravado to fight whatever was keeping her hidden from him.

All he wanted to do was walk, breathe in the cooling fall air, and chill out. Above, clouds ran in short, squat spoonfuls, white on the tops and sea-gray on the bottoms. He'd do anything to just float away with them. He and Penelope often lay in her backyard and watched the clouds. Her dad called it cloud-bursting. But together, he remembered it as a moment to daydream and open their unbridled imaginations. So many times, Penelope would hold his hand and ask him to close his eyes. Then whole new worlds unfurled between them. He missed her something terrible. Since her death, he tried putting her out of his mind, but she always re-emerged to leave breadcrumbs across his memory.

He didn't keep track of the time. Didn't care, for that matter. He had walked all the way through the suburban downtown of Alton. When his stomach grumbled, he stopped at Donny's Pie Shop, the best pizzeria in 20 square miles, for a slice, and he kept walking as he ate it.

It was almost 1:30 PM when he finally checked his phone for the time, ignoring the five unread text messages from his parents. By then, he had completely traversed the town. Oblivious, he had meandered into the parking lot of Evangeline Lutheran Church, the Archers' church, where off in the back of the lot, past rows of aspen and white pine lay the cemetery.

Penelope.

Even though he had spent the majority of her funeral in a daze, he remembered her casket, draped in violets. A sea of black-clad mourners squinting in the midday sun. The quiet sniffles and sobs punctuated by the monotonous words of the pastor. Ian walked between the headstones until he found her. Up close, he noticed her gravestone was ground to a smooth reflective finish. Glittery pink flecks within the stone added a sparkle that he was pretty sure Penelope would have never wanted. She didn't even like pink. He imagined her mom, Alexandra, kneeling by the stone with Windex and a roll of paper towels.

Her name hit him the hardest. The dates. Each letter carved perfectly into the stone. It all seemed so finite. Bleak.

When he stood above her grave, he popped his ear buds out and stowed them in his pocket. Swept the front of his hair with his hand, as if she could see him. After a few moments of shifting his weight from foot to foot, he thought he should say something. But when he started, his voice cracked and squeaked. Instead, he just spoke silently in his head and hoped that the spirit Penelope could read minds.

Sorry for not speaking out loud. Of course, you know that it takes me three kinds of forever to get up the gumption to say anything... important. I just miss you. You probably know that. You were always the smart one. I guess I'm just scared.

Mom and Dad are super worried. Mom's being a trouper. She cleaned up my puke this morning. Yeah, I know. Gross, huh?

Pete Stamdahl kicks my bus seat every morning. I still don't know why he has it out for me. Though, he did mention you the other day. I don't know. Maybe he liked you and hated me for taking all your time. I don't know. I wish I could talk to you again. Feel you.

Nothing has gone right since you...left. Here, there, everywhere. I met this guy Steve from a different dimension trying to get me to help you...er, I mean your alternates. He says the worlds we played in actually exist, but they're mutated, or something, now. We went to the Islas Encantadas. It's not right. Everything is backwards. Noface is king and you and I, we're, uh...either dead, or missing, or captured, or something. Those worlds are nothing like how we thought they were. I don't want to go back. But if I don't, Steve says each of your alternates will be in danger. I wish none of this ever happened.

Ian paused a moment. He pursed his lips in worry. Hesitating, he found a raised corner on a scrap of sod and poked at it with the toe of his shoe.

What did happen, Penelope? Steve said you were a traveler. What is that? Did you know what you were? What you could do? It wasn't the Smudge World, was it? You didn't think you could fix it? Or rescue those people, did you? Things are hard enough back home. I can barely keep one world straight. The only thing I know is that until you…left, everything was going great. At least I thought it was. We, uh, were closer than ever. I just wish I could be more like the other Ian Wilders. Those guys have no problems making split decisions, putting their bodies and emotions on the line. Perhaps I'm the alternate of one of them? Who knows? Just know that I still love you and wish you were here. Nothing works without you.

Ian looked at his phone again. 2:11 PM.

I should go. It'll take me an hour to walk home. Boy, Mom and Dad will be pissed. Probably already are. Well, goodbye Penelope. I miss you.

CHAPTER 17

ACROSS THE DROP-DEAD BRIDGE

At 3:25 PM, Ian turned the corner and saw his dad's Yukon parked in the driveway. He was home early. As he walked up the driveway, hot liquids and metal in the engine cooled in a series of pings and gurgles. His dad sat on the front stoop, still in his suit, his gray suitcoat draped over the porch rail. As Ian approached, he looked up and said, "How's Penelope doing?"

Ian stopped, startled. "What are you talking about?"

His dad held up his phone. "Phone-tracker app. I saw that you went on a long walk. Ended up at Evangeline's Cemetery."

Ian let out a breath like a breeching dolphin. "Still gone," he replied.

Harold scooted to the right on the stoop, making some room for Ian and patted the cold cement. "Have a seat."

Ian took off his backpack, set it on the walk, and sat next to his dad. "Is Mom upset?"

"Let's just say it's best not to go in there yet."

Ian rubbed his head. "I meant to go to school, Dad. I really did. But I ended up walking past the school and into town. By the time

I cleared my head, I was at Donny's Pie Shop and third period was over."

Harold nodded. "Losing someone close is terribly hard to overcome. Did I ever tell you what I did when your Uncle Paul died?"

Ian shook his head.

"I skipped out on work. Took a bottle of Southern Comfort to the Deer Run Dam north of Camden. I leaned against that rail and drank and watched the water roar under my feet and crash into the river below."

Ian watched his father's face. He'd been six, maybe seven when Uncle Paul died.

"It was exhilarating. The feel of it. The vibrations of the water. The smell of mud, the earth, raw and bare. And being one railing away from my own death. I stood there all day, trying to make sense of why my brother had to die and the rest of the world got to keep going. Then I saw the baby ducks," he said.

Ian squinched his face into a question. "Ducks?"

"Yes. Ducks. Three or four little ones. They swam too close to the falls and were about to be drowned."

"Did they?" Ian asked.

"No," his father said. "I ran to the shore and picked my way around the large rocks to get to them. I don't know what I was thinking. Maybe I figured I needed to save something after losing my brother. But I was determined to get to those ducks and keep them from being sucked under the falls."

Ian sat in trepidation. "Did you save them?"

Harold shook his head, dipped his chin to his chest. "No. I didn't. But their mother did. I got about an arm's length away, when she flew in and paddled them back to shore with her wings."

Ian took a breath. "So what's the big lesson? The moral of the story?"

Harold looked at his phone and shook his head. "I don't know, son. I still haven't figured it out, and maybe there is no moral. I just wanted you to know that it's okay. We understand that you need some time and space. Just make sure you tell us what you're doing so we don't worry, okay? Your mom and I want to help, but if you don't talk to us, we can't do much." Harold paused and turned his head to stretch his neck. "Now you'd better go in there and apologize to your mother. Maybe offer to make dinner."

Ian grabbed his backpack. "But I only know how to make spaghetti."

Harold slowly got up from the stoop. Stretched his back. "Spaghetti sounds just fine."

Later, Ian made his world-famous Ragu spaghetti, making sure to serve both his parents like a waiter. He was even able to find two mismatched candles for the table. And although his mother didn't eat much, she managed a small smile and kissed him on the cheek before going to the living room. His father nodded his approval.

After loading the dishwasher, he climbed the stairs and fell into his bed. There, he paged through the contents of his journal. As one hand spread out the page to read, the other meticulously felt each colored bead on the necklace Penelope had made for him. Again, his fingers journeyed across the beads and their etched symbols. A waning crescent. The moon. Like the one hanging over Schwarzwald. An elongated x below a small circle. The skull and crossbones. The pirate world of Islas Encantadas. His fingertips ended on the larger turquoise bead—their getaway world.

He focused on the information from their adventures in the Islas Encantadas, the quest for the Ruby Spyglass, the mutiny of the Wicked Crow, and Captain Noface himself.

He hadn't been there long, when a blue light traced down the seam to his closet doors and Steve, still fully dressed in his pirate gear, burst through them. "Sulking in your room, I take it."

"I'm not sulking," Ian said. "I'm just tired. Major damage control back home here."

Steve shook his head and said, "I never told you to skip school, pal. I even re-arranged my schedule so you could keep your stories straight."

"It's so hard! Between the pirates and my parents going off the deep-end, I don't know if I should save the ducks or let the mother save them!"

The corner of Steve's lip curled up in an expression of confusion. "What do ducks have to do with any of this?"

Ian grunted and flopped over on his bed, burying his face into his pillow.

"Listen," Steve said. "I don't know about any ducks, but I do know that you spent nearly an hour at the grave of your dead girlfriend today. Her alternate is waiting on the other side of these doors. And she's being tracked and hunted down by that malig. She won't know it's coming, and we're the only ones who can save her, Ian."

A muffled, unintelligible response leaked out of Ian's pillow.

"What?" Steve asked.

Ian turned his head and with a scowl, said, "I know!"

"Then get your pantaloons on and man up," Steve said.

"There it is," Jacob the fisherman said, sitting atop the driver's bench of his wagon. He pointed to an island in the sea. "Drop-Dead Island. The last resting place of Captain Lopper."

"Cap'n Sopper, I heard," said Gargle.

Boils chimed in. "I heard it be Cap'n Topper."

"Whatever you believe, take your provisions, your lamps," said Jacob. "It's time to part ways."

Ian and Steve unloaded the wagon of the few things they packed. High above them, a muted shriek cut through the air followed by a quick dark flash of shadow. Steve looked upwards, shielding his eyes. "That damn condor is keeping pretty close."

Ian followed Steve's gaze. Saw the thin brushstroke of the bird circling overhead in lazy loops. "Unless it can talk," Ian said, "I don't think we need to worry."

"I don't know," Steve said. "Longbottoms was pretty chummy with that thing."

Once unloaded, Jacob and the wagon rolled away leaving Steve, Ian, and their chaperones on the lip of a windy bluff, where the entrance to an old rope bridge lay before them. Numerous weathered signs painted with words of warning were staked into the ground before the entrance:

Beware!
Go Back!!!
Death Awaits Ye!
The Rocks Take Your Bones!
The Ghost Takes Your Soul!

Ian and Steve stepped to the edge and leaned over it to get the view. Below, the bluff descended a good two hundred feet straight down to the craggy shore below. A flock of crows squawked and chattered while picking at the rocks below.

"Great," Steve said. "This looks safe."

"How do you build a bridge like this?" Ian asked as they examined the bridge. "It's impossible!" Constructed of thick, but fraying rope, the walkway had hundreds of three-foot planks, many of which had broken, sending their travelers to their deaths below. At the end of the bridge on the other side, sat a tropical island and the gaping cavern from Penelope's drawing. Around the island sprang a sharp volcanic reef. Boils pointed. "That reef looks like the jaws of a shark!"

"Never a chance a long boat makes it through without bein' torn to shreds," Gargle added.

But Ian wasn't looking at the reef. He stood hypnotized by the wide entrance to the cavern at the opposite end of the rope bridge above the crashing surf below. The winds between the bluff and the island swirled upward violently, only to switch within a heartbeat to a crosswind or a downdraft. The play of the winds made the cavern wail like a ghostly breath over the top of a bottle—just like he heard when he first saw Penelope's painting in the classroom.

"Come on," Gargle shouted. "That girl is the key to the cap'n's victory." Gargle took a broad step over the first few busted planks in the bridge and set his foot on the first available step.

"No, wait!" Ian shouted.

But when Gargle put his foot down, he did not break through.

"I thought there was a code to the bridge?" Steve asked.

"There's no stinkin' code," Gargle shouted. "All a bunch of horse apples." But when he turned on his heel and took the next step, the plank broke and sent Gargle screaming to the rocks below with a mushy crunch.

The crows scattered briefly, before converging on Gargle's body, their new, tenderized meal strewn before them. Steve and Ian looked down in horror, and then at each other, eyes wide.

Boils pointed his pistola at them. "You two go first from now on. And get a move on."

Ian stood at the bridge's entrance, both hands clinging to the posts against the whipping wind. What was he thinking? He couldn't do this. He was just a stupid kid. Maybe pirate Ian ran across rope bridges like they were sidewalks, but this was for real. One wrong step and game over. Ian took a deep breath and risked a hand to wipe the cold sweat from his brow. The distance to the first step was almost three and a half feet. It seemed so small, yet so wide. Down the length of the bridge, numerous planks had broken, sending their victims to the depths. Ian crouched down to keep his vertigo from toppling him. Steve crouched next to him. "Do you know the code?"

Ian shook his head. "No. I don't."

"Come on, you two," Boils shouted. "Time's a wastin'." Then he shoved Ian over the gap. Flailing and off-balance, Ian fell onto the planks on the other side. Thankfully, they held, but his feet dangled through the gap. Ian gripped the planks out of white-knuckle fear, pulling the lower half of his body up onto the bridge. He lay there for a moment to steady himself, gulping at the air and trying to quiet the thump racing in his chest and temples. He closed his eyes. He felt a warm wetness in his pants. Thankfully, the other two couldn't see the dark spot that bloomed there. When the knot in his throat shrunk enough to swallow safely, he opened his eyes.

At first, he thought he was seeing things; the planks looked like they had markings on them. But after focusing more closely, he could make out faint scorings on the first plank. He pushed himself up on all fours and looked on the next plank. More scoring symbols. On his knees, he reached up to the rope rails and looked down the bridge. Each plank he could see had a faint, but specific marking; an entire codex of symbols. But he didn't know what they meant. He had never seen this language before. Behind him, the pistola cracked a shot into the air. Ian ducked for cover.

"On with it!" Boils bellowed.

The knot grew in Ian's throat again. A stiff wind caught the bridge and sent it swaying. He gulped hard in panic and gripped at the rope railings. He ducked his head to his chest to compose himself, and he felt the necklace Penelope had given him tighten around his throat. Wait a minute. Ian cautiously let one hand go from the rope rail and blindly touched the etched beads of the necklace. He remembered them, the symbols, each one etched to represent a story. Was this the answer? Did she leave him a coded message? A language only he could understand? The symbols on the necklace had to be the code. Penelope wanted him to find it.

"I know it!" he shouted back to Steve.

Ian crouched down to inspect the closest intact plank. It had a skull-and-crossbones etched into it. Pirates. It was on the necklace, Ian thought, so it had to be safe. But when his foot hit the plank, it shattered and he stumbled. In his fear-soaked flailing, he managed to hook his armpit on the lower rope rail. His bladder fully released, soaking his pants. "Oh my god, Steve!!! Oh my god!!!" Ian screamed, before his voice caught with a whimper in this throat. Ian couldn't help but look down at the surf crashing against black rocks. Ian thought about his dad's story. The dam. The crashing water below his feet. His arms and shoulders trembled to support his weight.

"It's okay," Steve called. "Just pull yourself up!"

"Not likely!" Ian yelled back. He remembered how, each year during the school fitness exams, he struggled to get half-way up to the bar, his skinny, video-game-playing arms shaking terribly under the strain. "I've never actually done a pull-up before, Steve!"

Steve sidled onto the left side of the bridge, his feet on the bottom rope and his hands on the top rope. With his and Ian's weight to the left side and the updrafting wind, the bridge almost twisted upside down.

"Just lay across the good plank!" Ian yelled.

"Are you insane?" Steve said but lay on his belly across the good plank. A curling downdraft jerked at the bridge. Steve slid to the right, but maintained his hold on the planks. "You have to be a monkey with four hands to do this without falling to your death!" he yelled. Steve reached down and grabbed Ian's pants and pulled. With Steve's help and a furious set of kicks, Ian pulled himself up to the next plank, adorned with a symbol of Saturn.

It did not break.

Trying to catch his breath, Steve yelled, "Figure this out, because I do not want to do that again!"

Grasping the rope rail, Ian panted. His lungs and heart rapped wildly against his ribs. The wind whipped through his spine, chilling him. "Of course," he gasped. "Using the skull and crossbones in a pirate world is too easy. It must be all her symbols except the skull and crossbones." With half his weight on the good plank, he reached over three other planks to the next one he knew: a longhorn skull.

It held.

"Okay," he called to Steve and Boils. "Watch my feet carefully and only step on the planks I step on. Step on any others and you're dessert for those crows down there."

For the remaining hours of the afternoon, they maneuvered their way across the bridge. Ian's whole body throbbed from his falls and from gripping the ropes so tightly, but he kept focused on each plank ahead of him. When Steve and Boils met him at the entrance to the cavern, they looked back towards the bluff, where the sky burned off its indigo for the night.

"That's a long way back," Steve said, only to get thumped in the temple by Boils and his pistola.

"Close your trap and get to walking," Boils said. "Let's find your girl and get back to the cap'n."

Steve and Ian took two steps forward to the mouth of the cavern, but Boils did not. A dark red spot bloomed through the bandanna on his forehead and dribbled down his face. Boils staggered forward, sprawling dead on ground, the echoing report of a musket rattling through the cavern. Once the echo faded, a new sound filled the void.

Footsteps.

With the clanging of chains.

Ian swallowed. The ghost of Captain Lopper. They had passed the bridge. Now they had to pass the ghost.

CHAPTER 18

THE GHOST OF CAPTAIN LOPPER

Ian and Steve stood in fright, the footsteps and chains crashing closer. When he first heard the stories, Ian was skeptical. But in the cavern, with the metallic rattle bouncing off the walls and the harsh footfalls marching toward him, he believed. Boy, did he believe. In a panic, Ian scanned the ground for Boils' pistola, but saw nothing gun-shaped in the waning sunlight.

A light glowed from the cavern darkness, small and dull, but growing brighter with each loud footstep and chain rattle. The stories of the villagers heaved in Ian's mind. Ghost, murderer, whatever it was, it approached. When the light become its brightest, almost blinding, it stopped before them and swayed.

An oil lamp.

A face appeared in the shadows behind the lamp. Scarred and wind-burnt from the sea, the man otherwise appeared young. Maybe a year or two older than Ian. With a mop of long, greasy hair and a short, patchy beard, the stranger wore what must have once been a magnificent set of pirate leathers, but they had grown cracked, worn, and tattered. He carried a musket slung over his back and held an oil lamp connected to a rusty length of chain in his left hand. In the other, there was nothing, not even a hand. Only a knotty wrist stump remained.

When the stranger held the lamp up to Ian's face, he gasped and lowered it quickly. "What have ye come here for?"

Terrified, Ian looked at Steve for advice, but he was without answers. Ian couldn't swallow. He could have really used an ice-cold soda. Anything. And he couldn't help but stare at the pirate's missing hand.

"Out with it now," the pirate said.

"We've," Ian started and stuttered, looking intently at the pirate. There was something familiar about him that Ian couldn't place. "We've come to f-find Ms. Penelope Archer. We b-believe she's in danger."

"Sorry to say, boys," the pirate grumbled. "But you've come a long way for nothin'. You see, Ms. Archer surely is in danger, but she's not here."

Ian shook his head. She had to be there. The drawing? The bridge? "What do you mean? She drew this picture," Ian pulled out the sketch from Ms. White's class and showed him. "She coded those planks," Ian gestured toward the bridge. "She has to be here!"

"Well, she's not!" the pirate raised his voice. "And no amount a sayin' it will bring her back."

Steve stepped in and asked gently, "How do you know?"

The oil lamp swung around and followed the pirate as he walked away into the darkened cavern. "Because she took my place so I could go free," he said.

"Why would she do that? Who are you?" Ian called after him.

In the darkness, the pirate's voice cracked. "I'm Captain Ian Wilder."

Torches sputtered in the cavern drafts around Ian, Steve, and Captain Wilder, illuminating a wide living quarters, complete with piles of pirate gear and plunder. Steve and Ian sat in velvet-cushioned, high-back chairs that the captain had pulled from the plunder. Captain Wilder apologized for the accommodations; he didn't have many guests. He sat sideways in a wooden throne, a low, beautiful mosaic table between him and Ian and Steve. With his left hand, the captain rotated a spit skewered with a large haunch of wild boar. Between their words, embers in the fire popped and crackled.

Awestruck, Ian found himself staring at the captain like he had just met a celebrity. The captain was everything he was not: six inches taller, cut from stone, a square jaw, tattoos, and scars, and he had enough swagger for both of them. He even found it difficult to talk to him. "So you've lived here all this time?" Ian asked.

"Since her rescue, yes," the captain said. The spit handle creaked on every half turn. "For years she fought gallantly by my side as we crossed Noface in every port. She was there when I swam to the bottom of the sea to retrieve the Neverblade. When we stopped his armada from finding the Ruby Spyglass. Even when I dueled Noface on Hagshead Peak and threw him over the edge."

Ian remembered his dream on Hagshead Peak. The storm. The gargoyle statues flashing in the lightning. The ceremonial bowl, spilling over with water. The glee in Noface's eyes as he lay Penelope dead at his feet. He shook his head to clear the horrible dream and reached across the table to nab a chunk of pineapple from a shoddy wooden bowl. "So everything was going great."

The captain turned the spit, silent a moment. Each squeak of the handle was amplified in this cavern. "It was. Not anymore. Nothin's been right since. I have no zest. No vigor. Together, the world bowed to us. No horizon seemed too far, no sea too deep." Captain Wilder paused again, staring into the fire. "It's not the same without her. There's no point." He ceased rotating the spit momentarily to lift a flask of wine to his lips, drinking long and hard. "What little joy I find is from dispatching the looters after our treasure. But so few of them make it past her traps. Even I can't figure them out. I almost fell to my death thrice on that vile roped bridge."

Ian took another piece of pineapple. "So she left you here to protect you?"

"I have no idea. Maybe. Everywhere we went, and everything we did, we did together. Then one day she goes mad and tells me we're through. And I never saw her again, until the day she came to save me."

"From Noface's prison?" Steve asked.

"Aye," the captain answered.

Ian swallowed and looked at the captain lounging in the throne across from them. In the flickering glow of the torches, he didn't see much of himself in him. The captain's hair was far longer. His arms and legs bulged thicker. Even his voice came from a different land. And his hand. Ian couldn't imagine ever losing a piece of his body. But right when he had the thought, his own wrist felt the pain, like a phantom blade worked between his wrist bones, prying his hand from his arm.

Steve chimed in. "You must have upset her."

Captain Wilder lurched his head to Steve and said, "What? How? How did I upset her? I gave her everything."

Steve shook his head and said, "What about the credit? While you were out there playing the hero and doing all the good stuff, did you ever give her any of the glory? Was it ever her name chanted in the background of all those celebrations?"

The captain pouted his lips in thought. "I have no idea," he said finally. "Perhaps not. I suppose that might get her a little cranky."

"You two were supposed to be in love," Ian said, a little judgmentally.

Captain Wilder cackled. "Let's not get ahead of ourselves, lads. Trust me, there was plenty o' love between Penelope and me, that much I can assure you."

Ian stood up in a huff. "Don't talk about her like that!"

The captain chuckled again. "Oh, looky here. The little man thinks he's big." Captain Wilder stood up and confronted Ian. He looked down on Ian and poked a finger into his chest. "I saved your measly life, friend. That no good scally was goin' to shoot the both of you after you found Penelope. All a' Longbottoms' crew is that way."

Steve squeezed himself between the two and gently separated them. "Thank you, Captain. We really do appreciate that. Right, Ian?" Steve nodded at Ian to concede. After a beat, Ian nodded. Both of the Ian Wilders returned to their seats.

Captain Wilder took up the spit again. "So since I told you my story, I believe you should tell me yours. Like why do you look like my uglier little brother?" he asked, pointing to Ian.

"Our story...is a little more complex," Steve told the captain. "Let's just say that it's imperative that we find Penelope as soon as possible."

"That's a pretty big word, there, Stevo," the captain chuckled.

"Do you know where she is?" Steve implored.

"Of course I know where she is," the captain replied. "But you can't get to her without a ship and a crew. And I have neither. Not to mention, if it came to crossin' blades, you're going to have to do that yourself, because I'm a bit short at the moment." To emphasize his point, the captain thrust up the stub of his right arm to show them his missing sword hand.

"That's fine," Ian said, leaning forward. "All we need is the Neverblade. It grants its wielder the skill and abilities of all its former handlers. So simply give me your sword, and I can take your place."

The captain chuckled again. "I don't have it anymore."

Ian scrunched his nose in confusion. "What do you mean? It's your sword. We...I mean, you swam to the bottom of the sea to retrieve it."

"I know that," the captain said. "What do you think Penelope had to trade in order to let me out?"

Ian sat back in shock. "He has the Ruby Spyglass and the Neverblade?"

The captain reached to tear a shred of pork from the roasting haunch and said, "That's what I'm tryin' to tell you. You have no chance." The captain ate the roast pork and continued. "Besides, what makes you think Penelope wants to be rescued? A blimey skiver I dumped on the rocks some weeks ago told me his ship was taken by the Wicked Crow. Only Noface wasn't at the helm. A young woman was. Your precious Penelope. Noface sits on the throne, but she sails his fleet."

Ian shuddered, trying to make sense of it all. How was it possible? Why would she save him and then take up with Noface? Was it under duress, or had this despicable version of himself driven Penelope to switch sides? Or did she simply recognize the winning side and decide to save her own skin with Noface? Could he blame her? After seeing three days of this world, he didn't want to live here anymore either. But wait…was this Penelope at all, or the malig? The one who had come to visit him the day of Penelope's funeral?

Steve grabbed Ian by the shoulders, and that's when Ian realized he was shaking. "Maybe we should take a load off for a while," he whispered into Ian's ear. "Get a good meal, drink a little wine, and get some shut-eye. We'll tackle a new plan tomorrow, okay?" Captain Wilder watched this exchange with interest while carving the boar.

The three ate roast pork and island fruit and drank wine. Though, when Ian tried to refill his goblet the second time, Steve put his hand over it and shook his head. Ian did sneak another glass when Steve went to the mouth of the cavern to pee.

Steve and the captain swapped stories, while Ian went back and forth from listening to getting lost in his own blurry thoughts. He vaguely heard Steve try to explain the concept of infinity to the captain, but it didn't go well. The captain reveled in stories of hunting hogs and dispatching the vagabonds that managed to make it to the island. At every instance, Steve followed the captain's stories with probing questions, determined to get to the bottom of things. Ian saw how Steve encouraged the captain to drink more wine while he himself nursed his third glass. The captain appeared to be cozier with the bottle than Ian imagined an alternate of himself to be, so it worked.

Before long, the captain revealed that he never figured out or understood why Penelope had exchanged her life for his own. "She never said why," he slurred, slurping wine. "But I saw it in her eyes."

"What?" Steve asked.

"Fear," the captain replied. "Something or someone scared her into it."

After the wine, with a full belly, Ian wasn't sure he cared what had motivated Penelope to set him/the captain free. As far as he could tell, this world had rotted so far away from what he thought it was, it wasn't worth salvaging, even if it meant not seeing Penelope again. And now he had no backup plan. No thoughts on what to do. He was exhausted, apathetic, and buzzed. He just wanted to be home, in bed, snuggled into those fantastic pajamas his mother had gotten him.

The night ended when Ian's snoring became louder than Steve and the captain felt like talking. "Easy there, cowboy," Steve told Ian as he helped him to a nearby pile of robes and blankets. "Get some shut-eye, kid," he whispered. "I think I know what we need to do now. We'll see you tomorrow."

Ian burrowed into the pile and fell into a full sleep.

❀ ❀ ❀

Ian kneels aboard the deck of the Wicked Crow once more. A storm rages in the distance, and cold rain strikes his back like a volley of arrows. His belly is shriveled to a husk, and the quake of hunger distracts from the looming mask of Captain Noface.

Before him, Ian's right hand is chained to a block. The wind rises, and waves rock the ship. "For crimes against the crown," Noface's voice booms. And as he speaks, his usual black leather tricorn hat morphs into a golden king's crown. "I grant thee punishment of dismemberment and a lifetime in my brig!"

Lightning glazes the sky, and Noface draws his sword. Only it isn't Noface's sword, it's Ian's—the silver glimmer of the Neverblade. Ian catches his own reflection in it: filthy and dressed in beggar's clothes, his face and body almost skeletal. Panicking, he yanks his hand against the chains. But it only opens the blisters and sores where the manacle digs into his skin. There is nothing he can do.

Noface swings the sword down, cleanly severing Ian's hand from his wrist. Pain splinters up his arm as he cries out. He pulls free of the chains and holds the gory stump in his good hand. His whole body drums, beats with the rhythm of a hundred hearts. As blood pumps from his wrist, he feels his existence go with it. As he collapses forward, his blood pools on the ship's deck, where the rain patters at it until it washes between the boards and mixes perfectly into the sea.

CHAPTER 19

A HELPING HAND

Ian awoke in a frightened, sweaty gasp. He bolted to sitting and grasped for his right hand with his left. The dream seemed so real, he just assumed that he, too, had lost his hand like his counterpart. Relieved to find himself intact, he sprawled back out in the heap of robes and blankets, rubbing his right hand with the left.

He had to pee. He crept as quietly as he could from the warm pile to avoid waking Steve, who was snoring at the other end. He stood and nearly toppled over from the pain. Oof, he was sore and stiff. Yesterday's exertions on the bridge had caught up with him. He stretched in the darkness, gasping at the ache in muscles he didn't know he had.

After he felt a bit more limber, Ian took his cell phone from his pocket to light his way. Across the cavern, Captain Ian Wilder lay tangled amid stolen silk sheets and a satin coverlet on a four-poster mahogany bed. His bare, hair-covered chest rose and fell, while his handless arm lay above his head on a faded velvet pillow. Ian lifted the neck of his shirt and shined the phone down at his chest. Just three sparse hairs, struggling to make a go at it.

After peeing at the mouth of the cavern, Ian took the opportunity to check out the place, looking at all the loot Penelope and Captain Wilder had stowed away for the future. He wondered how she had gotten the furniture in. Carrying a bed that size across the bridge was not an option. But knowing Penelope, she would find a way.

The captain's musket, affixed with an old spyglass, leaned against the stolen throne. Ian imagined his counterpart spying through it to pick off Boils at a distance. Ian shined his phone on an oval table behind the throne, where six pistols lay in various stages of reload. A dusty barrel of swords and cutlasses sat on the other side of the table, likely holding little interest for the captain since he was once in possession of the Neverblade. Ian drew out a cutlass with a metallic swipe and quickly slashed the air in front of him. No problem, he thought.

Using the rusted cutlass as a walking stick, Ian stepped about the cavern, inspecting chests filled with silver candlesticks, heirloom brooches, and golden jewelry. He found a barrel of apples and carrots and grabbed an apple to snack on as he walked about. He found an old coffin along the back wall of the cavern, standing upright next to a handcart and a wagon. Curious, he pulled back the lid, which creaked like a creepy coffin should.

Only what he saw was not a decomposed body or skeleton, but a secret passageway carved into the cavern wall. Ian used his phone to light the way and walked up the steps carved into the narrow tunnel. Curious, Ian checked behind him to see if anyone had seen his discovery. Where did this passageway lead? He sensed a secret ahead. A plot twist he and Steve hadn't anticipated. He followed the tunnel for many yards, before a ladder of lashed branches and roots emerged. Climbing the steps, he came to a thatched cover that detached easily enough. Stashing the lid off to the side, Ian pulled himself up to the topside of the island, which spooled out in rolling, grassy hills and tropical forest.

Overhead, the multitude of birds and chattering monkeys told him Penelope had chosen her island well. With the pineapple bushes, the coconut and papaya trees, plus the wild game on the island, Penelope could have lived a long, bountiful life here. He followed one of the animal trails to the forest's edge, where the island swooped downwards into a black gorge filled with craggy old lava flows. Finding his way carefully through the gorge, Ian discovered it emptied out onto a black sand beach, where his boots sunk deep into the fine silt. Ian stabbed his cutlass into the sand and removed his boots, stepping out to meet the waves as they rolled in. He could feel the sea mist on his face.

Ian shielded his eyes with his hand and gazed to the sea. About a hundred yards out, the jagged reef crown circling the island jutted upwards, slashing the incoming sea to ribbons. Just like shark teeth, as Boils had said. The dead pirates were right. Any boat would have trouble crossing that reef without shredding its hull. A lone sailor might be able to wash up on shore alive with some luck, but likely not without injury.

Penelope had found a virtually inescapable and unbreachable island fortress. Captain Ian Wilder was right; whatever or whomever it was she feared, it frightened her enough to secure this hideaway.

The beach filled him with a happiness he hadn't felt in a long time. Ian sat cross-legged and picked up fine black sand and let it run through his hands. He had always marveled at the tactile sensation of sand. When his parents took him to the beach as a child, he never built castles or dug trenches. He just sat, feet dug in, and felt the sand sift through his fingers, handful by handful. Ian closed his eyes and listened to the steady cascade of waves at the shore, felt the sun kissing the back of his neck, and inhaled the fresh smell of sea foam. Ian had found his nirvana.

With everything that had happened, Ian enjoyed the break from the insanity. He let his mind and body relax, could feel the tension and soreness leave his aching muscles. It felt so good, he lost track of time. When he opened his eyes and looked out to the sea, a dark brushstroke of a ship lolled on the waves. Ian rubbed his eyes to be sure of what he saw. He could only see the ship's profile, but he would recognize it anywhere. It was the Wicked Crow.

Fearful that Captain…no…King Noface would send a longboat full of his finest to run him through, Ian quickly scrambled for cover behind a nearby stash of driftwood. But after a second or two, he remembered things were different here. Noface sat atop the throne now and Penelope, the pirate version, commanded his fleet!

Ian stumbled out of hiding and jumped about the beach, waving his hands in a near frenzy to get the ship's attention. Using all the power in his lungs, he screamed her name. The thought of her being so close, yet so far, filled his veins with searing electricity. He had to get closer. He ran into the surf and battled the waves. He tried to swim past the riptide and current. But with each head-bob above the water, he saw the Wicked Crow sailing farther and farther away. He hadn't even made it a quarter of the way to the reef before the ship turned into a dot on the horizon and then disappeared. Dejected and exhausted, Ian lay on his back and let the waves push him back into shore. He wondered if Penelope had even looked at the island.

She had to. This island was hers.

As he floated, Ian imagined her at the helm of the ship, passing by the secret refuge and extending her spyglass for a brief glimpse, a quick shuddering image of him. Ian couldn't believe that things were that bad between her and him…er…the captain that she wouldn't still care for him. Ian was sure she had seen what she wanted to see: the captain alive and well. Now, she could go about her business.

Ian slogged out of the water and back onto the sand. What if that has been his only chance to save her? The thought depressed him. The malig could be anywhere, working her way to Penelope. She could get to Penelope before them. And he had wasted his one chance because he couldn't swim fast enough or shout loud enough to get her to notice.

Soaked and standing in the sea breeze, he grew chilled. He'd better head back. Steve would probably be worried. Ian put on his boots and grabbed the cutlass before trudging up the black gorge and back onto the top of the island. The way up was more taxing than the way down, and he was out of breath when he reached the secret entrance. He climbed down into the passageway making sure to affix the thatched grass cover over the hole. He reached for his phone to light the tunnel.

His phone!

Patting around his wet pantaloons, he found it and pulled it out of his pocket. The phone refused to light up or turn on. Fried. Ian shook his head. One more thing to add to the list of screw-ups. Swearing to himself, he felt his way down the stone stairs and, arriving inside the cavern, closed the coffin lid behind him.

Both the captain and Steve were up and talking at the table. Over the fire, Steve tended to a pot of boiling liquid that smelled like coffee. The captain drank from a steaming tin cup. "And this will help?" he asked. To which Steve responded, "With as much as you drank last night, it certainly won't hurt." Steve looked up from the cooking pot and saw Ian. "There you are! Where did you disappear to?"

Ian stowed his cutlass back in the barrel with the rest of them. "I think I saw the Wicked Crow."

"Did you now?" Captain Wilder said. "She used to come every week. Then every month. Lately it's been hit or miss. But she's still checking up on me."

"Sure." Ian nodded and sat down. He couldn't help but think of pirate Penelope, oblivious to the hidden assassin stalking her.

"Your friend and I have been talking," the captain said. "He told me the whole story."

Ian looked at Steve, wide-eyed. "The whole story?"

Steve nodded his head. "You know. About the assassin from the Eastern Isles, Malig Chen, a Lin Kuei warrior."

The captain drained his tin cup of coffee and wiped his mouth with the back of his hand. "If this warrior is as formidable as your friend says, we must waste no time. We must get aboard the Wicked Crow." The captain smiled.

Ian recognized something in his smile—a slyness, a cockiness that he remembered, perhaps from his own incarnations of the character. "But why now?" Ian asked. "You've been holed up here, drinking, sleeping, watching the days go by as Penelope took your place on the Crow. Why now?"

The captain paused and stared at Ian. "Because I finally see it," he said. "My mistake. My weakness. I've been feeling miserable about losin' my hand, feeling unable to do anything but watch the Crow ease around the island with her on it." He paused to look back at his reflection hiding inside his cup. "But there's no need for it. Noface rules the land and sea, yet the Wicked Crow and its new cap'n slide by every month or so, sculling just close enough to get a gaze through a spyglass. She gave up everything for me. Everything. And I let her. And I've sat here doing nothing."

"She still loves you," Ian realized.

"Aye, she does. And I haven't been brave enough to do anythin' about it. Until now."

Steve shook his head and stirred the coffee in the pot.

Ian said, "What brought on this change of heart?"

The captain stood up and slid a cutlass from the barrel and slashed the air clumsily with his left hand. "You," he said, pointing the sword at Ian. "You're an odd chap. I see a bit o' my old self in you. A brash innocence, or maybe ignorance about you. You've travelled all this way to find a girl you hardly know, to save her life. That sounds like the kind of stupid thing I used to do all the time. And it's about time I did it again."

A zest like fresh-grated lemons rippled through Ian. For the first time since he arrived in this reality, something sounded like the world he and Penelope played in for so many years. Like a strobe from a lighthouse, the captain's words cut through the fog and showed them a path. Even Steve looked more excited than normal. Ian couldn't contain his smile. All the remorse he felt for failing on the beach had been swept away. "So what's our plan?"

Captain Wilder again slashed his sword gracelessly with his left hand. "We have to get her attention."

"How do we do that?" Ian asked.

Captain Wilder grinned broadly and winked at him. "By sinking a few of her ships."

Steve eased back on the controls of the faux Millennium Falcon and released the closet doors, exposing Ian's dark bedroom. "Don't worry about the plan," he told Ian. "It's better than anything we've come up with so far."

Ian stood up from his co-pilot's chair. "He just seems overly confident."

Steve shook his head. "Of course, he does. He's everything you're not, right?"

Ian looked down at the floor. The metallic paneling of the ship blended into the carpeting of his room. "Right."

"He knows that world far better than we do, and having him around could be, well, handy."

Ian shot Steve a scowl.

"Too early?" Steve grinned. "I've been dying to use it since we met him."

"No more hand jokes," Ian said.

"Fine. Get some rest. The captain has plans for you. And good luck with the phone."

Ian stepped into his room, and the doors slid shut behind him. Next to his bed, his alarm clock read 10:23 PM, a scant 3.5 minutes since he had left. Ian still didn't understand the crazy quickness of the time differential. He spent days in the Islas Encantadas, yet only a few minutes passed here. Steve had told him that, like the traditional three dimensions of space, a spot in time could be plotted and traveled to as well. His brain hurt when he tried thinking about it. Stay out of the quantum mechanics, Steve had told him. Ian rubbed his eyes and lay on his bed. As much as he wanted to, he couldn't sleep. He took his phone out of his pocket and set it on his nightstand.

Still fried.

He'd have to deal with that later. He opened his journal and paged through it, wondering if somewhere within it lay answers to his problems. But as hard as he looked, he found none. Their adventures played fresh in his head. It seemed so long ago since that afternoon in the treehouse, yet he knew it was a matter of weeks. He wished things were the way they used to be, where Penelope was alive, their days were full of love and adventure, and he was innocent of the Infiniuum swirling around him. Finding no answers in the sketches and stories, he closed the cover and stared at the ceiling until he fell asleep.

CHAPTER 20

A BALANCE OF BOTH WORLDS

After what felt like thirty minutes, Ian's alarm clock blared before he swatted it off. Dragging himself off the bed, he showered and brushed his teeth. Hell, he even flossed, which he never did. Without thinking much, Ian put on a lavender polo shirt and some khakis rather than jeans and a hoodie. When he packed his backpack, he decided to stuff his journal in too. Just in case.

Downstairs, he fixed his normal breakfast of three types of cereal and joined his parents at the table. His mother sat dressed for her pottery classes at the community center and spooned out sections of a grapefruit. His father ate egg whites and some turkey bacon. "My," his mother said, looking him over. "Don't you look dapper?"

His father folded the newspaper down and gave him an approving look. "When I played basketball," he said, "we wore suits and ties to school on game day. What's the occasion?"

Ian chewed his cereal and shrugged his shoulders. "I don't know."

"Well, you look good, Ian," his mother said. "Handsome."

Ian noticed that her voice had changed for that last word—the way a parent says something that obviously means something else; translation: he looked sane, normal, better, or not-screwed-up.

"Thanks," he mumbled.

"Straight home after school tonight, Ian," his father said from behind the paper.

Ian scrunched up his face. "Why?"

His father folded the paper down again. "It's Friday. Movie night. You remember, the action picture?"

"Wait, is it Friday already?" Ian asked. He had forgotten that he threw out movie night to make it up to them for all the craziness. "Great."

Both his parents eyed him, and his father said, "Of course it is."

Looking to the ceiling for help, he tried to count off the days of the week in his head. Why had he thought it was only Wednesday? The days seemed to blend into one. "Right," Ian recovered. "That's right. See you tonight then."

On the school bus, Ian did his best to slouch down in his seat and avoid eye contact. But he couldn't help but notice Heidi Flugalmann with those braces and starry eyes, staring him down. He put in his ear buds and reached for his phone, but it wouldn't turn on. A residual drop of water worked its way out of the casing and wetted Ian's hand. Right. Fried.

Almost on cue, a quick swat came to the back of his head. Pete Stamdahl.

"Hey, psycho," Pete said. "Patti Reinbarth said her mom saw you at the cemetery the other day."

"So?" Ian sighed.

"So," Pete said. "What? You miss your girlfriend?"

Ian pulled out his ear buds to put them away. "I do, yeah. What's it matter to you?"

"Did you cry, freak boy?"

Ian ignored the question.

"What? Were you reciting poetry to dear Penelope?"

Ugh. "No."

Pete tried grabbing Ian's journal from his backpack as he stashed the earbuds. Luckily, Ian pulled it away just in time. "Were you comparing notes in your diaries?" Pete put on a mock emotional face. "Penny, I miss you so much. Why'd you have to go? I wish everything was back to normal."

Ian found it odd that Pete quoted almost exactly what he thought standing over Penelope's grave. "I didn't actually say anything to her," he mumbled.

"Figures," Pete said, making another grab for the journal. "You two weren't talkers. Always keeping notes in your little wussy diaries." He reverted to his mocking tone, wringing his hands near his heart. "I secretly love Ian. And I secretly love Penny. We're super-secret lovebirds who play secret pretend and enjoy being dorks."

The veins in Ian's temples throbbed. His fingers formed fists around his bag straps. He imagined what Captain Wilder would have done. Even without his sword hand, he would have popped Pete in the chin and jabbed a dirk into him.

Ian smiled.

He could see it all play out on the bus: the punch, a quick twist of a hand, and the blade slipping between Pete's ribs with a short, juicy slice. He imagined Pete pausing, his lips a surprised rictus as the captain held Pete's shoulder with his stump and jabbed the blade deeper with his good hand. Pete would slump into a puddle of his own urine and blood, never to bother him again.

"You're not even listening!" Pete shouted. "Off in la-la land again. What a loser." Frustrated, Pete walked to the back of the bus and high-fived his friends.

Ian attended every class, the day passing quickly. In art, he stared at the empty space on the wall where the watercolor painting of the cavern had hung. Even though it was no longer there, the void among all the other pieces made the vacuum worse. It was even harder to believe he'd been there. In that cave.

At home, his parents greeted him happily. Ian showed his phone to his mom and made up a story about dropping it in the toilet on accident. After stashing the wet phone in a plastic bag of dry rice to draw out the moisture, they whisked him off to the mall, where they ate dinner in the food court and bought tickets for the latest action movie. Ian's parents let him get whatever he wanted at the concessions counter. Ian ordered popcorn, nachos, Junior Mints, and a Cherry Coke.

"Really?" his dad asked, removing his wallet from his back pocket.

Ian nodded and his dad handed two twenties to the cashier. "I wish I could eat garbage again," he told his wife, watching Ian carefully balancing his smorgasbord.

Maggie shook her head. "He has a teenage boy's metabolism, Harold."

The Wilder family watched the hero punch, stab, and intimidate his way through a revolving door of Euro bad guys. About 45 minutes in, Ian stepped out to get a Cherry Coke refill. At the concessions counter, Ian was shocked to see Steve wearing a movie theater uniform and a name tag that said "Bethany."

"The costume thing still floors me," Ian asked. "You can find a movie theater uniform, but not some decent pirate duds."

Steve scrunched his lips into a frown. "It helps to know where you're going."

"What are you doing here?"

"Refilling your Cherry Coke," Steve said. "You downed 48 ounces in 45 minutes."

"I was thirsty."

"You are going to piss like a racehorse tonight, pal," Steve said, handing Ian his refill. "I came to ask if you're really ready."

Ian took a sip. "Ready for what?"

"The final leg," Steve said. "This is when it gets a bit...ah, squishy."

"Squishy? How so?"

"The investigative and detective work is done. Now it's time for action. And I know you have reservations about your ability to act."

Ian looked at Steve, almost offended, but he had a point. "I guess I hadn't thought about it too much."

"Really?" Steve asked. "We're going to be in the fray this time, buddy. We're stealing a frickin' pirate ship! We're going to take on the Wicked Crow. I'm certainly worried about it!"

"Sorry," Ian said, looking down at his soda. "I've had a lot on my mind lately."

Steve wiped the counter. "Well, spend a little time thinking about this one, would you? My life, job, and existence depend on this too, you know."

Ian slurped his soda. "I will."

"Good!" Steve said. "The captain is busy prepping your training, so come prepared."

"Training?"

"Yeah," Steve said. "He can't do it on his own. Noface took his sword-hand, remember?"

Reflexively, Ian's right hand made a fist, reinforcing its own existence at the end of his arm. "Right."

"Go finish your movie."

On the walk back to the theater, Ian thought about the training and the upcoming clash. Could he do this? He couldn't even stand up to Pete Stamdahl. How would he be able to best Captain Longbottoms, bizarro-Penelope, or King Noface? None of the adventures he and Penelope created in their backyards ever had real stakes and consequences. They always made it out alive and uninjured. That's how fiction worked. He already had a few cuts and bruises he couldn't really explain. Worse, he doubted he could even complete one step of this crazy plan. Hell, he'd have his hands full simply taking out a deckhand.

Down the long hall of the theater, he gazed at the photographic mural displaying prominent heroes and villains throughout cinema history: the Joker, Superman, Captain Hook, Luke Skywalker, Scout

Finch, Hannibal Lector, Inigo Montoya, and others. He frowned at them all. They had it easy. They had their stories predetermined, written down. They knew their ends.

Ian did not.

He understood now that stories were never simply hero beats villain. Time changes. Worlds change. People deserving of long lives are taken early and those who should be rubbed from the parchment of existence are allowed long lives. As far as he knew, Captain Wilder would kill him in training. His mind flooded with doubt as he stepped into the darkened theater.

CHAPTER 21

TRAINING WITH CAPTAIN IAN WILDER

Clashing steel rang against Ian's ears, complicated by the sudden pain blistering through his back and head from the fall. His arms screamed at their hinges. His legs wobbled like they were filled with overstretched rubber bands. A bead of sweat rolled from his brow, stinging his left eye closed.

Lying there, beaten, exhausted, and tortured, Ian exhaled and tried to find the fluffy bunnies and swans amidst the buttermilk clouds in the Islas Encantadas sky. Before his ears recovered, the captain's gravelly voice barked across the hilltops of Drop-Dead Island. "I have no idea what's worse, your footwork o' your lack of attention. Over here, daydreamer."

Ian turned his head from the clouds to the captain's cracked and worn pirate leathers. He wanted to respond with the killer of all comeback lines, but nothing came to mind. His head ached. Even his hair hurt. Ian staggered back up and retrieved his rusty cutlass from the grass. Under his breath he muttered, "If we had the Neverblade, we wouldn't need any of this."

"What'd you say?"

With a start, Ian said, "Nothing. Let's get back to it."

"If we had the Neverblade, this wouldn't be necessary. Unfortunately we don't, so we'll have to make do!" the captain snarled.

Captain Wilder assumed a left-handed sword stance and approached Ian with three quick steps, thrusting his cutlass at him each time. Ian followed, taking three steps backward and deflecting the attacks with his own cutlass.

"Sloppy and slow," the captain yelled. He approached Ian with a bold attack, alternating high and low, finishing with a slash to Ian's belly. Driven backward, Ian blocked most of the attacks, but ultimately fell over his feet and back to the ground.

"And this is with my LEFT hand," the captain taunted. "Perhaps this plan will be harder than I thought."

Ian gnashed his teeth. His chest heaved in exhaustion. The muscles through his brow grew taut. A headache brewed. He needed caffeine. He had lost track of the days already. At least three straight days, he figured, of listening to this mutated blowhard of an alternate him. His wits at an end, he imagined, if one person was to annoy him to the point of actually taking a life, it would be his very own doppelgänger, Captain Ian Wilder.

Basic Seamanship

Captain Ian Wilder held a length of gnarly rope in his hand. Using his stump to hold the rope against his knee, he wove with his left hand to and fro, then pulled the rope tight for a fine, perfect sheepshank knot. He handed another length of rope to Ian.

Ian stuck out his tongue at the corner of his mouth and wove his hands inside and out, looping the rope through a space and pulling it tight.

Egads. Terrible.

"That's not even half-way to a half-hitch," the captain said.

Rudimentary Artillery

Atop the island, two barnacle-clad, rusty cannons sat in the sunlight. One-handed, the captain ladled in his powder bag, stamped down the wad, then inserted the shot in his cannon.

Across from him, Ian yanked on his rammer to clear the breech, but it wouldn't budge. Wedged. Giving up after numerous tugs, he slumped in misery between the cannons with his elbows on his knees.

The captain sparked his primer, setting off the cannon in a cloud of smoke. Ian nearly leapt from his skin in surprise.

Beginning Firearms

The captain guided Ian as he loaded a musket: first powder, then wad, and finally, shot. Ian tamped the rammer through the muzzle. Finished, the captain inspected the work and handed the long firearm back to the boy and gestured for him to shoot at a dummy stationed thirty yards away.

Ian, with his tongue stuck out the corner of his mouth, pulled the hammer back, took aim, and squeezed the trigger.

But nothing happened.

A second later a small jet of smoke ejected from the rear of the breech, and the shot slowly rolled out of the barrel.

The captain pointed at the end of the musket and bent over in laughter.

Intermediate Melee Combat

Again, on the top of the island, Ian and the captain traded glancing blows of their cutlasses. Although Ian got in an attack or two, the captain still owned the show.

Intro to Navigation

In the torch-lit cavern, the captain had rigged up a fake helm from an old table and some cabinet handles. As the captain barked steering changes, Ian spun the wheel one-quarter turn, a half, a third.

This way and that, Ian spun the wheel to the captain's commands. At one juncture, the captain stepped in, fixed the course on the wheel, and pointed to the modifications to show Ian.

Artillery 101

Cannon smoke cleared as Ian wormed out the breech, ladled in the powder, packed the wad, and inserted the shot. As fast as he could, he tamped it all with the rammer and yanked out the rod, just as the captain sparked the primer and blasted the cannon, nearly taking Ian's arm with it.

"What the hell?!" Ian screamed.

"Have to move faster!" the captain boomed.

Celestial Navigation 101

From the black sand beach, Ian and the captain watched the last whisper of the sun sink beneath the horizon. Stars poked dully from the waning lavender but emerged bright-eyed from the growing navy of the night. Among them all, one star shined brighter than the rest. Ian remembered that star from the first night they spent here. The imaginary fishing line tied to the small of his back tugged at him.

Home.

"Have a destination?" the captain asked. He sat on a snag of driftwood behind a weathered crate. A whale-oil lamp balanced on the crate flickered in the gentle sea breeze, poorly illuminating the charts and logbooks scattered about.

Ian looked up to the home star. "Yes."

"Give me a compass reading."

Ian pointed the compass to the star. The captain held the lamp over it, and Ian waited for the needle to settle. "243 degrees. Southwest."

"Quadrant bearing?"

Ian squinted at the compass and did the math in his head. "South 63 degrees West."

The captain turned to his charts and scribbled down the readings. He handed Ian a sextant and took out his pocket watch. "The time is 9:34 PM." The captain paused to unroll a seamstress measuring tape and measured the height from Ian's feet to his eyes. "Sight height is 5 feet, 6 inches. A bit short if you ask me."

Ian turned away from the sextant and glowered at the captain.

"Get off it, sprout. It's a measurement from your feet to your eyes. Give the reading on that star of yours. An' don't short-change it again. Use the vernier to get an accurate measurement this time."

Ian peered through the sextant's telescope. Then, through his teeth, Ian muttered, "53 degrees, 14 feet."

The captain held the lamp to the sextant, inspected the readings. "13 feet, lad."

Advanced Firearms

Ian stood 30 yards away from the stuffed dummy. On his belt hung four loaded pistolas. At the captain's signal, he drew one and fired, hitting the knee of the dummy.

In the next moment, he stowed the empty pistola and drew the second, aiming and firing quickly. An upper thigh hit.

A third draw and the dummy's right wrist burst open.

On the last draw, he rushed it, and the shot missed.

The captain stepped in and, using his cutlass as a pointer, raised the pistola in Ian's hand and steadied his shot. With his stump hand he motioned in a circular fashion at Ian's diaphragm. "Breath and draw, hold and shoot," he lectured.

Fluid Melee Tactics

Inside the cavern, the captain and Ian traded steel again. This time Ian lasted longer on the offensive than the defensive, trading blows and clashes with the captain. Ian's footwork over the rocky terrain had improved and he now paid attention to every movement his opponent made.

When the captain whirled about to slash at him, Ian had disappeared. From behind him, Ian thrust his cutlass and poked the captain in the butt-cheek. Yelping in pain, the captain quickly turned and chased Ian throughout the cavern, redoubling his efforts to best him again.

"Finally!" the captain barked.

Advanced Boarding

On top of the island, ropes were fastened to trees hanging over the black lava-rock gorge. The captain held a rope in his one hand, ran backward, and then screamed at the top of his lungs as he raced down the gorge and flung himself up to the other side.

Ian backed up and followed, arcing downward through the gorge and then back up into the sunlight, where he let go and jettisoned himself upward and to the grassy slopes on the opposite side.

"We might just make a pirate outta you yet!" Captain Ian Wilder hollered. His slap to Ian's back was so hard, it sent the boy toppling into the knee-high grasses.

Long-Range Artillery

Again, Ian tamped in the cannon shot and removed the rammer. He reached down and made changes to the adjustment screws and eyed out his target on the hillside over a hundred yards away: a pineapple sitting on a stump.

He sparked the primer and the cannon fired, volleying the shot up the hill and destroying the stump underneath the fruit. In the sprinkling aftermath of wooden shards, the pineapple tottered end-over-end down the hill.

Deadly Drawing 601

Ian stood across from the target dummy again, his four pistolas tucked snugly in his belt. Behind him, the captain tapped his foot, awaiting the outcome. With a fluid motion, Ian drew the first pistol, fired, stowed, and drew the next within seconds. The aiming and breathing came together as Ian took the third and finally fourth draw. The reports of the shots echoed through the nearby gorge.

When the target dummy finished bouncing, the captain saw the results. Three hit their mark squarely in the victim's chest, while the fourth and last shot took off the top of the dummy's burlap-stuffed head.

"Not bad at all," the captain said.

Steve eventually found them on the black sand beach beneath the gorge. Ian Wilder and his otherworldly alternate, Captain Ian Wilder, sat cross-legged, eyes closed, taking up handfuls of sand and letting it fall between their fingers. Although dressed differently, they looked much more alike than Steve had ever noticed before. The beach had a resonance to it. The gentle electric hum of two disparate dimensions coming together at a focal point.

Wiping his sweaty brow, Steve tossed a large gunny sack onto the beach beside Ian and sat down on a nearby rock. "I got everything you asked for. And Jacob the fisherman will bring us there for coin. A lot of coin." When the captain did not respond, Steve said, "Did you hear that, Stubs?" Ian stood and turned around first, projecting the new scowl he had close to perfected. Steve raised his hands and hunched his shoulders. "Sorry. I couldn't help myself."

Ian rummaged through the large sack. Captain Wilder hung back on the beach, content to lift handfuls of sand and let the grains slip through his fingers. Ian withdrew a long, polished, black scabbard with a gleaming silver hilt. Red-stained leather lashings wove around the hilt to form a one-handed grip. Ian recognized it from his very own stories—the Neverblade.

Excited, he held the scabbard and quickly unsheathed the sword. The sun caught the shimmer of metal and shined it back in Ian's face. Carefully, he slid his fingers down the flat side of the blade, where intricate etchings of twisting vines and leaves ran from haft to tip. Ian admired the blade for so long, he forgot to breathe and quickly inhaled like a drowning man breeching water.

Steve wiped his brow again and said, "Easy, kid. It's not the real deal. It's just a knockoff."

Ian turned, sword in hand, and looked at the captain, who still played with the sand, his back turned to them. His eyes closed, the captain said, "I've found in my experience that sometimes a lil awe and wonder can be the sliver of chance you need to get the upper hand."

Ian sheathed the sword and set it aside. Reaching into the large sack, he pulled out a brand-new set of pirate leathers. A perfect match to the captain's. Ian looked at them and then back at the captain.

"Think you can forego the wallowy sad-sack routine long enough to be a REAL pirate? To be me?" the captain asked, sifting another handful of sand through his lone set of fingers.

Ian swallowed. His stomach quivered, and his knees wobbled.

Sensing Ian's nervousness, Steve patted his shoulder. "Longbottoms thinks you're the real deal. But in order to pull this off, we needed a few props."

Ian looked at Steve and then at the captain with a quizzical expression. "What exactly are we pulling off?"

Captain Wilder stood and turned to them. "Commandeering the Leaping Lizard, that's all."

CHAPTER 22

STICK TO THE PLAN

Panic set in. Masquerading as a pirate was one thing, but commandeering a pirate ship? No way. Ian felt as though a strange wind had blown by and pulled the air from his lungs. He grew light-headed and dizzy. His upper body swayed and the beach reached up to him. Steve caught him before he fell over.

The captain frowned. "What's the matter with him? Longbottoms is a puppy compared to Noface. He should save his fainting for him."

Steve looked up at the captain. "Cut him some slack. He isn't you. He may look like you and share some similarities, but that's where it ends."

Ian slouched against Steve, unable to keep his legs under him. The last thing Ian remembered was the captain muttering, "Gonna need a wing an' a prayer for this one, mate."

❀ ❀ ❀

Ian floats through an aimless void. There he bobs in the gloom until it grows lighter, the tint of an evergreen pond. A distant sound trickles to his ears, but at every turn, the creeping murk hides it from him.

Is it a scream?

A shout?

Ian slowly rotates in place. He feels his head expanding like the oxygen in his brain has stretched too thin. He's underwater! Frightened, he kicks his legs and pushes the water down, propels himself until he breaches the surface. There, he gulps at the air. The still, moonlit sky stretches above, and the sea tosses around him. Two mighty galleys trade cannon shots nearby. Wooden shards and splinters pelt him from every angle.

Sailors and pirates clash on the decks above. They swap steel, some standing, others shrieking into the depths. Scallies and powder monkeys swing across the gap on ropes. Their pistols flash in palls of smoke. Bodies collide on the ropes above him. Some smash into the sides of the ships before slipping into the water.

Ian swims to the side of the Wicked Crow, navigating around the dead and drowning. He shimmies up the rails and onboard. Across the deck, the crews scuffle in a brutal, blood-curdling dance. Nearby, a misdirected shot splits through the fighting, catching a pirate's forearm. Ian draws his cutlass and dashes past a sailor getting gutted by a dirk.

Ian climbs the stairs to the aft and slips in a streak of blood, falling to the deck. Lying on his side, he sees Captain Ian Wilder duel Penelope by the helm. But something is different about her. Back on his feet, Ian peers through the clouds of gunpowder to get a better look. It can't be her—she's wearing Noface's very own burned-black pirate gear.

Ian scrambles toward the two, pushing men out of his way. But he is too late. Captain Ian Wilder miscalculates a block, and Penelope thrusts her steel forward, just under his chin and into the side of his neck. With a flick of her wrist, she spills his carotid. The sickening sound of arterial spray against the deck skids Ian to a stop. For a second, the sounds and winds of the fray fall silent around him. Captain Wilder crumples to his knees. He grasps for his neck, desperately trying to cover the jetting wound, but it is pointless. His body wavers briefly with the tossing of the waves before he tumbles face-first onto the deck in a twitching spasm. Frozen in shock, Ian stares stupidly at the captain's dead body.

"Just the one I was looking for," Penelope shouts to him over the battle. Her voice is changed; her words no longer end with a smile, like he remembers. This smile has a sharp, serrated edge.

"I'm supposed to be looking for you!" he calls. "I came all the way here to save you!"

Penelope smirks—a sly, jagged thing he doesn't recognize. While Ian falters, she storms him with her cutlass. He clumsily responds to block her attack, pinning her blade down between them. He leans in closer, his face inches from hers.

"Not sure if you noticed," she said, "but I don't need saving." She jerks him toward her for a kiss. Ian wants nothing more than to kiss her, to be with her, hold her against him again. But he remembers that smile: Penelope's funeral. When she came back from the dead. When the malig kissed him.

Ian shoves her away before her lips greet his. "You!" he howls. "Where is she?"

Penelope hacks at him with her cutlass. Ian bars her advances and retaliates with an attack of his own. But Penelope is just too good. She slashes away his thrusts and counters with a sequence of ripostes that catch Ian off-guard. Their blades cross, her face hovers inches from his. "You think I'm holding her in some brig or tower, waiting for you to come and rescue her?" she asks. She winks at him. "Come on, I know you loved it the first time."

A fiery anger erupts in Ian, and he boots Penelope away, sprawling her backwards and onto the deck. Quickly he straddles her, his silver sword at her neck. "Where is she?" Ian roars.

Her answer comes with that barbed smile. A thorn-like pain wraps around his ribcage when the realization hits.

He is too late.

The malig has already killed this Penelope.

His grip weakens on his sword. He has failed. All the work, all the insanity; it was for nothing.

"Not for nothing," the malig said, wrenching him by the collar and locking her lips to his. His body shivers in bewilderment, but reacts to her. It craves more: her tongue, her breasts, everything. But while those parts lust for Penelope to linger with him forever, his mind senses the malig slither through him, stitching into his synapses, into his nerves, his brain, and then dissolving into the bluish ribbon of the Infiniuum.

❈　❈　❈

"You have to realize," Steve told Ian, safe in the confines of the faux Millennium Falcon, "This was never going to be easy. And I'm not just talking about learning all the pirate stuff and braving the scruff of battle, kid. That's just simple logistics." He leaned back in the pilot chair, arms behind his head. "You've been exposed to a whole horde of mind-bending, seemingly impossible things. I mean a minute ago you were sitting on a beach with an alternate pirate version of yourself. How crazy is that?"

"It's not actually that crazy," Ian admitted.

"Not anymore, but that's what I'm saying. Your mind is in a constant state of adjusting, adapting to the new existential phenomena you encounter."

Ian rubbed a hand through his hair. "That's why my dreams are so nuts?"

"Probably," Steve offered.

"Probably?" Ian questioned. "Shouldn't you be a little more…I don't know…sure of things? You're a feron. You deal with this all the time. There should be an instructional guide or something."

Steve sighed. "If anyone had all the answers, I don't think there'd even be an Infiniuum."

Ian nodded. Point taken. "But you should at least know where she is, the malig," Ian said. "If my parents can track me through my cell phone, you should be able to find her. Don't you have some app or something that can just draw a bead on her?"

Steve shook his head. "I wish it were that easy, kid. I have yet to find an interdimensional tracking app, I'm afraid. Like I said before, maligs and ferons are cut from the same cloth. Beings of pure plasmic energy. Negative to positive. I can sense her simply by the cosmic interference."

Ian huffed. "So you're the tracking app. Great."

Steve shrugged his shoulders. "Sorry."

"So what's the plan?" Ian asked.

"Get to Penelope and wait for the malig to make her move. She will be having just as much trouble finding her as we are. There's a chance we're ahead of her."

"Right," Ian said, doubtfully. "Ahead of her."

Steve patted Ian's knee. "You'd be surprised at how effective the biological response is in detecting plausibility."

"In English."

"What's your gut say?" Steve asked.

Ian's gut never told him anything good. "It says we're doing fine," Ian lied. "Just fine."

CHAPTER 23

A LITTLE BIT OF
BREAKING AND ENTERING

"Get in there and dig that spike," said Mr. Wasserbaum.

P.E. Ian's favorite period. Topping off his nearly week-long ice cream sundae of pirate boot camp, Wasserbaum had the whole class playing volleyball. Every action involved bumping the ball with his sensitive forearms, setting with his worn and swollen fingers, or jumping as high as he could to slam his palm into the ball for a spike. None of it was very tempting. "Dig it?" Ian asked.

Wasserbaum looked back at him as if he just realized he had been talking to a parrot. "Is there an echo?" he asked. "Yeah. I said dig that shot, Wilder." Wasserbaum put his forearms together and got in a deep squat to demonstrate, then straightened his elbows. "Simple. Don't be afraid of the ball."

Okay. Dig it. This wasn't that hard. Really. Besides, he had just completed hardcore pirate training boot camp. Dig it? Consider it buried, Wasserbaum.

Ian lined up with his classmates and watched as his team served. The opposing team, led by Kit Cambridge, resident dreamboat and JV football captain, waited for the kill. His teammate set the ball up for him. Then Kit was able to vault up on his well-chiseled calves and spike the ball across the net. Right at Ian.

Dig it. Dig it. Dig it. Wasserbaum's voice boomed in his mind.

So Ian did that. Everything in his head went according to plan: he squatted to the floor, extended his arms, and tried to dig the shot and give his team a chance for a return. But he leaned too far forward. When his sweaty skin hit that parquet floor, he stuttered across the wood grain. The pain was intolerable. The sound was worse, hovering between a sneaker squeak and a fart. The volleyball hit the floor a good two feet in front of Ian.

His pirate training did not translate to the volleyball court, of that much he was certain. Maybe if he had a cutlass to skewer the stupid ball, or, better yet, just shoot the damn thing with a pistola.

"Wilder!" Wasserbaum shouted. "What in the hell was that?"

The teams reset and continued play. In the rotation, Ian moved to the front line. Front line was easy: set, spike, and block. But in a worrisome panic, he almost always resorted to setting the ball up to a teammate or, worse, simply setting it back over the net for the opponent. Luckily on the first serve from Kit's team, the ball didn't come near him, so his teammates were able to set it up and win a point by spiking it past Marly Chang.

On the next serve, Ian and crew managed to set it up and over. But Kit's team dug it, set it up, and spiked it back over. Nervous, Ian lost the trajectory of the ball. Kit hit it so hard, he swore the ball disintegrated. But it didn't. It whistled over the net and "faced" him, which, in the hallowed halls of high school lore, meant a ball or other sporting implement that hit a face so completely, the red mark left no square inch uncovered.

Ian sat on the locker room bench after showering and pulled his t-shirt over his head. Ouch. Even the cottony fabric felt like a rusted strand of barbed wire being pulled down his sensitive pink face. Still, as long as Ian ignored the throbbing and didn't touch it, it wasn't that bad.

After a brief stop at his locker and a quick 03-11-25 on the dial, he was out the school doors.

"Ian," Dr. Caulderon said, adjusting his briefcase to his other hand to shake hands. "Good to see you!"

Ian shook hands and reluctantly spun around and walked back into the school. He accompanied the doctor to Ms. Sutter's old office. Ian set his backpack on one of the chairs and slouched himself in the other across from the desk.

Caulderon noticed Ian's face. "Volleyball?"

Ian cocked his head in surprise. "Yeah. How did you know?"

The doctor took off his coat and sat down. "I've faced a volleyball or two in my day." He paused, framing his thoughts before speaking. "How are things going? Your parents mentioned some vomiting and erratic conversations." He said 'erratic' like it was a word given to him by someone else.

"Which one do you want first?" Ian asked.

"I don't know. Vomiting."

Ian reached into his backpack and pulled out a can of soda, popped the top, and took a long pull. "I drink maybe eight of these a day," he said.

The doctor's upper lip curled subconsciously in disgust.

"Yeah," Ian continued. "Gross, huh?"

The doctor cleared his throat. "Talking to yourself."

Ian took another drink of soda. "Online gaming. *Halo. Call of Duty*. Virtually any other game. You have to talk to your team to win, right?" Dr. Caulderon nodded. "Should I explain it some more?"

"No," the doctor said. "No need. That should do nicely." There was that pause again. "I'm more interested in things that trouble you."

Now it was Ian's turn to pause, and he figured giving it a long spell with a little head-scratching might be better, so he dragged it out. "Dreams," Ian said.

Dr. Caulderon leaned forward, his eyes widening. "What about them?"

Ian thought about it for a moment, making sure all his i's were dotted and t's crossed. "Say your dog ran away. And you've spent weeks looking for him and can't find him." The doctor nodded. "Then say one night you have a dream where you finally found him, but it wasn't him."

The doctor squinted in thought. "Not him? How so?"

"He had changed. Became feral, unfriendly."

"Interesting," the doctor said. "Dreams themselves are largely unexplainable, but some theories suggest the dream state is simply different areas of the brain working things out. In this case, perhaps the feral nature of your dog symbolizes the repugnant nature of decay and decomposition you would logically find if your dog had gone missing and died. Perhaps your psyche, your id, forbids you to find your dog for fear of having to deal with its death." He ended with a crescendo on the word death.

Ian looked about the room and contemplated what Caulderon had to say. Ian knew what he was doing—trying to tie everything back to Penelope's death. "What if, in my dreams, the universe as we know it is infinite and therefore everything we can think of, even the existence of multiple versions of yourself, exists somewhere... out there?"

Caulderon smiled the way people do to mask an inadvertent laugh. He leaned forward over the desk and said, "Ian, I'm not a theoretical physicist, but what I can say is that a belief like that may symbolize a fear of accepting the truth. Sure, in some far-off place, I may be a metropolitan playboy, but that doesn't change the fact that, right here, right now, I am not."

Ian piped in and said, "Technically it wouldn't be you."

The doctor squinted in confusion. "What do you mean?"

"The playboy," Ian said. "Technically, it wouldn't be you. It would be an alternate you. Someone who looks almost like you, has some of the same qualities, but with minor differences."

The doctor nodded. "I see. The fact remains, this alternate is not me. I am not the alternate. The sooner I face the truth in my reality, the better I can cope with it. We aren't living in a Green Lantern comic book."

Green Lantern? The good doctor had been doing his research.

"Your parents said you visited Penelope this week. Did you have anything to say to her?"

Ian thought about his cemetery visit and his silent, mental conversation. They already thought he was talking to himself; he didn't want to admit having a one-sided conversation with his dead girlfriend. "I don't know," he said.

Caulderon folded his hands in front of his chest. "How did your visit to Penelope's grave make you feel?"

Ian shifted in his seat and continued. "Um, sad I guess."

"Did you tell her that?"

"No. I just…told her stuff, that's all," Ian admitted.

"Do you mind sharing, just a bit?" the doctor asked gently.

"I told her I loved her," he said. "I told her the whole world is screwed up without her in it. That I wanted it all to go back to what it was before."

The doctor nodded. "That's very good, Ian."

"I guess I miss what we could have had together," Ian continued. "College. Marriage. Kids. A full life together." He paused. Was he saying too much?

Dr. Caulderon leaned forward, almost as if he cared about what Ian just said. Hell, maybe he did. "I'm so sorry, Ian. I can imagine that would weigh heavily on you."

"We had sex," Ian said. The words just burst out of him like a broken dam. "It was just before she died." Ian paused to rub his head. "It was our first time. Probably not good, but…I probably shouldn't have said that."

"No, it's fine, Ian," the doctor said, leaning back in his chair. "It's a natural step for a couple who has an intimate emotional connection.

Hearts yearn for love, and bodies crave physical intimacy. That's why a death like this can affect people so much."

After a moment of thoughtful silence, Dr. Caulderon asked if there was anything else Ian felt like discussing today, or if he had any questions. "Um…nope. I guess that's about it," Ian replied.

Rubbing his hands together, the doctor said, "Well, I think that should do it then. We covered a lot of ground today."

Ian looked at the clock on the wall. "But it's only been fourteen minutes. The hour isn't up yet."

Caulderon smiled. "I think you've earned some time to focus on yourself today." He reached out to Ian for his closing handshake.

Suspicious, Ian stood and grabbed his backpack, giving the doctor's hand a quick shake. He felt like at any moment, a team of attendants would burst in, wrap him in bubble wrap, and administer sedatives to him with pneumatic injection guns. But there was no one in the hall when Caulderon held the door for him. With a trickle of confidence burbling through him, Ian said, "Take it easy, Dr. C," on his way out.

On the activities bus ride home, he did his best to ignore Pete Stamdahl. Though, with the morose overtones of the *Braveheart* soundtrack piping through his ear buds, wild visions of painted-face swordplay with Pete made him smile. At home he managed through the dull banter required at dinner where his parents performed their thinly veiled daily "sanity checks" on him. Afterward, he stowed away in his room behind his desk, struggling mightily with his math homework.

Imaginary numbers.

At first, he thought the subject might be interesting, but he quickly figured out that the numbers weren't that much more imaginative than normal numbers and were grossly complex. In the middle of a particularly difficult problem, he looked over to his plump journal and decided he'd had enough math for the night. Paging through the journal, he found the map he and Penelope scribbled out of the Islas Encantadas and unfolded it on the desk.

To the north, lay the Silver Isle, home to the king, now Noface. He traced his finger down to Port Paveo, where he and Steve had first landed. That's where Longbottoms' ship had been. It may still be moored there. He followed the island's coast north and east, following the wagon trail that Jacob had brought them along to cross over to Drop-Dead Island. But it wasn't on the map. He checked all the other islands, thinking perhaps he had his bearings wrong. But no. He rechecked the route and pointed at the empty spot in the ocean where Drop-Dead Island existed in that reality.

Confused, he leaned back in his chair. Why wasn't it on the map? If their imagination allowed them access to see that world and map it out in this reality, it should be there. He felt like he should know the answer—that it was closer than he realized, but he couldn't make the connection. What was it? All night he stewed about the missing island. Past dark, he lay on his bed and stared at the ceiling. Maybe Penelope had a different map of the islands. If only he could get to it.

At 12:30 AM, the lights at the Archer house next door had been out for more than an hour. He opened his bedroom window and crawled down to the fence between his house and Penelope's. If he remembered right, he could pull himself onto the roof from a certain spot on the fence. Carefully, he balanced across the fence and, using a nearby tree branch for leverage, pulled himself up onto the Archers' roof. He nearly cried out as his sore muscles strained further. As quietly as he could, he stepped across the shingles until he reached the second-floor windows. He hoped the screen was still loose from their summer night meetings. Sure enough, Penelope had simply left it sitting in place and not secured. Now, the window. A quick pull and it slid to the side. It was almost too easy.

Once in, he paused for a moment, taking in Penelope's room with the light of his cell phone. The Archers had kept it almost entirely like it was when Penelope was alive. Her paintings and drawings decorated the walls of her room. From pencil to pastels to watercolor, she had every manner of character profile, landscape, and creature created. She had even rendered a large drawing of

Labyrinth the dragon, etched in thick carbon pencil. A watercolor of Cactusback Flats hung on another wall. The vibrant, rusty canyons of Moonshine Valley laid out before a setting sun.

Even the portrait of Whiskey Joe Firesky looked authentic in acrylic on canvas. On all four walls hung maps from their worlds, large and rustling in the breeze from the window. But the map for Islas Encantadas wasn't there. He paged carefully through a pile of paintings, sketches, and portraits that clung to the slanted tabletop of her art desk.

There, he found the map and pulled it out. Flattening it over the rest of the pictures, he realized her map of the islands had been filled in. Where his map had highlighted a few key areas, hers looked almost complete, with towns, roads, shipping lines, and islands. North of Port Paveo, he followed Jacob's path. Sure enough, it led straight to a bridge symbol and to Drop-Dead Island. He folded up the map, and just as he put it in his pocket, lights lit up the room. Ian gasped in fright.

In the doorway stood Penelope's parents, Tim and Alexandra, groggily assessing the strange, strange situation. "Ian! Is there anything we can help you with?" Ms. Archer asked, her tone polite, but firm. He had to think. What is the one thing that could explain why he snuck into their dead daughter's bedroom in the middle of the night? What would Captain Ian Wilder say? But the longer he waited, the weirder it got. "It's not what it looks like."

Stupid.

Twenty minutes later, he stood at his front door facing his parents, who looked both concerned and horrified. Ian still couldn't think of anything better. "It's not what it looks like," he said again. But their faces said everything he needed to know. Ian's mother burst into tears.

His dad did his best to cover, smiling politely and reaching out to touch Ms. Archer's shoulder. "I'm so sorry, Alexandra. Tim," he said, shaking Mr. Archer's hand. Then he turned to Ian. "Please get to bed," he said quietly. "School tomorrow."

Ian stepped forward, afraid to say another word. He knew he should apologize to the Archers, or at least comfort his mother, but he had to escape. Hide. At the top of the stairs and out of sight, he heard his dad say, "He's really struggling with losing her." Ms. Archer sucked up a sniffle, and he imagined Mr. Archer wrapped his arm around her shoulder. Ian stopped to listen. "I understand, Harold," Mr. Archer said. "This whole thing has thrown everyone for a loop."

In his room, Ian closed the door and leaned forward until his forehead rested against it.

"What's up, man?" Steve said behind him.

Ian didn't even turn to greet him. "Not now."

"Sure."

After a few deep breaths, Ian turned to Steve, who sat at Ian's desk and paged through his math book. "Imaginary numbers," Steve said. "Ironic."

Ian yanked the book away from Steve. "How so? Because you are imaginary and I'm crazy, or maybe this is my real life and the one with my parents and school is imaginary?"

Taken aback, Steve stood up. "What's got your panties in a twist?"

Ian stowed his books in his backpack in a semi-fury. "I did something stupid."

"I gathered as much," Steve said. "What level of stupidity are we looking at?"

Ian turned to Steve, chastened. "I snuck into Penelope's room and got caught."

Steve's eyes bulged. "What? Are you crazy?!"

"I'm starting to believe so, yes." Ian sighed as he sat on the bed, head in his hands.

Steve paced the floor and rubbed his chin. "Of all the stupid things to do. Her parents are probably mega creeped out. You're lucky they didn't call the cops, pal."

Ian fell back on the bed. "They felt sorry for me and said they understood."

Steve clapped his hands together. "Well, good! You played the pity card on them."

"No, not good. My mom is crying, and Dad thinks I'm a lunatic."

Steve waved off Ian's comment. "That's all fixable, kid. Easy-peasy, lemon-squeezy. Unless," he paused to look over at Ian with suspicion. "Unless you went over there to…"

Ian looked at him and said, "What?"

"You know…"

"No, I don't."

"You weren't going through any drawers or closets were you?" Steve asked. "Please tell me you didn't touch any undergarments."

"I did nothing like that," he said in a low, intense voice, glaring at Steve.

Steve relaxed. "Good. What were you doing anyway?"

Ian dug in his pocket and unfolded Penelope's map. He showed Steve the missing island on his map, against hers. "I don't get it," Steve said. "Why would it not be on your map, but exist on hers?"

Ian folded up his map and tucked it in his journal. "I think Penelope was keeping secrets from me. She didn't want me to know about that island."

CHAPTER 24

ALL THAT AND
THREE BARRELS OF FISH

"That's your plan?" Ian asked. "Stow away in fish barrels?"

Captain Ian Wilder lounged in his throne, a pewter goblet of wine in his hand and a steaming bowl of freshly cracked crab claws sitting on the arm rest. Steve sat next to Ian at the table, his tin plate covered in a mound of empty crab casings. Ian's plate held a few pieces of pineapple and nothing else. Ever since getting caught snooping around Penelope's room, his appetite had shriveled. The captain sucked crab meat from a claw. "You have a better idea?"

Steve looked at Ian, giving him the benefit of the doubt, but Ian didn't answer.

"Like I said, ships have to stock up for their raids," the captain continued. "An' part of that is food for their crew. Any fisherman up and down the coast will tell you, they don' care who buys their fish, as long as they got coin."

Steve nodded and pulled more crabmeat from a leg on his plate. "Jacob, the fisherman who helped us before. He'll stow us away for the right shine."

The captain pointed a crab leg at Ian. "See, there you have it. Once we're aboard, we wait until nightfall. Dispatch the guard, quiet-like, and enter the captain's chambers. From there, it's as simple as placin' a shot behind his ear. After that, we have the ship and crew."

"Then what?" Ian asked.

The captain guffawed. "Well, what do you think? We sail for Silver Isle to find your wayward lass. That was the whole point, wasn't it?" The captain gestured at Ian's empty plate with his stump. "You better fill your belly. Once we're in the barrels, I can't guarantee when we'll get out. And if we're under watch, a gurgling gut will give you away."

Following the captain's orders, Ian ate some crab and fruit. Afterward, Steve and Ian dressed for their raid as the captain organized their weaponry. Ian's whole ensemble was black leather stitched with burgundy thread, except for the linen shirt. The long coat bore smooth pearly buttons dyed like blood. His black tricorn hat had a band of shark's teeth sewn around it.

Once in the ensemble, Ian looked down at himself and felt the supple leather clinging to his body like a second skin. "Good fit," he mumbled. "Kind of cool."

Steve straightened his ratty, blue long coat. He had not gotten new clothes. His looked like the captain had ripped them from a buried corpse on the island. "Does it smell as bad as it looks?" Ian asked.

"Funny," Steve said. Then he held up a salt-stained, black bandanna and a faded, light-brown leather hat and said, "Hat or bandanna?"

"We're going to be stuffed in a barrel. Better go with the bandanna," Ian said.

Steve pointed at him. "But you get a hat."

"I'm shorter. More room in the barrel."

Steve nodded and tied his bandanna around his forehead. "You okay, buddy? You were a bit moody at dinner."

Ian sat on the stool, hooking his booted feet in the rungs. "Between home, here, and my crazy dreams, I'm starting to wonder if it's all too much for my brain. I'm waiting for the moment my head explodes."

Steve finished the knot in his bandanna and turned to Ian. "You've lasted a lot longer than others," he said. "Most lose it way earlier. You're a tough kid. Tougher than you think, anyway." Steve looked around, as if hoping to spot a mirror, and then remembered where they stood. "It's natural to question your environment. That's what keeps you safe, and half of what makes the imagination so powerful. Without doubt or self-exploration, the Infiniuum wouldn't exist."

Captain Wilder strode in, interrupting their conversation. "You blokes ready yet?" When the captain saw Ian, dressed head-to-toe like himself, he took a step back. "Blimey. It's like looking into the past." Slowly, he walked around Ian and looked him over, prodding the leathers here and there. "A fine, fine replica, my lad!" He quickly looked Steve up and down. "And that'll do just fine. Come! I have your effects ready to go."

The table now held an array of weapons. The captain handed Ian the faux Neverblade and two pistolas. "A backup, in case plans drown in the tide pools. You should only need one shot," he told Ian. For Steve, he pointed to the cutlass, dirk, and pistol lying on the table. "From what you showed me last week, you'll be able to provide him some backup."

Ian looked to Steve. "What did you show him?"

Steve shrugged. "I'm a polymorphic organism." Ian stared blankly at him. "Learning and adapting are my strengths," Steve said, rolling his eyes.

"What are you bringing?" he asked the captain. Captain Wilder reached his stub hand over his shoulder and tapped the barrel of his musket, the one outfitted with a spyglass.

"Will that fit into a fish barrel?" Ian questioned.

The captain responded by yanking the musket over his shoulder and, with a stunning precision, broke the musket down into its composite pieces one-handedly. He pointed to Ian. "You're the one who needs to do the dirty work for this, not me."

"He'll provide the long-range backup," Steve said. "If we need it."

"And you shouldn't," the captain added. "Now grab your gear, and let's go."

The three of them trekked out of the cavern, Ian and Steve carrying torches to light the way. More than once, Ian noted their eerie flickering in the darkness and the looming shadows they created. As they got closer to the entrance, Ian could hear the wail of the winds circling in and around the cavern. He thought about Penelope's painting, how the mouth of the cave opened wide, consuming the viewer, and an erratic shiver bolted down his spine. Ahead, he could see a glow in the cloudless sky above. The captain led them out of the cavern but stopped as he arrived at the rope bridge. "Why is he stopping?" Ian asked Steve.

"He's never known the code," Steve said softly. "He's been trapped on this island since he was marooned."

"That doesn't make any sense," Ian whispered.

"He's an alternate of you, Ian. He's not you. He wouldn't know the code that your Penelope gave you."

The captain ushered Ian to the bridge. "Lead us across." Ian placed his free hand on the rough rope rail. He waved the torch over the boards to find the symbols. "Only step on the boards I step on," Ian said to Captain Wilder. "I'll call out the symbol to you, and Steve and I can help light your way. Got it?" The captain nodded. Ian leaned outward and stepped on a board with a faint longhorn symbol. With the step supporting his weight, he called out the symbol, searched the next one, and moved on. The captain followed him, and Steve made up the rear. In the dark, it took them nearly an hour to navigate the coded bridge safely. Nearing the end, Ian saw a torch up on the bluff, the light illuminating the imposing build of Jacob the fisherman standing in wait for them.

When they arrived, Jacob called out to Steve, "Yer late," in greeting.

In the torchlight, Jacob squinted at Ian and the captain. "What? Are ye relations?"

"Half-brothers," Ian replied.

"We should be shoving off," Steve said, avoiding further scrutiny.

"In the barrels first," Jacob said.

"We talked about getting barreled up closer to town," Steve said.

"Longbottoms got people looking for ye," Jacob said. "Yer three days expired long ago, an' I'm not getting my throat slit on yer account." He held out his hand. "My coin?"

"Fine." Steve lifted a small cloth purse from his belt and handed it to the fisherman. "Our boarding fee and a bonus."

Jacob took the purse. "Much obliged. I'll show ye to yer rooms." In the back of the wagon sat a dozen barrels packed with smoked fish. The three barrels at the end of the wagon were empty. He waved his torch over them. "It'll be tight, but if ye want to make it aboard unseen, this will do it. Water yer lilies, and loose your bowels," he said, waving to the long grasses lining the rutted road. "It not be a short trip."

Relieved and prepared for the ride, Steve and the captain stepped up onto the wagon and slid into the oversized barrels. Both struggled to squeeze into them. Ian followed, taking the barrel between them. The smallest of the three, even Ian had to twist and bend his appendages to fit in. Through his opened top, a barrage of fishy-smelling objects rained down on him. "What's your problem?" Ian sputtered, trying to clear the gunk from his face.

"If ye aim to be a barrel of fish, ye damn well better smell like one!" Jacob called, as he poured smoked fish into the other two barrels. Ian heard Steve groan before Jacob fitted the top to Steve's barrel, gently pounding it in. "Now, these tops be not sealed," said Jacob. "So they should pop up with a good heave ho." Jacob's fleshy face appeared over Ian's barrel. "Good luck to ye, kid," he said, before Ian's world went dark. After a dozen gentle taps on the lid, the fisherman moved to the captain's barrel and repeated the process.

Within minutes, Jacob mushed his horses down the path as Ian steadied himself against the walls of the barrel. Ian's backside quickly fell numb, and the aches and pains in his joints slowly worsened. After an hour, he nearly gagged from the smell and the queasiness in his jostled stomach. He had to quell the claustrophobic panic rising inside him. With each turn and bump of the wagon, the vibrations jarred his bones ten-fold in his wooden tomb.

To distract himself from the torture of the trip, he thought about Penelope's map. The more he thought about it, the more his mind lingered on the possibility that perhaps Penelope, if she were indeed a traveler, had escaped from their reality and entered one of these. But he saw her in the casket at her funeral. The charm bracelet he'd given her was on her wrist. His mind searched for any explanation possible, but his discomfort pried against him at every angle, so much so that his body simply shut down, and he passed out.

It's night. An orange light glimmers through the open windows of the treehouse back in Alton, Minnesota. A light rain patters outside. A wavering wind ushers through, rustling the drawings, sketches, and maps clinging to the walls with tape and thumbtacks. Candles flicker around them, and shadows cling to the corners of the treehouse. Like the two Ians in the Islas Encantadas, two Penelopes sit in the same time and space. One from Alton, Minnesota, with milky white skin and soft, suburban hands has swapped her high school clothing for buccaneer gear. The other, the Penelope from the Islas Encantadas with a tanned face, sun-drenched hair, and tears in her eyes, wears jeans and pulls an Alton High School sweatshirt over her head.

"I know you're scared," says the Penelope in pirate gear, "But you need to take my place here, in my world. You know what's at stake for us. For our other sisters across the stars." She unclasps the bracelet dangling at her wrist and hands it to the other Penelope. The Penelope in the Alton High sweatshirt tries clasping the bracelet to her wrist but her hands tremble and shake. She heaves in sobs. The Penelope in the pirate gear leans over to help. When the bracelet is clasped, she pats it. "They'll come for me," she says. "They need to believe they killed me. This is the only way. Out of all of us, you are the bravest."

The Penelope in the sweatshirt wipes away her tears and nods. "Look after my Ian. Please."

The Penelope in pirate gear leans into her cosmic doppelgänger and hugs her. She too cries under the weight of it all. "Watch after my father."

The swap complete, the Penelope in pirate gear wipes her tears and sniffles. When they part, they hold hands, reluctant to let go, until their fingers finally lose their grasp on one another.

Penelope switched places!

Waking with a start, Ian cried out, the pains in his muscles and joints woke as well. Anxious and in pain, Ian twisted, trying to readjust, rocking his barrel. The claustrophobia set back in, as if the entire universe had entered his brain and demanded to be free. He remembered Penelope in her casket, how different she had looked in death, and all that makeup. Funeral homes were notorious for caking on makeup. That's why she looked different! With that much makeup on, no one would have noticed the difference, not even her mom! A muscle spasm wracked Ian's body, and again, he moaned as he tossed and turned in his barrel.

"Whoa! Buddy?! Pal?!" Steve called. "What the hell are you doing?"

"She's here, Steve!" Ian called to him. "I figured it out. Penelope! She's here!"

"Shut your pie hole," the captain growled from his barrel. "You're going to blow our cover!"

"I don't care," Ian shouted. "She switched places with the Penelope from here! She knew she was being hunted, and she must have convinced the pirate Penelope to switch spots. That's why she hid the island from me. That was a solitary fortress for herself. To protect herself from the malig."

"Whoa, whoa, whoa!" Steve called from his barrel. "Ix-nay on the Alig-may, man."

"Shut up, the both of you," the captain interjected.

Steve continued. "I know you're tired and exhausted, Ian, but think clearly. Is this true? Or is it something you want to be true so badly you're making it fit? If that island is a fortress for her, why is she sailing under Noface's banners?"

"I don't know."

"And if she knew something was wrong, why didn't she bring you with her? You were her boyfriend. You knew these worlds as well as she did. Don't you think with a quest of this magnitude, she could have used all the help she could get? It would be stupid not to bring you, right?"

Ian grew silent. When he worked up the courage to respond, he admitted, "Yes. She would have brought me with."

"See," Steve leveled with him. "You're tired. Exhausted. Answers pop into your head, and they're very convincing, but you have to be diligent and ask yourself, is it real, or is it simply something you want to be real?"

"Quiet, ye bloody monkeys!" yelled Jacob. "We're almost to the pier!"

CHAPTER 25

THE RAID OF THE LEAPING LIZARD

The wagon had slowed to a traipse, and through the barrels they heard squeaking hoists, cargo being loaded, and maties heaving pulley ropes. Near the shore, water lapped against wooden hulls in slaps and gurgles. Across the docks, bosuns called out, barking orders to lackeys and deckhands. The wagon stopped in the middle of the commotion, where Jacob stepped down and unloaded them from the wagon. "Quartermaster! I got yer order here. Five barrels of smoked cod and mackerel!" he shouted.

In a flurry, the Leaping Lizard quartermaster approached and completed the order. Purses were exchanged and lots tallied. Someone hoisted up Ian's barrel and carried it up a dock. As Ian drew closer to the deck of the ship, he picked up other sounds: scrub brushes shushing across deck boards, hammers repairing shoddy rails, boots and peg-legs scampering this way and that. Eventually his barrel was lowered into the hold and stowed against the wall.

After several moments, the hold grew silent, and Ian waited for the captain's signal. But none came, so he waited. His arms and legs seized up in the tight confines. He didn't remember dozing, but when he woke to a rap to the head, he quickly noticed that his legs and arms had fallen asleep in his cramped barrel. Above him, the top had been removed, and Steve's shadowy face stared down at him. Moonlight leaked from the deck boards above. "Get up, kid," he said, reaching his arm in to give him a hand. "We must have dozed off in these stinky barrels."

Ian struggled to climb out, his muscles tingling and then screaming from being cramped in the barrel. The ship had gone quiet. "Where's Captain Wilder?" Ian asked, as he stretched, grimacing in pain.

"I have no idea."

"What do you mean you have no idea?" Ian fumbled for his cell phone, which worked now thanks to his mom's handy rice trick, to give them some light.

"It means exactly that," Steve said, handing Ian a flask of water. "I have no idea. This wasn't the plan. He said he would let us out and we'd take Longbottoms real quiet-like in his chambers."

Ian took deep gulps of the tepid water. It tasted like mud and iron, but it was wet, and he was thirstier than he'd ever been in his life. Ian tested his legs. The needling sensations passed as blood refreshed them. "What do we do now?"

Steve grabbed his arm and pulled him forward to some cover near a stairwell. "You have to ask? We're taking the ship."

"Still?"

"What do you think the captain has been training you for?" Steve asked. "With or without him, we need this ship to find Penelope. It's time for you to be...well...you. I mean, Captain Ian Wilder, the pirate of the Neverblade."

As blood rushed to his sleepy limbs, Ian's muscles shook and quivered. He took a deep breath. Steve was right. He couldn't hesitate any longer. He had to do this, and now, or they'd be found. Quickly, he made fists with his hands to stop their shaking. "Okay. Let's do this," Ian said.

Between shafts of moonlight, Ian and Steve ducked upstairs and peered around corners. Most of the deckhands snored noisily in their hammocks. Above, a few guards roamed tiredly abroad the decks.

Quietly, Steve and Ian moved while the guards' backs were turned, slipping from shadow to shadow to the captain's quarters. Miraculously, the door was unlocked. They slipped in and silently shut the door behind them. Inside, a few nubby candles flickered on the large dining table, casting a shadowed glow across the room.

The two slid around the table to peek into the captain's bed chamber. There, Captain Longbottoms snored dully in his large bed underneath layers of silken blankets. Steve hung by the door and pointed his pistol at the bed. Ian swallowed. It felt like a cactus had been shoved down his throat. He gingerly drew one of his pistolas and stepped forward into the room. Nervous, he looked back to Steve, who gestured him to keep going as he kept watch.

Ian wiped his brow. Sweat rolled from his neck and ears. The pirate leathers clung to his legs. With a shaking hand he wobbled the barrel of the pistola to the sleeping head of the captain. *It's not real. It's just an imaginary world. You're not really killing anyone.'* When his pistola nearly touched the captain's skull, the man rolled over and sat up.

Even in the dark candlelight, Ian could tell that it was not the captain. "You again," said a sour, rum-soaked voice.

Ian backed away as the fat pirate in the blue and white striped shirt climbed out of bed. Ian aimed the pistola at the pirate's face, but it wobbled wildly. All he had to do was pull the trigger. Pull it. Pull it. He could hear Mr. Wasserbaum's voice in his head saying, "Dig it! Dig it!" But instead, he ran for the door, Steve calling after him, "What are you doing?"

Ian barged through the door, tripped on the molding, and sprawled himself out onto the quarterdeck. When he looked up, he saw the horizon had grown brighter as the sun rose and knew that the entire ship was waking. Before him, stepped Captain Longbottoms, his scimitar still sheathed and his pistol undrawn. His long, bare legs accentuated his tall frame, and his broad, bare chest finished the imposing nature of the captain. The loincloth around his waist contained fresh blood stains. Above him, perched in the rigging, sat Abigail the condor, her shriek a sinister cackle. "Well, well," Longbottoms said. "Where's my girl?"

Ian sat up to see all the crooked pirate smiles laughing at him, their stubbled chins and golden earrings exaggerated in their sneers. It was supposed to be simple. It was supposed to be as easy as a shot behind his ear. His stomach curdled, and he felt light-headed and dizzy. Why had Captain Wilder abandoned him? He needed him now more than ever.

"Such a pity," Captain Longbottoms said. "I expected more from the great Captain Ian Wilder." Behind the captain, the crew boiled in boisterous laughter.

An electricity gripped Ian. He didn't know where it came from, but it felt like someone much braver than him controlled his body. In a quick, deft move, he sprung up and drew his pistola on the captain. Again, it wobbled in front of Longbottoms' face, eliciting a laugh from him and the crew.

"A bit shaky on the draw, Captain," Longbottoms chuckled. "Don't be foolish. My men would cut you down." He paused and looked at his pirate brethren behind him. "Besides, I don't think you have it in you anymore. Too many years chained up in Noface's brig."

"We're taking the ship!" Ian yelled.

More chortling. The captain held his hand over his mouth to stifle his laugh. "You and your friend are going to take my ship? All by yourself?"

Ian thought about it. More than 50 pirates against the two of them. He swallowed another cactus-like gulp and said, "Yes." He tried to steady his aim on the pistola, but it wasn't helping. Why couldn't he do this?

Longbottoms raised his arms above his head and, with a snarky sneer, said, "Then by all means, take it!"

Ian's finger dithered on the trigger. He tried to convince himself that Longbottoms didn't really exist. He was just a character in his imagination, even if this was a separate, real universe. There was nothing wrong in doing what he needed to do to save the Penelope of this world. But then wouldn't she be imaginary too? Sweat beaded and ran down the curve of his back. His arm grew tired and twitchy. He felt wobbly and dizzy.

Then Longbottoms' forehead burst in front of him, splattering bone, blood, and brains over Ian's face. An echoing pop followed. As the dead captain's body teetered and fell to the deck beside Ian, the condor screeched once, flapped its wings, and flew off. Around them, the crew no longer laughed, but gazed in amazement at the gore covering Ian. In the silent few seconds after the confusion, Steve stepped next to Ian and whispered into his ear, "Draw the sword, kid. Show them the Neverblade."

His ears throbbing, Ian listened, mindless. The Neverblade rang out of the sheath, and he held it to the rising sun, the light from the blade flashing over the entire crew. There was no retaliation. No melee. No clashing of swords. To his bewilderment, the crew bowed to his blade. Steve whispered to him, "Way to go, kid. You did it."

As Steve hollered to the crew, Ian sheathed the fake Neverblade and held up his pistola. The shot remained. He hadn't fired at all. What had happened?

Then, as if he answered himself, Captain Ian Wilder swung down from the crow's nest and landed next to him, his trusty modified musket slung over his shoulder, still smelling of spent gunpowder. He shoved Ian in the shoulder "Ne'er hesitate. Never. You won't always have me around—"

Behind Captain Wilder a screaming black arrow darted toward him from the sky. Steve and Ian opened their mouths to warn the captain, but he had already drawn Steve's pistol, turned, and shot. Abigail, the once vicious condor, exploded in a cloud of feathers and dropped straight to the deck, skidding into a heap against the deck rail.

The captain stowed the pistol back in Steve's belt and finished, "—to back you up."

A red diamond repeated in Ian's mind.

That's what slowly opened up above the bridge of Captain Longbottoms' nose. A dark red diamond that expelled hot blood and gritty bone fragments. Ian replayed every frame. The sun had just blinked over the horizon. His hand wobbled terribly. His finger twitched, his arm ached. Then a blood diamond opened the captain's forehead, blood and matter stinging Ian's face in a hot spray. The blood salty on his lips as it cooled in the sea breeze.

His ears rang.

Longbottoms fell like an axed timber.

Ian had stepped aside to avoid the falling man, yet knew he hadn't willed his body to move. His mind felt thrust into catatonia again, like a ship stalled in the doldrums. Steve whispered instructions into his ear, but Ian never actually heard them. His blade rose above the chaos and flashed over the crew. Somewhere, Captain Ian Wilder arrived, his musket hot.

The captain had taken the shot, not Ian.

That's why his pistola didn't flare. What did the captain tell him? He thought it was important. "Never hesitate," he had said. "Never."

CHAPTER 26

NEVER HESITATE

Ian gasped and sat up in his bed. Frantic, he wiped away the blood and bone fragments from his face, but his hands came back clean. His bedroom unfolded around him in darkness. The curtains at his window fanned and unfurled with a tender early October breeze. He checked his alarm clock. 2:43 AM. He didn't even remember Steve bringing him back. He must have been in shock.

Chilled, he got up to close his window. Across the fence, the Archer house sat dark. His flashlight still sat nestled on the windowsill. He pointed it across to Penelope's window and turned it on and off, half hoping to see her light flash back, but of course, it didn't.

He lay back down and exhaled a long breath. What was he doing? The closer he came to Penelope in one reality, the farther he slipped away from his life in the other. There had to be a way to do justice to both. He had to prove to his parents he wasn't falling head-first into a tarry pool of mental illness. He had messed up a lot recently. And stealing over to the Archers' house to look for some silly made-up map was one too many apples on the teetering applecart.

He had to try harder. A lot harder.

His mom was the priority. An idea struck him.

He sprang from his bed and tip-toed downstairs into the kitchen. With the dimmer switch turned low, he opened the fridge and checked out the situation: eggs, whole-wheat bread, a large bowl of cabbage salad, sandwich meat, a bottle of Bailey's Irish Cream, some English muffins, American cheese, milk, butter, and some other random staples. Next, he took out a frozen package of Canadian bacon and set it on the counter. Finally, he searched three cupboards before he found the quick sauce and gravy packets, whispering, "Yes," to himself. Excited, he turned off the kitchen light and snuck back upstairs. He set his alarm clock for 5:00 AM and rolled back into his covers and tried to sleep.

At 5:20 AM, Ian stood downstairs in the kitchen, wearing his mother's mermaid apron. He scrolled through his phone, double-checking an online recipe. Hollandaise sauce thickened in a small saucepan. Water boiled in a larger stockpot. Canadian bacon sizzled in a frying pan. Ian cracked four eggs into the stockpot for poaching. Then he inserted English muffin halves into the toaster.

Eggs Benedict. His mother's favorite breakfast.

Ian was checking on the poaching eggs when his father stepped into the kitchen. "Ian? What are you doing?"

Ian wheeled around. "Making you and Mom some breakfast. Figured after last night, it's the least I could do."

Harold Wilder rubbed his bed-head and said, "Yeah, what was that all about?" But before he could linger on that topic, he added, "Is that eggs Benedict?" With widening eyes, he walked over to the stove and hovered over each pan, inhaling the aromas: caramelizing Canadian bacon, rich Hollandaise, toasty English muffins.

"I think I just really missed her last night," Ian told his dad. Sure, it wasn't the total truth, but it sounded the sanest.

The muffins popped up from the toaster. Ian's dad handed him a plate. "I understand you miss her, son. But last night wasn't just criminal, it was creepy. What were you doing in there? You didn't lie down in her bed, did you?"

Ian slid two slices of Canadian bacon over the muffins, remembering Steve's accusations. "No, Dad!" Ian said. "I just—I needed to be there. See her drawings. Her paintings. It sounds weird, but when I see them, I feel closer to her."

His dad moved the plate toward the egg pot and gestured for Ian to serve them up. "As long as you weren't going through her closet or dresser." He paused to let Ian ladle on the Hollandaise sauce. "You didn't touch her clothes, did you?"

Ian turned to his dad and frowned. "Dad…"

"Good." His dad took his plate to the table and began digging in.

Ian watched him ravenously mow into the eggs Benedict. "What about your diet?"

His dad looked up, a spot of sauce on his lower lip. "One dance with eggs Benedict does not spoil the prom, kiddo."

Ian began fixing a plate for his mother. "Where's Mom? She's usually down by now."

"She's not feeling too well. She's not teaching today."

Ian turned around in frustration. "But I made all of this for her."

His father dredged English muffin across his saucy plate. "Then maybe you should bring it to her."

Ian carried a tray topped with his mom's breakfast, a cup of coffee, and a glass of orange juice upstairs. He opened his parents' bedroom door, carefully balancing the tray on one knee. A pile of wadded up tissues had formed at the base of the nightstand, where an empty tissue box sat.

When he slid the tray onto the other nightstand, his mother woke with a start, another tissue wadded up in her hand. "Oh, darling," she said, groggily. "Why are you up so early?"

"I couldn't sleep. So I made your favorite."

She sat up to look over the meal. "Thanks, sweetheart. But I'm not hungry right now." She looked up at him with bloodshot eyes.

"Oh," Ian said, a bit disappointed. Though, he should have known better than to think he could fix his mistakes with food. Seeing his disappointment, she offered him a pained smile. "It looks very good, though."

Ian sat on the foot of the bed. "I just thought it was the least I could do."

His mom scooted closer to him. "I'm not upset about that, honey. I mean, you can't make a habit of breaking into the Archers', but…" she paused and fumbled with the tissue in her hand. "I'm upset because I know how hard it must be to deal with this. You forget, but I watched you and Penelope grow up together. Play together. Make up those fantastical stories together." She took his hand and shook it a bit, smiling. "Remember those cowboy outfits I made for both of you? With the little brown hats and the fringed chaps?" Ian nodded. "I know how close you two were, and it crushes me each time I think about it. Last night was just…well, I thought I had it under control, but I don't."

Ian cocked his head to his mom. "So you're not mad at me for going over there?"

"No. I'm just sad." She paused to dab her nose with the tissue. "You know, before I met your dad, I got pregnant. My college boyfriend and I got careless a few times, and it just happened."

Shocked, Ian said, "You have another kid?"

"Well, sweetheart, yes and no. The baby was stillborn. A girl. Her name was Emily."

Ian held his breath. Like a cog gumming up an elaborate grandfather clock, his body seemed to stutter to a stop. In the breath of a few words, his sister was born and then simultaneously snuffed out. The muscles around his chest grew tight and painful. He'd always wanted a sibling, but he'd had Penelope. Now he had neither. "Does Dad know?"

His mom smiled. "Of course. It was his reaction to that very story that made me want to marry him." She dabbed her eyes with the tissue and continued. "After Emily, it was very hard for me to try again. I was so afraid it would happen again. It felt futile to have the power to generate a life, only to have it born into the world dead. For years, I put off trying again. Until your father convinced me."

"How'd he do that?"

His mother smiled and looked Ian in the eyes. "He told me that if I let death rule my life, then I didn't really have much of a life at all.?" Ian rolled the words in his brain like a jawbreaker lolling across a tongue, tasting them. Although his mom's story wasn't a full parallel to his own experience, he felt a kinship, a likeness, between himself and her.

His mother nodded and wiped her nose. "It took a few months, years actually, to gather the courage, but I did. And then I became pregnant with you. And even though I was terrified of the same result, you came into this world screaming like a banshee across the Scottish moors. And I couldn't have been happier."

Ian forced a smiled. Guilt welled up inside him. This whole breakfast-in-bed thing was meant to take care of his mom, but somehow, she was always taking care of him. Still, maybe getting that off her chest had made her feel better too.

Maggie threw the tissue into the pile on the floor, then looked at the tray. "Eggs Benedict, huh?" she said.

"I know it's your favorite."

His mother hugged him tight. "Thank you."

On the bus ride to school, Ian forgot to put his ear buds in. Forgot about music entirely. Instead, he slumped in his seat thinking about his conversation with his mother. It explained so much. Why his parents had been married so long before having him. Why he was an only child. He tried picturing Emily's pink, infant face and how she would have looked had she gotten the chance he had been given. He didn't know when she was born or how much older she would have been. He wondered how his life would have been different had she lived and been his older sister. More so, had she lived, would he even exist? Would his mom have met his dad? Would she have had him?

The Infiniuum chattered with possibility around him. He knew somewhere within its eternal confines, Emily's alternates had lived a long good life. Something about that idea soothed him.

Behind him, the caterwauling of Pete Stamdahl and his loyal band of toadies grew to a din, but he ignored them. He pulled his math homework out of his backpack and opened it. After struggling through the first three problems, Ian gave his eyes a break. In the seat across the aisle, Heidi Flugalmann watched, not daring to say a word.

Then something strange happened.

Ian didn't know if it was the void he felt with Penelope gone, or if it was his alternate's advice to never hesitate, but Ian asked Heidi, "You know anything about imaginary numbers?"

Surprised, yet pleased, Heidi blazed him a braces-filled smile. "Do I?" she said in a mousy voice, then grabbed her backpack and moved into the seat with Ian, shoving him to the window. "I'm in the math club, silly!"

Immediately, she tore into his homework and began explaining it like a Nobel laureate. He missed the vast majority of what she said. The whole scenario amazed him. Since kindergarten, Heidi had nothing much to offer except quick, weird, furtive glances. But who was he kidding? It was nice to have someone to talk to. Sure, she was skinny as a Popsicle stick, had a ton of freckles, long curly ginger hair, and braces that could light up Sycamore Street, but really, she wasn't half bad, and obviously, incredibly smart. By the time the bus pulled into the school parking lot he had finished his homework, with Heidi's help, of course.

While waiting to exit the bus, Pete Stamdahl and his toadies laid into them. "Wilder and Flugalmann—a match made in Crazyville! Talk about a trade down, Wilder! With your nuts and her ginger, you'll make one hell of a cookie."

Ian tried to ignore them, but like before, a change took over him. Pete's words foamed rabid in Ian's head, repeatedly. From the old taunts about him and Penelope to these new ones, he just couldn't take it anymore. Never hesitate. He thought back to every other juncture in his life that had been marred by indecision; the results that weren't results at all. Nothing happened. He never dared to do anything. His life wasn't a life at all, but simply a series of safe choices.

Then he thought about his mom. How devastated she must have been after losing her daughter. But her life had changed dramatically for the better by simply making the risky choice, by taking a chance on getting hurt again for a shot at something greater.

After they stepped off the bus, Ian waited off to the side instead of rushing into school.

"Just let them be idiots," Heidi told him at his side, her pink backpack hanging off her shoulders. Ian didn't say anything. He simply waited. Pete was the first of his goblin crew off the bus, and Ian swung around and punched him in the gut. It felt like punching a steel-belted tire through three layers of unbaked pizza dough, but it did the trick. Pete doubled over in surprise and as his head went down, Ian slugged him in the nose with his left fist.

He expected Pete's toadies to raise a ruckus, but they didn't. They just helped Pete to his feet and walked with him into the school. A warm, fiery satisfaction burned through Ian. But when his brain finally took hold and thought it through, those flames were dowsed. What if Pete or someone else reported it? The principal would call Ian to his office. His parents would be called. Dr. Caulderon would be called, and he'd be shipped off to juvy—if they even had juvies anymore.

Feeling stupid, he looked to Heidi at his side. Her face smoldered in happiness, but she hid it quickly and said, "You didn't have to do that for me. I get called names all the time."

Ian hadn't really done it for her; he did it for himself. "It just felt right," he said. "I never used to do things like that."

"Your hand!" she said, lifting Ian's left hand and inspecting it.

"Just a split," Ian said, looking at his knuckles.

"Hold on," Heidi said, pulling him to the sidewalk. She removed a pink first aid kit from her backpack. Inside the kit was an assortment of ointments and bandages. She slathered some ointment on a Hello Kitty bandage.

"Oh, that's…cute," Ian said.

Heidi placed the bandage over Ian's split knuckle. "I have a thing about Japanese popular culture icons," she said, patting down the bandage. "So how is it working?" Heidi asked.

Ian flexed his hand and admired the Hello Kitty bandage. "Just fine."

"Not that," she said. "Doing new things."

"I don't know yet," he said, smiling at her. "I guess we'll find out."

CHAPTER 27

A Convergence of Worlds

Pete Stamdahl did not rat him out. Nor did anyone else. Sure, a knot twisted in Ian's gut regarding the moral and ethical use of violence to solve problems, but it was probably the best day he'd had since Penelope's death. Pete Stamdahl had been silenced, at least momentarily, and Ian had a taunt-free day, the first as far as he could remember. And he smiled thinking about Heidi Flugalmann's kindness and her tender care for his split knuckle.

The air hung cool around him as he walked home from the bus stop. Leaves at the tops of trees had begun turning. It seemed like he'd turned a corner of some kind. Like maybe things were stabilizing into a new normal.

When he got home, he hung up his backpack and headed to the kitchen, where his mom peeled potatoes for dinner. Ian popped open a soda and drained half of it in one gulp. "Can we get takeout tonight? I was thinking Japanese. Oh, and I invited Heidi Flugalmann to dinner. Hope that's okay."

His mom stopped peeling. "You haven't had Japanese food before. Well, except the sushi. And we all remember how that ended. Are you sure?"

Ian downed the last of his soda and squeezed the can until it crinkled in on itself. "I'm sure," Ian said. "I'm trying new things now."

Maggie Wilder stowed the potatoes in a pan. "I'll call your dad and have him bring some home." She paused, then continued. "You know, if you're trying new things, maybe you should entertain the idea of cleaning your room or kicking the soda habit."

Ian chuckled. "Yeah, that's a riot, Mom."

Two hours later, Harold Wilder struggled through the front door, carrying three large bags of Japanese food. Once in, he used his foot to shut the front door. He set down the food and his briefcase and then kissed his wife as she set the table. "Remember the last time we had Japanese food?" he whispered into her ear.

She set out four plates. "Of course I do. But I didn't make this request. Ian did."

Harold stepped back. "Ian? Didn't he throw up after trying sashimi for the first time?"

"Yes. It was quite colorful." Maggie laid out four sets of chopsticks from the bag.

Harold followed her and counted the table settings. "Who is coming over for dinner?"

She placed napkins at each setting. "Ian's new friend."

Harold screwed his face into astonishment. "New friend?"

Maggie stepped to the top of the stairs leading into the basement and called, "Kids, dinner's ready."

Harold watched Ian emerge from the stairs, followed by a ginger-haired girl with braces and freckles. Heidi approached Harold, shook his hand, and said, "Nice to meet you, Mr. Wilder. I'm Heidi Flugalmann. We were playing video games. Hey, are you related to Almanzo Wilder from the *Little House on the Prairie* books?"

Slow on the uptake, Harold tried processing all her words. She was a talkative one. "No, we are not related to Almanzo Wilder," Harold said with a welcoming smile.

"I told you," Ian said to Heidi, then sat down at the table.

Heidi took the remaining seat. "Did you get miso? I love miso."

Harold nodded and handed her a large Styrofoam carton of soup. "But it's got tofu."

"Bonus!" Heidi said.

"What else do we have?" Ian asked.

Harold pointed to the cartons in order and said, "Nabe Yaki Udon, noodles with shrimp tempura, mushrooms, and spinach. Yaki Nuku-Don, beef sautéed with yellow onion and hibachi sauce—your mom's favorite. Vegetable Soba, noodles, and vegetables. And some ramen, for you, since the last time, you—"

"Dad," Ian interrupted, sending a toe into his father's shin under the table. "I'll try the soup and the thing with the shrimp."

Ian ate and kept down the food. Much of it was pretty tasty, despite his initial fears. He liked this "new things" approach he had going on. So far it seemed to be working. After eating, Ian asked to be excused, and he and Heidi found their way to the basement again, leaving both parents bewildered, yet relieved that Ian was socializing again.

Downstairs, Ian and Heidi fired up *Call of Duty* and played split-screen. Ian never knew Heidi liked video games. Then again, you'd be hard-pressed to find anyone in the tenth grade who didn't. Still, she had a knack for the sniper rifle and sent Ian out on scouting runs to bring their online opponents into her web of long-range death.

Between games, she migrated back and forth from playing on the floor to sprawling on the couch where Ian sat. However, as the matches wore on, Ian noticed each time she switched back to the couch, she got closer and closer until, on her last migration, she jumped up after sniping an unsuspecting opponent, said, "Hells yeah!" and sat on the couch right next to him.

He immediately thought he should get up and move, maybe give her some space. But he stopped. That was old Ian. New Ian would see how things shook out. Maybe this one decision would break off a completely different future, creating something other than this recent mess.

New things.

Let it ride.

So he did. For the remainder of the night, she stayed next to him thigh-to-thigh. After a few more games, she got quieter. Her celebrations on long-distance shots no longer had a spunky shout or an upright fist. The space between them grew unstable, humid. The eerie calm before an ozone-soaked strike of lightning. Her thigh muscled twitched like a ripple on a pond. He felt it against his skin. His heartbeat reached the rate of an Indonesian howler monkey, the one fact he retained on their field trip to the zoo last year. The latest match took forever to upload, leaving them in some dreaded, thigh-twitching unbroken awkwardness.

Heidi broke first, leaning in to kiss Ian.

Now, to his defense, his last kiss had come from an interdimensional baddy who had likely just killed his girlfriend, so Ian's first instinct was to turn away. But Heidi lost her balance and toppled into him. Not only did their lips crash into each other, but so did their chests. Together for that brief moment, they shared much more than they intended. For one brief second all their undulations, their intimate curves and grooves, matched in perfection.

Ian had never imagined Heidi Flugalmann's lips to be that soft. It was a significant trade-up from the hard, probing tongue of the malig Penelope.

But as quickly as it started, it ended. Heidi pushed herself from Ian's chest and sprung up, embarrassed. Her eyes darted around the room for the fastest escape. With her hair, freckles, and now blushing cheeks, she looked as if a fire had ignited from within. "I'm sorry, Ian. That was weird."

Ian sat forward. Sudden, yes. Weird, no. If anything, he wanted another crack at it. Unless the weird was him. Maybe he screwed it up? Though he had done enough of it with Penelope to know he didn't totally suck at it. "Yes, weird," he said. "But it's fine, really."

Heidi cocked her head and looked at him. "It's too soon, isn't it?" she asked. "I should have waited. You're still grieving. That was rude of me."

Ian shook his head. "No. It really is fine, Heidi."

Heidi frowned. "I'm so sorry, Ian. I should go." She dashed up the steps.

"Wait," Ian called, rising from the couch to catch up to her, but when he stood the room had changed into the faux Millennium Falcon.

"Who's the sparkly red-head?" Steve stood in the entryway of the cockpit, blocking Ian.

"A friend," Ian said. "I have to go get her."

Steve stepped forward and grabbed Ian's arm. Hard. "What do you mean you have to go?"

Ian looked down at Steve's hand. Steve had never grabbed him like that before.

"You and I have to go. Remember Penelope, sea-crusted pirates, murderous malig, that whole bit?"

"I can't right now," Ian said, breaking free from Steve's hold. He dashed out of the cockpit and found the basement stairs leading up to the kitchen. He needed to talk to Heidi.

But when he reached the top, rather than spilling out into the kitchen, Ian found himself back in the faux Millennium Falcon again with Steve sitting in the pilot's seat.

"What are you doing, pal? We have unfinished business."

Ian ignored him and opened the doors to the cockpit, where the living room sprawled onward to the front door. He ran and opened it, ready to yell for Heidi to wait up, only it led back to the faux Millennium Falcon again.

Steve again sat in his pilot's seat, his feet up on the console. "I can do this all night, man."

Angry, Ian said, "So can I."

Ian tore open the doors to the cockpit and stepped out to the front steps. Down the street, Heidi walked hurriedly under a streetlight and into the night. "Heidi, wait," he called. "It's okay." But after a few steps, he came back into the cabin of the starship again.

"You're making this a lot harder than it has to be," Steve said.

Ian threw open the cockpit doors and ran. Only, after a few paces, he emerged into the cabin of the Falcon again.

Steve stood up calling after Ian, "You're losing focus, man! You need to get it back!"

"No, I don't!" Ian shouted. Again, he threw open the doors and dashed back into his neighborhood. He followed Heidi who tramped through her yard and onto her front step, canopied in an ivy-covered trellis.

Ian was almost to her yard before he emptied back into the faux Falcon once more.

"Look," Steve said. "I don't know what your play is here, kid, but we need to get back there. Penelope needs us!"

For the first time since he had thrown a spasmodic fit after Penelope's death, Ian let his emotions completely go. "Penelope's dead, Steve! Dead! I can't do anything for her now! It's all a complete waste of time! Now leave me alone!" Only after he said it did he realize what had unraveled from his mouth—a slick black snake of anger and contempt. He already regretted it, but there it was, coiled in the corner.

Silence fell aboard the cockpit. Only the artificial air flow from the vents above filled the gaps. Steve's face slouched. His eyes tired, he slinked back to his seat and sat down. "Okay, pal. You're the captain."

Ian threw open the doors to the starship and ran. He half-expected to end up back in the cockpit again, but he didn't. Even though each step took him closer to Heidi, his anger at Steve filled a hollow within him. Maybe this new philosophy, the new things, was a way to escape the pain in his life. Was he simply covering his pain with a shiny new rug to hide it?

His hand hovered over the Flugalmann's doorbell, hesitant, when he heard a voice from the porch swing.

"You didn't have to come after me," Heidi said, swinging gently, one foot toeing the porch to keep the swing in line.

Ian joined her, making sure their thighs touched again. "I didn't know what else to do."

"It wasn't you," she said, her eyes down. "When I said it was weird. I meant me."

"You? Weird? No, trust me. It was me," Ian said. "I'm terrible with girls. Always have been."

"No, I meant," she paused in thought. "When I kissed you, I could tell."

"Tell what?"

"That I wasn't Penelope."

"So?"

Heidi wiped a tear building in the corner of her right eye. "I'll never be able to replace her."

Ian exhaled a loud puff of air. "I don't expect you to."

"Still," she said. "You two were perfect for each other. It felt like I was intruding on something."

Ian didn't know what to say. Why did girls have to be so complicated? The only thing that came to mind was his dad's story about the ducks. "My dad told me this story once," he began. "It was right after his brother died. Things were rough, and he couldn't really deal with it all. So he got drunk at some dam and stood at the rail over the gushing water and just watched it. I think he was looking for answers or something, but while he was there, he saw a family of baby ducks in the river below. They couldn't get out of the backflow. He thought they'd drown. So he left his bottle and crawled over the rocks and down the shore. He thought if he could do something for them, he should. He got about ten feet away from the ducklings when the mother duck flew in and paddled them all out."

Heidi looked at him, waiting for him to go on. When he didn't, her eyebrows knitted in confusion. "What does that mean?"

Ian shook his head. "I don't know. I think it means, just because your action had no effect on the results, doesn't mean it wasn't worth a try."

Puzzled, Heidi forced a smile and laughed a little. "I have no idea how that fits with what just happened."

"Yeah, it doesn't," Ian sighed. "I think the story was just meant for me, actually."

The sounds of crickets filled their ears. "Thanks, Ian," Heidi said after a pause. "For running after me. I shouldn't need it, but sometimes a girl just likes to have someone run after her."

He walked her to the door, where she told him that she'd see him on the bus the next morning. Then she kissed him on the cheek and went in.

When Ian got home, his parents were sitting on the living room couch watching a reality cooking show. His dad read a Vince Flynn novel, and his mother struggled desperately at a needlepoint project she had been working on.

When he passed through, they asked about Heidi. He told them everything, leaving out the incessant badgering of his interdimensional friend, Steve, of course. They seemed worried about Heidi, but after he told them about their talk on the porch, they relaxed. Before he went to his room, he stopped to watch them for a secret moment. Their family felt balanced again, in harmony. Energized, he ran up the stairs two at a time.

In his room, he flung open the closet doors, only to find sweaters, dress shirts, jeans, and dress pants hanging in the back. As urgent as Steve had sounded, he expected him to be waiting. Ian closed the doors and opened them again, but still the closet remained.

Odd.

He remembered the hollow he felt earlier. His blow-up with Steve. A worry wriggled into his brain. Steve looked really dejected. Was this his way of getting back at him? The interdimensional silent treatment? For a third time, he flung open the closet doors, hoping to catch Steve by surprise. But again, only his clothes.

Resigned, Ian crawled onto his bed and lay on his back. He shouldn't have shouted at Steve, should have never told him there was nothing more he could do for Penelope. His eyes fluttered in sleepiness, caught in that mist between waking and drifting. A yawn fumbled out of his mouth.

Ian climbs down a rocky shore. Overhead, a dam roars. Muddy water tosses around him. This time it is Penelope who is caught in the undertow.

Her hands slap at the water. Gasps usher from her mouth. Panic. Frantic. Her head bobs under and back up. Her eyes crash about, searching the shoreline for anything, anyone to help. When she sees Ian, she yells, "Ian! Help me! I'm so tired. I can't hold out much longer!"

As nimbly as he can, Ian scrambles over the rocks and into the water. The churn of the water drowns out her violent coughs and gags.

Ian swims. Kicks his legs until they spark in twisted cramps. The water feels thick, like swimming in mud.

"Hurry!" she screams. He tries to swim faster, even with the painful knots in his legs. Between the rushing water and his own gulps of air, her wail falls silent—a siren drowned by an incoming storm. Her screams stop, and only the deafening churn remains.

Ian scans the water but cannot find her. Beneath his feet, the undertow pulls at him. He kicks and paddles until his muscles feel ripped from his bones. But it isn't enough. A hundred thousand gallons of water plunge him deep into the silt. His mouth fills with the fetid taste of rotten, water-logged corpses.

CHAPTER 28

ENTER THE WICKED CROW

Ian awoke with a cough, half-expecting to spew up an entire river. But it was just another dream. When had he fallen asleep? He rolled off his bed and stood up to creaking floorboards. His balance off kilter, he spilled to the floor. Only when his face hit, it wasn't the carpet of his bedroom—it was the musty, floorboards of a ship.

Ian sprung up in shock. Around him unfolded the chambers of Captain Longbottoms. The ship tossed to the side, and Ian was dumped to the floor again. His knees and elbows smarted from his tumbles. How did he get here? He didn't remember Steve transporting him. He had checked the closet and found nothing but clothes. Did Steve come to get him as he slept? Getting up a second time, he found his balance still tenuous, so he steadied himself with the bedpost. He noted that the bed was bolted to the floor.

They were at sea.

Quickly, he looked about the room for his clothes. He craned his neck and found all his pirate gear piled on the desk. As he tugged on his leather pants, the ship rocked again. He and the clothes fell to the floor. While there, he wriggled into the pants and buckled them. He pulled the linen shirt over his head and was reaching for his long coat when the port side of the captain's chambers exploded in wooden shards. A gaping stripe had been caved in by a cannonball. Shaken, he threw on his coat and grabbed his hat.

What in the hell?

Scrambling to the chamber door, he opened it to chaos. The whole crew heaved at ropes and adjusted canvas. Below decks, gunners readied the cannons. And at the helm, Steve and Captain Ian Wilder argued with each other over the calamity of the attack. "Hard to port and take her head on!" yelled the captain.

"Are you nuts?" Steve yelled. "Give her a broadside shot when she's already peppered our hull?"

"I don't care."

"Well, I do," Steve shot back.

Finally, both realized Ian was standing there. "What are you doing here?" they yelled in unison.

"You brought me here," Ian yelled to Steve.

"I did not," he said. "You made it abundantly clear I was on my own for this!"

The captain got in Ian's face. "Everythin' I did for you and you abandon us?"

Ian looked to Steve. "If you didn't bring me, how did I get here?"

Steve shrugged. "Beats the hell outta me, kid. Welcome to the Infiniuum."

Ian stepped back and let them continue their argument. What was happening? Was this a dream, too? Did he just navigate the Infiniuum on his own without Steve or the faux Falcon? The ship rocked, but his legs found their equilibrium and balance, acting on their own pure instinct.

He looked up and past the bow. An island came into view portside. He grabbed the spyglass from the captain's belt and extended it for a look.

Oasis Island. A bean-shaped landmass about three miles long and one mile wide. The island had long been festooned with hot springs and lava flows, creating a perpetual cloud of fog, smoke, or both around the island.

Ian shut the spyglass and threw it to the captain. He barked out to the crew, "Take us around the east side of that island!"

"Aye!" the crew shouted in confirmation.

The captain grabbed Ian. "By the time we go 'round the island, she'll have undercut us on the inside. When we come out of the fog we'll be chum in the water."

Ian smiled. "Precisely why once we're under the cover of fog, we kick it out starboard and come up behind them when they think they're undercutting us. They'll be the chum."

The captain smiled back. "Now you're startin' to sound like me. 'Bout time."

Ian adjusted his hat "Who's tailing us anyway? An ally to Longbottoms?"

"The Wicked Crow, who else?"

Ian looked to Steve, who threw up his hands. "That's what I was trying to tell you when you told me to shove off!"

Ian paced the deck. "Sorry, man," Steve said. "We barely got out of port when Penelope came down on us. We thought we'd have to go out and find her, but she must have a bee in her bonnet, because she found us instead."

"That doesn't make sense," Ian said.

The Leaping Lizard approached the island to the east. The cannon fire from the Wicked Crow had stopped.

Ian thought about it. Perhaps Longbottoms' plan to use Penelope against Noface had gotten out. That would explain why Penelope had sought out the Leaping Lizard. That was the only reason for her showing up like this. Right? A shiver wriggled down Ian's spine like a cuttlefish. Why did nothing ever go according to plan here?

Without thinking, he yelled to the crew, "They're assessing our move. Tack it to portside. Slowly. We really need to sell it!" The ship swayed to port and, in the distance, the Wicked Crow slowed its pursuit. Fog rolled down the island hills and over the waves, enveloping them. "Easy now!" Ian yelled. "Wait until we're in the fog. Easy. A little longer. Now! Hard to starboard! Go! Go! Go!"

Sails fell and lifted. Ropes ran up new canvas and caught the wind again, pulling the ship in the opposite direction.

"Now we see if your ploy worked," Captain Ian Wilder said.

Ahead, the fog floated thick. The crew fell silent in anticipation. "This will either be the naval maneuver of the millennium or the fastest scuttling ever," Steve said nervously. Around them the mist swirled and eddied. Without their sight, the crew skittered about to noises. A swoop overhead. A ping against the hull. A distant splash. Some looked over the rail, only to see more fog and a glimpse of rushing sea beside them.

After five minutes of sailing, the Leaping Lizard emerged from the fog, and the Wicked Crow no longer sat in her place. "Spyglass," Ian said to the captain. Ian spied the edge of the island. Sure enough, a wake lay just beyond it. The Wicked Crow had chosen to undercut their original route.

Ian stood at the bridge and yelled down to the crew, "Slow and steady now. No eddy or sound. Keep her keen to the fog. We aim to sneak up on her. Boarding party, prepare for interception." Ian turned to Steve and the captain. "No cannon fire. We're here to get on board, not to kill anyone."

Captain Wilder rolled his eyes.

"We just need to talk to her," Ian reminded him. "Explain what's going on so she understands." Ian watched across the horizon for the Wicked Crow. It had to be lying in wait at the other end of the island now, cannons at the ready. The captain stood on his left. A satisfied little smile split his face, and his left hand stood ready on the hilt of his sword, his modified musket still strung over his back.

To his right, Steve watched over the bow as well, his body against the rail. He opened and closed his hand, revealing the bottle-cap-sized hole open to the cosmos of the Infiniuum.

Open and closed.

Open and closed.

"Everything okay?" Ian asked

For the first time since he had met him, Steve looked truly worried. "Huh?" he glanced at Ian. Steve shook his head to clear his thoughts. "I mean, yeah. Fine." He tightened his fist and shook it.

"You look nervous."

Steve looked up at him. His eyes had lost their shine. His thin lips tried to turn upwards into a smile but failed. "I'm getting warm."

Ian looked up, trying to find the sun above the fog. "It is warm. I feel like a busted grape in this ridiculous leather outfit." Ian said, thinking maybe a joke would ease the tension.

A fleeting smirk faded on Steve's face. "Not the weather," he said. "Me." He opened his hand and showed Ian the Infiniuum through the hole in his hand, nebulas and galaxies swirled beyond them. "Cosmic interference. This whole trip it has grown. Instant by instant. The malig's anticipation is growing. It must know we're here. Trying to throw me off. Casting arcs of interference around her. But she's close."

"You can tell all that by a feeling?" Ian asked.

Steve squinted his eyes at Ian. "Your kind built technology because you lacked a higher insight. You still think this is about technology? Gizmos and gadgets? The Infiniuum isn't about sleek, metallic star cruisers or laser swords. It isn't even about smartphones and mobile apps. The Infiniuum is life—the all-spinning, pulsating fiery plasma of the cosmos, kid. The primordial ooze of an infinity of galaxies, systems, and planets. The steadfast marching onward of a cornucopia of organisms. All connected by the same matter and energy that started it all."

Steve held his hand against Ian's forehead. Ian felt the heat of the cosmos but so much more. He couldn't describe it. It was like the entire Infiniuum had a heartbeat and he felt it racing, screaming like an air raid siren. In that moment he felt a multitude of unseen realities flowing through him like a tapestry of energy being woven not only inside him, but across everything. He felt a sense of connectedness with a whole. A vast whole he could not see, hear, identify, or perceive, but he felt it. He understood what Steve told him much earlier. "I feel it," Ian said.

"Finally," Steve said. "Took you long enough."

Ian gazed upward, where an albatross dipped in the wind. "God, right?"

"God is just a semantic concoction to explain the unknown," Steve said. "Life is God. From the infinitely small discharge of protons and electrons to the massive existence-shredding appetite of a black hole, everything is connected: the wood in this ship, the water beneath us, the whales and porpoises below that. We're all one big organism. Each doing their part in unison."

Ian looked down to the decking and back up to the albatross. The bird soared on the currents like a kite.

"We're always in constant communication," Steve said. "Whether we know it or not. It's just a matter of being able to tune in to it. And every organism can, if they understand those connections: feelings, dreams, sensations, emotions. Those are the 1's and 0's of the Infiniuum. Not some fabricated piece of silicon junk. What you call technology is simply organic life creating overly complicated work-arounds to true communication. Maligs and ferons, we're like opposite ends of the same battery. We cancel each other out. Maligs corrupt the Infiniuum. Ferons try to protect it."

Ian nodded at Steve. "Alright. Sorry I brought it up."

Steve wiped the sweat off his forehead and looked at his feet. "I'm sorry. I'm just...anxious. I hate being this close and yet so far away."

"We'll have to be careful," Ian said. "If we don't know who or what the malig is, being closer to Penelope will give us the best vantage."

Steve exhaled. "Yes. That's probably the wisest move."

Ian tried opening his mind to the hidden possibilities of the malig. Was it a shark circling the ship? The albatross soaring above? A deckhand below leaning into the cargo netting? Or was it someone on the Wicked Crow? Noface? Ian even turned to Steve. It couldn't be Steve. He had been with him the whole time. Not after all this. Embarrassed for thinking it, Ian turned away, squinted ahead to take his mind off the idea. They had to be coming up to the Wicked Crow shortly if their ruse had worked.

Ian's skin grew cold, clammy. A quaking uneasiness rippled through his gut. His heart fluttered off-rhythm and rose in his throat.

The malig was close. He could feel it too.

Off in the distance, a black object loomed in the fog. As they approached, a mast and sails emerged like a great black hand reaching up from the ocean. There was the Wicked Crow. The breeze carried a concoction of brine, smoke, and peaches.

Penelope.

For so long he had wanted to smell her again. He imagined Penelope meeting him on the deck of the Crow, her smile like a cascade of notes from a harp. She would leap to him, wrap her body around his. They would gaze into each other's eyes and the entire universe that had separated them would disintegrate, powder to the deck like spring pollen, and her kisses would drown him.

The captain's voice broke through Ian's delirium. "I have a shot." He stood against the rail, his eye to the spyglass mounted on his musket, which was aimed and ready to fire.

Almost a hundred yards out, the Wicked Crow emerged like an oily wraith set about the sea.

"Stand down, Captain," Ian told him. "We're not here for blood. We're here to talk."

"Ne'er hesitate, boy."

"Not this time."

The captain cocked the hammer back to his flintlock.

Ian stepped quickly to him and ordered, "Do not take that shot, Captain!"

From behind his weapon, the captain loosed a sly smile, while squeezing his trigger finger. "Too late."

CHAPTER 29

THE MALIC UNMASKED

But before Captain Wilder could pull the trigger, a soft pop cut from afar. The captain shrieked as the spyglass atop his musket exploded in his face. "Ah, hell," he screamed, dropping the destroyed weapon.

Ian and Steve rushed to his aid amid a hailstorm of shots upon their ship. The captain held his face. Blood gorged through his hand, and he kicked the rail in pain. Ian's stomach lurched, seeing the gore, the shards of glass embedded in the captain's face. More musket balls ripped through the sails. On the verge of retching, Ian peered over the rail. The Crow didn't have the angle for cannons yet, but she was quickly correcting herself.

"She shot out my eye!" the captain yelled.

Ian braved the fire overhead and yelled down to the crew, "Prepare to board!" The captain, Ian, and Steve stumbled down the stairs to the main deck with the crew.

"Are you going to be okay?" Ian asked.

The captain looked at him with his one eye, a jagged grin on his face. "I'm still standin'." The captain grabbed a rope and continued. "But how about you? You almost tossed your apples back there."

The jagged grin again. It stopped Ian for a moment as he groped for a boarding rope. In his hesitation, cannon fire tore into the side of the ship. His balance lost, Ian pulled on a rope, but the throng of his crew pressed against him, toppling him over the edge and into the sea. He hit head-first and cut through the waves, into a muted silence.

Shots sliced through the water around him, losing their velocity and sinking to the ocean floor like harmless coins. Above, cannons flashed. Both ships exchanged fire. Bodies fell flat and limp against the sea. Shards of wood careened into the surf. One of the ships burned, which one he couldn't tell. There in the green murk, he remembered he had seen all of this before.

His dream.

His lungs burned, and his head felt swollen as he sunk further under. Kick, he told himself. Get to the surface. Rising, Ian thought back to the dream: his duel with a malig-infested Penelope. It couldn't be, could it? Not after all this. He kicked his legs and breached the surface, gasping for air. His ears immediately rang with volleys of cannon fire. A pirate fell from a boarding rope and splashed in front of him. He gathered his bearings and swam for the Wicked Crow.

Climbing the cargo netting up the side, he scampered onto the deck and drew his faux Neverblade. All around, steel clashed with steel. Some of the blades met flesh in spitting gurgles. Others tore through shirts and leggings. At the bow, Steve clashed with three Crow sailors himself. His cutlass struck so quick and sure, Ian thought it almost silly, like those lame movies from the fifties with poorly painted sets. He almost laughed, but they caught each other's eyes. Steve pointed his cutlass to the aft, before swiping it across his opponent's face.

Ian looked aft.

At the rear of the deck, Captain Wilder dueled Penelope. Ian's chest tightened, and he lost sight of the captain's blade crossing hers. All he saw was this world's Penelope. Not his version of her from home, but the pirate version here. She looked exactly like he remembered from her paintings, dressed in burgundy pirate gear and cavalier hat with a long, elegant wine-colored plume. Her skin tanned and her long brown hair sun-bleached and wind-tossed. She looked so much like his Penelope, he couldn't help but soak his eyes with her. A smile bloomed on Ian's face. A stupid, smitten smile that had no place in this world of spilled blood and double-crosses. It took a trio of battling pirates to knock him over for Ian to get his bearings.

Why was the captain attacking Penelope?

Ian sprang up and dashed to the stairs. He wasn't thinking clearly. This was no time to be caught up in his emotions. He strode to the aft deck and slipped, his face sliding into a patch of thick, warm blood. He wiped his cheek and looked at the red on his hand. It was happening again. The dream. Rolling onto his feet, he ran to Penelope between fighting seadogs and skewered deckhands. Shoving his way through, he emerged and saw Penelope block the captain's attack. He recognized her sword: gleaming silver, ivy etchings. The real Neverblade. She had kept it!

The captain assaulted Penelope again, but she defended herself easily. Ian yelled to the captain above the din, "What are you doing?"

"Aye, you survived. Good. Wouldn't want you to miss this," he said, between blade strokes.

Penelope pressed back, pushing the captain to the rail.

"I'm so glad to see you!" Ian shouted to her.

With the captain at bay, Penelope reared back and punched Ian in the nose. "After all my work to keep it locked up on that island, you let it out!" The captain lunged, and Penelope engaged him once more.

What? Ian stopped, feeling blood trickle from his nose. Let what out? Confused, Ian tried to find Steve, but he was nowhere to be found. Penelope and the captain crashed into him and knocked him over. Again. What was going on?

He got to his feet, just as Captain Wilder cornered pirate Penelope and went in for a killing stroke. But before the captain struck, he waggled his handless stump at her and said, "Had you killed your love when you had the chance, you wouldn't have to die now. Just give me the spyglass, and I'll let the annoyin' whelp live!"

This was madness. Ian had to do something. He leapt at the captain and tackled him. Straddling the pirate captain version of himself, Ian said, "What are you doing?"

The captain smiled that jagged smile again. "Really? Still haven't thought it through? Why would she love an imbecile like you?" He reached up with a hidden dirk and slashed at Ian's chest but caught his right forearm as Ian tried to protect himself. The blade split the skin and blood burbled out. Before the pain cut a fiery beeline to Ian's brain, the captain shoved him off. "Don't die right away," he smiled again. "I'd like you to see this."

Ian watched from his back on the deck. His forearm burned like a hive of hornets burrowed beneath the skin, and the sight of the blood made him dizzy. He couldn't think. His mind kept flashing back to the captain's smile. Why did it bother him so much? And then it hit him, stealing the breath from his lungs.

The malig.

The captain was the malig.

Of course. After the funeral. The kiss. The malig had used him as a bridge to this alternate reality. It burrowed into his mind and used Ian's memories to bring itself here, into this reality, into his alternate here! Captain Wilder claimed that Penelope had put him on that island to keep him safe, but she'd put him there to protect herself. No wonder he'd been so willing to help them find her! That's why he trained him so hard. He needed every advantage to take the Leaping Lizard. He used them to find her. Ian felt sick. Instead of protecting Penelope from the malig, he'd brought the malig right to her. A hollow cavity ached in his stomach. He felt like throwing up so violently it would turn himself inside-out.

Across the deck, the captain harassed Penelope, who lunged, and parried, and scrambled about exhaustively to defend herself. Even with his left hand, Captain Wilder was outmatching her. But she had the Neverblade; she could channel all the past users if she wanted. Where was her vigor? Her fight? Why such a lackluster performance?

When she hesitated on a killing blow, the captain took advantage, skewering her sword arm between the radius and ulna. In agony, pirate Penelope dropped her weapon and fell to the deck. The captain threw his rusted blade overboard and picked up the Neverblade. Penelope slid backwards into a corner, her left hand applying pressure to her wound. Her eyes searched the captain's face, seeking something lost inside him.

Still woozy and bleeding, Ian could only watch. Why couldn't she fight him?

"Such a crude organism," the captain told her. "Soft, pink, pointless. What did she tell you? Did she make you a promise? Pledge to remake an unmade world? Right all the wrongs? 'Tis but a fantasy, lassie!"

Penelope looked around for an escape. "Yet here you are, looking for her and that spyglass."

The captain stepped closer. "You know we'll find her. We are one, we are all. And when we're done, missy. I'll come back here to—"

Love.

It struck Ian dumb. This world's Penelope couldn't fight Captain Wilder because she still loved him—the man, not the malig burrowing around his brain. That's why she lost. Ian tried to imagine in those brief seconds how painful it was for her to see the person she spent her entire life with about to cut her down. No wonder she hesitated and held back. Ian wondered if he would respond any better if the situation were reversed. Would he be able to shove his feelings to the side and think rationally? Clearly? Not likely. It seemed impossible.

But this wasn't about him.

It was about her. And he could do what she could not.

With the faux Neverblade in hand, Ian lunged at the captain. As the captain turned, Ian's blade found the gap in the captain's ribs. Captain Wilder fell backward to the deck, his mouth upturned into that jagged smile. With a thick, clot-infested gargle to his voice, he said, "We are one, we are all."

The captain's mouth opened and out heaved a thick, bright yellow, glowing worm-like tentacle. It existed or moved in multiple dimensional planes. Its strange, elemental, almost organic beauty compelled Ian. Perception crackled and bent to its movements. The entirety of the Islas Encantadas shuddered around it. It reached for Ian's face, and at its end a bottle-cap-sized hole appeared and opened to the indigo cosmos beyond. He remembered that hole. The same window into the beyond Steve had shown him on his hand.

As much as he wanted to run or cut it down, Ian again froze, dumbly taking in the strange sight. The tentacle lurched at his face and landed over Ian's eye, knocking him down. With an electric tongue, it probed his retina, looking for a way in. Like when he first saw the Infiniuum expanded, the back of Ian's head crackled with pain. Ian felt if he stopped fighting it, the pain would go away.

But a bright flash blinded him, and his grasp of this reality shrunk to a pinpoint in a realm of darkness before a breath of heat blew over him. The probing stopped. The pain ebbed.

The pinpoint closed to darkness as he heard Steve's voice. "Ian?! You okay, buddy? Come on. Wake up!"

Ian awoke to the silence of the captain's chambers aboard the Wicked Crow. Three decks below, the hull lurched and groaned against the sea. Above, the crystal chandelier tinkled with each swell. Even without opening his eyes, he remembered the mermaid shapes dangling down into perfect droplets of glass. Between the curls of burnt beeswax and whale oil, the scent of sandalwood lingered.

Penelope.

Or at least this world's version of her.

Rolling over in the large bed, Ian felt the space behind his eye throb like a fistful of nails had been stuffed into it. A wormy twitch shot through his brain and sat him upright. The malig. Ian rubbed his face and pried open the fluttering eye, hoping that he had not lost his sight, or worse yet, the whole thing. He struggled to focus, finally producing fuzzy, dull images of the cabin: the hanging chandelier with nine beeswax candles aglow above the dining table, the ornately carved dragon-head legs, and even the hand-painted map of the world on the wall, complete with sea monster and treasure locations clearly marked. It brought a smile to his face. He had seen it all before in Penelope's paintings and drawings. Even the velvet-cushioned chairs around the chamber Penelope had painstakingly designed herself.

A stern, yet soft voice cut through his stupor. "As happy as I am to see your face, I regret you ever came 'ere."

Ian tracked the origin of the voice. She sat on one of the chairs, submerged in shadow.

"I'm sorry," Ian said. "I thought I was doing the right thing."

She stepped over to the bed and sat down beside him. In the candlelight, her face emerged tan and weathered, brown eyes, parched lips, and a golden nose ring. He wished her skin ran milky and smooth like the suburban version he had loved his entire life, but like everything else here, she too stood off-center to his expectations. Although this Penelope ignited the same fluttering feelings he always experienced around the Penelope he had known, he resisted the urge to lunge at her and kiss her. For all his recent trying of new things, he retreated into his former self, suddenly shy.

"You couldn't have known," she said. "And thank you fer doing it. He used to call me Barracuda for my blade." She laughed under her breath, her eyes glassy. "I spent so much time steeling myself for it, thinking I could cut him down if I 'ad to. If it came to that."

"I'm sorry it did," Ian said. "I just saw you. Saw her in you. And I couldn't hesitate any longer. I'm sorry."

Pirate Penelope wiped a tear from her eye. "'Tis the pact I made. 'Tis the future I rendered."

Ian recalled his dream, or vision. Hallucination likely. His Penelope trading places with this Penelope.

"Pact?" Ian asked. "She asked you to trade places with her, didn't she?"

Pirate Penelope shook her head. "No. She had another with her. She had other designs for me."

Ian grew excited. "So my Penelope. She didn't die. She traveled here. Instructed you to imprison the captain on that island. She knew they were coming for her." He paused to chew a fingernail. "She knew they'd use me to get to her."

Penelope exhaled and nodded. "Where she ventures no one dares go. She showed me things. Wondrous and dreadful places. Where we both shared worlds, lives, minds. How we were both the same. I felt it. Pieces of me were pieces of her. She said she only needed one thing."

"The Ruby Spyglass?" Ian asked. "But for what?"

Penelope shook her head. "I do not know. I was bewitched. We are the same, she and I. Like sisters. How do you say no to your sister?"

"You don't," Ian said. "This is nuts. Back home I wished so hard for it not to be true. That my Penelope didn't die. That it wasn't true. I thought I was going insane."

"Your Penelope convinced me that the imagination is a powerful thing, Ian. The doors it unlocks, the ideas. One glimpse into the imagination changes worlds. At first, I didn't believe her. Even about my captain. He still smelled of rum and leather. Still kissed like a horse thief. Fought like a rabid panther. But his smile was never the same. It was the one flaw in a majestic painting."

"You cut off his hand."

Pirate Penelope nodded. "Aye. I was to kill him, but I couldn't. So I stashed him on Drop-Dead Island."

"And my Penelope coded that bridge," Ian said. "She wanted me to find her."

Pirate Penelope sighed. "I rigged the bridge."

"That doesn't make sense," Ian said. "She wouldn't just leave me behind."

"That was her instruction," Pirate Penelope said. She placed her hand over his. A rough bracelet hung off her wrist and rested against his skin. Baling twine interwoven with small shells. The same symbols from his necklace, from his Penelope's bracelet, had been painted on the shells. "I knew I had to leave my Ian behind. But if your love for her was as great as mine was for him, I couldn't let her leave you behind."

"This doesn't make any sense," Ian said. "I need to know where she is."

Pirate Penelope stood up. "I know not where she went. No amount of wine or talk could pry that from her." She strolled to a lockbox across the room and, using a key hanging on her necklace, unlocked it and removed a small envelope. When she walked back to him, Ian followed her every move, feasting on her as if she were his Penelope. Her right arm had been bandaged. She sat down on the bed and handed him the envelope.

On the front, written in flowery handwriting was Ian's name.

"I managed to pry this from her journal," Pirate Penelope told him. "She may not have wanted you to follow, but she spoke of you often, and with heart. The one thing that did flow as easily as the rum was her sorrow for leaving you behind. Perhaps one of us can salvage love from this maelstrom."

CHAPTER 30

A FESTERING WOUND

"So that was you?" Ian asked, lounging comfortably in the co-pilot seat of the faux Falcon. He picked at the bandage on his forearm and lifted it to see a scrabbling patchwork of terribly executed stitches. "You released that thing?"

Steve sat in the pilot's chair, cuddled into Ian's blue flannel pajamas. "Yes. It's one with the Infiniuum now." He slapped Ian's hand. "And don't pick at those stitches. They took forever. Human bodies, sheesh."

"The entire Infiniuum at your literal fingertips," Ian said, "And you don't know how to do stitches."

"I'll have you know," Steve said, "Despite your pop culture's insistence, the universe is not filled with two-legged flesh tubes. All that aside, I'd probably get that wound looked at. You don't want that to get infected."

"I will," Ian said. "By the way, you looked pretty sharp with that sword."

Steve shrugged his shoulders. "Polymorphism. I'm just gifted that way." Steve gestured to the envelope from Pirate Penelope sitting on the dash. "You gonna read it?"

Ian looked at the envelope. He still couldn't fathom that Penelope hadn't died. The more he thought about it, the worse he felt. She had just left him behind. For something she had to do on her own. Ian didn't know what was worse, losing someone to death or losing them to their own decision. But he felt worse with the truth. Whatever she was doing, she felt the best path forward was without him. Another dark seed fell inside him and buried itself into the soil of his mind. "I don't know. Her death seemed to have less sting. Is that crazy?"

"Not when you put it that way." Steve picked up the envelope and smelled it. "Peaches."

Ian nodded. "Her favorite."

Steve set the envelope down. "You should read it. When you're ready."

"The malig is dead, right? We're all done?" Ian rubbed his eye.

Steve smiled. "Trust me. It wasn't my first time."

"Good," Ian said. He grabbed the envelope and moved to the doors of the starship. He paused at the exit, looking back at Steve. "Will I ever see you again?"

Steve stood. "I have to check on some things, but I think we're done."

Ian thought about his conversation with Pirate Penelope aboard the Wicked Crow. His Penelope's plan. Did Steve know? If he did, it certainly didn't seem to show. Ian debated whether to ask Steve about it.

"What?" Steve asked. "You need a frickin' hug or something? Fine." Steve stood and wrapped his thin arms around Ian and gave him a sturdy hug. When he broke the embrace, Ian said, "Right before Captain Wilder died, he said, 'We are one, we are all,' or something like that. What does that mean?"

Steve sighed. "I don't know. He was probably trying to scare you."

"Really?" Ian asked. "It felt weird. Cold. Like I'd heard it before."

"Like in *The Three Musketeers*," Steve said. "Don't worry about it." Steve patted Ian on the shoulder. "Welcome to having your life back." He sat back down at the control center. "And you're welcome, by the way."

Ian exhaled. "Thanks for the save." Ian stepped out into his bedroom and turned once more to Steve.

"You did well," Steve said. "Be proud of that. Don't overthink it too much, and you'll be happy. Got it?"

Ian nodded.

Steve smiled. "Excellent. Have a great life, pal. It was a pleasure doing business with you. Hasta lasagna."

The doors to Ian's closet closed, and the neon blue line between them faded and returned to blackness. Ian stood there in silence. The paper of the envelope felt smooth in his fingers. After a few moments, he reached out and opened the doors again, thinking Steve would still be there eating Cheez-Its, but only his own clothes hung there.

Tired, Ian fell onto his bed. He put the envelope on his nightstand behind his alarm clock. 2:39 AM. A yawn erupted in his mouth. He reached over to his pillow and opened his journal. Flipping through it, he found a sketch Penelope had drawn of the two of them dressed in their pirate clothes, fighting off pirate scallywags back-to-back. With his imagination, he filled in her colors: burgundy for the long coat, cream on her linen shirt, and a large, wine-colored plume extending from her cavalier hat. For him, he filled the shark teeth along his cap with grey and the engraved vines on the Neverblade in bold green. Finished, he lashed the journal closed and rolled over to sleep.

In the morning, he woke for school, brushed his teeth, and showered. He washed the tender wound on his forearm and rebandaged it before dressing in a long sleeve t-shirt and jeans. Downstairs, he assembled his usual bowl of three cereals and sat down between his parents.

His dad hid behind the morning paper, and his mother sat quietly with her thoughts. Ian crunched his cereal. "I'm glad everything turned out alright with Heidi," Harold said from behind the paper.

"Yeah," Ian said between bites. "Me too."

His mom sighed. "Such a sweet girl." She sipped her coffee. "I thought the worst when she ran out of here like that."

"Flugalmann?" his dad asked, folding the paper into a neat rectangle. "Her dad's the pharmacist, right?"

Ian nodded.

"Do you know what their life insurance situation is?"

Ian rolled his eyes. "It never came up, Dad."

"Right." His father nodded. "If you think about it, ask some time, would you?"

"Really? After all this, you want to hit them up for life insurance?"

"You're right, Ian," his father said. "We should have them over for dinner first."

After breakfast, Ian grabbed his backpack and ran out to catch the bus. Finding a seat near the front, Ian eyed Pete and, instead of receiving a taunt, Pete nodded and looked away. Relieved, Ian slouched into his seat. The morning definitely demanded tunes. *The Good, the Bad and the Ugly*, maybe.

In a soundtrack coma, he smiled with the music. When Heidi got on, he scooted over to make room for her and popped his ear buds out. She saw the vacancy and sat down. Ian couldn't be sure, but he thought she was wearing a bit of makeup. Her eyelashes were darker, and her lips were shiny. Another remarkable thing made him take notice.

Peaches.

She smelled of ripe peaches with just a hint of cream. "I like your perfume," he said.

"It's hand cream, actually," she corrected him. "My mother says it's got a ton of Vitamin E and it's good for the skin. We Flugalmanns have really fair skin, so we have to protect it all the time."

Ian smiled, and Heidi caught it.

"What?" she asked.

"You," he said. "We've gone to school together since kindergarten, and I think I've heard you talk more in the last two days than you have in the last nine years."

"Maybe you just haven't been listening, Ian," Heidi teased.

Ian laughed. "That's very possible," he said. "But I am now." Heidi blushed.

"What are you listening to?" She asked. Ian showed his phone screen. "Ooh, Clint Eastwood. That's neat. You know, many of his Westerns were based off early Japanese samurai films?"

"You don't think listening to movie soundtracks is weird?" Ian asked. "I always thought other people would think it's lame."

"Our weirdness defines us."

For the bus ride into school, they shared ear buds and listened to the lonesome, brooding score. All through school, Ian's arm itched. In biology, he stuck his pencil up his shirt and itched around the bandage. In art, he kept rubbing his sleeve to satisfy the itches. By the afternoon, the itching was incessant, but he made sure to scratch around the wound since it had grown painful to the touch.

When he got home, he locked himself in the bathroom and took off the bandage. The wound had grown swollen and red, and there were tiny red dots around it. A bit of pus leaked from the jagged stitches. He washed the wound with hot water, squeezed almost a whole tube of Neosporin on it, and redressed it. After a while it felt better.

After dinner, he texted Heidi and she came over. They spent the waning hours of the night in the backyard. First, they swung on his old childhood swing-set, which they were far too big for. They tried the hammock but kept falling out. Then, Heidi asked if they could go up in the treehouse. "Sure," Ian said, hesitating a moment. He hadn't been in the treehouse since his last time with Penelope. When they had sex, and then later, when she struggled with the Smudge World. Perhaps going up there would help him with closure.

He let Heidi climb the ladder first, then he followed. She sat down in one corner and he the other. "Cramped," she said.

Ian hadn't realized how much he had outgrown the place. "Yeah, I suppose."

"Now what?" Heidi asked expectantly.

Confusion settled over Ian. Why had they come up here? His forearm grew hot and painful again. "It's kind of dorky, but Penelope and I would spend hours up here, caught up in our own little worlds."

"That's not dorky," she said. "You two were creative and fun."

Ian pulled a board down from the ceiling and pulled out an old school pencil box and opened it. Inside were a variety of playing-card-sized cuts of tag board. On the front of each piece an elaborate portrait of a character was drawn in bright colored pencil and on the back was a written character profile. Heidi dug in and rifled through them. "You made these?"

"No," he said. "I mean, kinda."

"Did you draw these pictures?"

"No," Ian said. "I did the backs. Penelope did the drawing. I usually did the writing. Well, not good writing. Backstories, mainly."

Heidi stopped on one. "Redcrowne," she said. The portrait showed a well-muscled man wearing a tight white jumpsuit, a white cape, and a red hood over his entire head. Under the hood, several protrusions poked upwards at odd angles. "What's under the red hood?"

Ian smiled. "Redcrowne was experimenting with the ability to read minds. He fabricated a band that he could wear around his forehead that used psionic technology to read people's thoughts. The experiment failed horribly, though, searing the flesh off his head and permanently fusing the technology to his skull."

Heidi looked up and made a yuck face. "Ewww. That explains why he wears the hood."

"Exactly."

She shuffled through the others. She stopped on one of Penelope dressed head-to-toe in a fairy maiden's dress with an intricate leaf pattern design. "Princess Terralina. Wow. That dress is gorgeous. Penelope could have been a fashion designer."

Could have been. He was home, where everyone here knew her to be dead and not gallivanting across the Infiniuum on some mission. Nor would they ever believe the truth if he tried telling them. Penelope had left him here alone. But it was more than that. Now he had to lie for her. That's the legacy she left for him: to be a lonely liar. If it was him, he would have brought her. He wouldn't have left her behind. Together, they could tackle anything. But alone, he didn't know. Before he could stop it, his brow crumpled and his eyes spat out tears. Not bawling or whimpering, but a silent, gaped-mouth cry. He wasn't sad; he was angry.

Heidi's face fell. "I'm so sorry, Ian. I didn't mean to say that. I shouldn't have—"

Ian waved her off and wiped his eyes with his sleeve. "No," he stuttered. "It's fine." But the more he tried to stop it, the more it poured from him. Heidi leaned over and gave him a hug. He put his arms around her and hugged her back. She felt so warm, he hadn't realized how chilled he was.

"I'm sorry she's gone, Ian. She must have been a great friend."

Ian nodded and wiped his face. "Yeah," he said. "I'm sorry about this."

"Don't worry about it. My dad says everyone grieves in their own way."

"My dad says the same thing," Ian said, a small smile on his face.

Heidi patted his thigh. "They're right. This is just how you deal with it."

"By crying like a baby."

Heidi reached over and fixed the front of his disheveled hair. "It can be our little secret, okay?"

Ian liked that. He nodded. He dried his eyes and tried to sniff the snot back into his sinuses.

Heidi gazed out the cutout window as the sun set behind them. "The view definitely makes up for the space issues," she said.

Ian itched his arm and slid next to her to watch. All his life, he had figured he and Penelope would be together until they grew old. He assumed they'd get married, have kids, and retire on a lake or beach somewhere. All his images of the future had her in them. Now they wouldn't. Each imagined future flitted away from his memory like seeds from a dandelion. A whole lifetime of hopes and dreams, just gone. Ian's heartbeat pounded in his temples. He felt like his heart might burst.

When the last sliver of sun slinked under the horizon, Ian felt his insides collapse again, but he muscled through it. His arm ached, and he felt hot and cold at the same time. He was exhausted. "We should probably get going. It's getting late."

Heidi smiled at him. "Sure. Long day, huh?"

"Yeah," Ian said. "I'll climb down first and help you with the last step. It can be tricky.

Ian made it two steps down when the blood poisoning overtook him and he fell from the ladder. He never heard Heidi scream or felt his body hit the ground below. He never saw his parents run out to Heidi's screams and wasn't able to enjoy the adrenaline rush of the high-speed ambulance trip.

CHAPTER 31

Moving On

Rain.

Pitter-patter, pitter-patter.

Ian's ears roared with it. So much rain it drove him mad. He wanted to swear at it, but his eyelids were heavy in sleep. The rain consumed his mind in numbing, continuous sheets.

What happened? He remembered the treehouse and Heidi. He remembered a sunset. No clouds or rain. But now there was rain.

Pitter-patter, pitter-patter.

What the hell? He furiously put all his energy into his eyelids. He had to get them open. Another unconscious grunt.

Only a sliver. He tried again. More this time, but still too heavy. He imagined lifting something so heavy, his muscles came unbound from his bones, leaving him in a floppy mess. He remembered lifting a bag of water softener salt and farting suddenly under the exertion.

Pitter-patter, pitter-patter.

He heard voices.

His eyes rolled forward, and blurs moved before him. A blink. So heavy. He could feel his body again, but it felt buried, like being under those heavy x-ray blankets. Blink. One of the voices was female. Penelope? Mom? Heidi? The other was a man. Dad? Please be dad.

Pitter-patter, pitter-patter.

"We should get the doctor," his mom said.

"I'll be right back," the male voice said. It was definitely his dad. Somewhere in his brain, he felt a slight pop, like a bubble bursting, and everything around him gargled fresh, clear, and loud.

"He's awake!" his mother cried. On the other side of the hospital room, his dad and the nurse ran in.

"Excellent," the nurse said, shining a light into Ian's eyes. "You gave us quite a scare, Ian."

After checking Ian's eyes, the nurse gently took his right arm, where a new white bandage had been wrapped around his wound. Ian tried pulling his arm away but couldn't. "No," he said, only managing a whisper. His parents couldn't see the wound.

"I'll be gentle, Ian," the nurse said, mistaking his concern.

"No!" Ian yelled.

The nurse held down his arm, to check the dressing. Gone were the haphazard, puckered trails of stitches and swollen flesh, replaced by precise, professional ones. A spider web of red lines broke out from the wound.

She turned to Ian's parents. "His fever is breaking. The antibiotics are working. He just needs rest. A lot of rest." His mother gasped in relief, and his father's shoulders relaxed like he'd shed a cruise-liner's anchor. "But," the nurse said, moving them away from Ian, "his reaction to me checking the wound." She paused. "It's troubling. I know you said he just experienced a trauma, but I have to ask, is there any way he might have cut himself? On purpose?"

Maggie Wilder shook her head, tears running down her face. "No. No. He'd never do that."

Concern awash over her face, the nurse reassured them. "If he is cutting himself," she said, "he's going to need more than antibiotics."

Harold breathed deeply and said, "I understand. We've been working with Dr. Caulderon."

The nurse perked up. "Oh, he runs Oakhaven. The adolescent treatment residence just out of town. That's a great place."

Ian woke to Dr. Caulderon speaking to his parents in hushed tones. Ian closed his eyes again and pretended to sleep. The doctor approached the bed and patted Ian's hand.

Ian watched through slit eyes as Caulderon pulled a chair to the corner of the room and gestured for Ian's parents to join him. Sitting down, he said, "I'm happy to hear that Ian will be okay and his wound is healing. However, cutting is a very serious condition. It's self-mutilation and, as you can see, it can lead to serious medical issues. I understand you never found the instrument used for the original wound, but your sewing kit was disturbed, Mrs. Wilder?"

Wait, Ian thought. Cutting? What the hell was going on? He couldn't have done this to himself!

"The thread he used was the same as the thread from my needlepoint," Maggie confirmed. "A needle was missing, too," she said. His mom broke down and started to cry.

What?! Ian thought hard. He didn't think his mom sewed. Or did she? She didn't even have a sewing kit that he knew of. He wanted to speak up, to defend himself, but he also needed to know what they knew. What they thought was going on.

"Your family has had a lot to deal with in the last month." Dr. Caulderon paused to let Ian's mother collect herself. "I talked to the girl yesterday."

"Heidi Flugalmann," his father said. "They were new friends. We thought it was a good sign that he was interacting with other kids. Making new friends."

"Yes, it is a good step. When I talked with her, she told me that Ian broke down in the treehouse. Over the loss of Penny." He paused and said, "I think that's another good thing. He seems to be getting some closure on that front. But he may feel he's responsible for her death and is punishing himself for it. Or perhaps he's feeling so much internal pain, the physical pain from harming himself comes as a relief. A distraction, if you will."

Ian wanted to yell at the top of his lungs, scream at them about the truth: the Infiniuum, Steve, the malig, the complex multi-dimensionality of it all. He saved Penelope. Or at least one of the Penelopes across the Infiniuum. He had learned to use a cutlass, a musket, and a cannon. He fought pirates. He had killed himself to save her. At least an alternate version of himself.

This was the real story, not whatever Caulderon was spewing. But he couldn't very well say that, could he? It would sound crazy. Crazier than him cutting himself. His body tensed in frustration, and he clenched his fists at his sides. He couldn't win. If he could tell his side of the story without their unopened minds judging him, then they'd see. They'd see that there was nothing bad going on. It was all good and honorable. Right?

The room in his mind had emptied. He heard his own thoughts echo to a nonexistent audience. It did sound crazy, he admitted. But that didn't mean it wasn't real, right? Steve's words back on the Islas Encantadas slipped into his mind: is it real, or do you want it so badly that you believe it's real?

Could he have made it all up? Possibly, but had he? The existence of multiple and infinite dimensions and continuums? Was this something his imagination had concocted to take his mind off Penelope's death? To avoid dealing with it, processing it? It certainly seemed convenient. But it couldn't be just convenience. He and Penelope had wild, crazy imaginations. Together, they could access millions of worlds, billions of planets with colorful characters and stories. But he tried to see the situation from Dr. Caulderon's perspective, what he would say, and how he would prove Ian wrong:

Ian: Existence of multiple, connecting dimensions?

Dr. Caulderon: Wrong. Coping mechanism.

Ian: Interdimensional feron guide?

Dr. Caulderon: Nope. Your id.

Ian: Dueling pirates to save alternate Penelopes?

Dr. Caulderon: Afraid not. Your lack of acceptance of Penelope's death.

Ian: An alternate Penelope in her casket.

Dr. Caulderon: Really? Her parents confirmed the body.

Ian: The dueling wound in the forearm.

Dr. Caulderon: Wrong again. Cutting.

Ian: But Steve stitched me up.

Dr. Caulderon: Mom's sewing kit. Plus, look above. Steve is your id, which can't physically stitch you up. You had to have done it yourself.

Ian: I couldn't just make all of this up.

Dr. Caulderon: The mind is a tremendous thing. Capable of imaginative things.

The exercise exhausted him. For every point of proof he threw up, Caulderon would have an answer for it. Perhaps, he was even right.

Caulderon told the Wilders what he thought was best for Ian—a residence program for troubled teens at Oakhaven. He had the best staff, and his award-winning program was covered under their medical insurance. Ian watched through one eye as Caulderon pulled a professionally designed brochure out of his coat pocket and handed it to Ian's mother. She dried her eyes and opened it. His parents nodded and shook hands with the doctor. He affirmed their decision by telling them it was best for Ian.

Lying there, feeling numb, Ian accepted it. All of it. He had grown too tired of fighting it. Believing it. He really just wanted to rest. His eyelids were so heavy. Caulderon shook hands with his parents, then left. His parents came to his bedside. His mom ran her fingers through his hair, and his dad patted his shoulder. Ian wanted to say he was sorry, but his lips wouldn't move. He was too tired to speak or stay awake. The rain outside was overwhelming. As his eyes closed, he took a mental portrait of his parents' faces before lolling off into sleep again.

"Dr. Caulderon says you haven't spoken in two weeks," Heidi said. They sat on a plush sofa in Ian's residence hall at Oakhaven. The furniture in the communal living room had been cobbled together. Different styles. Different patterns. Different smells.

Heidi was right. He hadn't spoken since he got there. He felt betrayed. His parents. Caulderon. Penelope. No one understood him. No one knew the truth. And he couldn't simply tell the truth, because he himself was losing his grip on that. The entire thing was a cluster. No matter what he said, he couldn't win. So he just stopped talking. He also hated that his mom had found his journal and posted a dozen or so of Penelope's sketches and paintings on the walls for him to look at.

Ian felt cursed in a way. Not only was it hard enough to come to terms with him being completely delusional, but now he had a daily reminder. His mom had even found the envelope Penelope had left him and propped it up at his window, when he moved in here. That had been the last piece to rectify in his mind. He still vividly saw Pirate Penelope unlock it from her keepsake box and hand it to him. But for all he knew, he had made that up too. Maybe his Penelope's mom had dropped it off after the funeral. At first it had smelled like peaches, but had since faded. No one had opened the note, not daring to violate the privacy between Ian and Penelope.

"I saw your parents talking to the Archers the other day," Heidi said. She looked down at his right forearm, where the jagged scar of his 'cutting' was healing into a whorled line of scar tissue. "Don't tell them, but I snuck into your treehouse one day after school. It has such a good view." She paused, and he knew she was remembering the sunset the night he fell.

"Pete Stamdahl has become a model citizen now," she added. "He's actually kind of my enforcer. When others make fun of me for liking you, he stands up for me. He even punched one of his own toadies for lipping off without his permission. I don't know what it is between you two, but he always seems to like the girls you like. Weird. I think he wants me to ask him to the Sadie Hawkins dance, but I'm not going to. I'm asking you, even though you can't go. There's no one else I'd want to go with anyway."

She saw the unopened envelope from Pirate Penelope peeking out from his closed hand. It had become battered over the weeks from Ian holding it constantly. His name on the front had been smudged, from his fretting thumbs rubbing against the paper. "You still haven't read it, huh?"

Ian didn't respond.

Heidi reached across him and grabbed it. "Maybe we should just pull off this bandage."

"No," Ian said and swiped it back.

Heidi smiled. "Made you talk."

Ian shook his head. For weeks he went back and forth. What version was the truth? He knew, of course. But here in this world, he was locked into a falsehood, a fiction he didn't intend to write. Did he want to know what Penelope had to say before she left him behind? Yes, of course. But what would it change? She'd still left him. Made the conscious decision to leave him behind. He did not want to be held hostage by her words. If he had any hope of salvaging his life, he'd have to move on. But he also missed her. Terribly. And he felt he would never be able to scour that feeling from his mind and his memories.

"You know what," Ian said. "I am ready." He held up the envelope to show Heidi, but instead of opening it, he ripped it to pieces. The pieces fluttered to the floor like the oak leaves outside. "She's gone. I have to accept that."

"Why did you do that?" Heidi said. "You loved her!"

"I did," Ian said. "And she loved me. Past tense. Words won't change that."

Heidi stared out the bay window. Oakhaven had four large houses modified with eight small bedrooms and a common living room for therapy sessions in each. The building at the center of the compound was the community building with offices, a cafeteria, and a community room with televisions, arts and crafts, and games. They even had two community gardens, if the residents wanted to exercise their green thumbs. Sidewalks wove throughout the compound and between the treatment homes and the community facility. A late October breeze rustled in, and a shower of red, gold, and brown leaves fell from the oak trees planted along the path. "You got another great view here, Ian," she said. She took out her cellphone and checked the time. "I gotta go," she told him, leaning over and kissing his cheek. Ian felt a flash of her metal braces and tried a smile. "I'll see you next week," she said and left the residence home.

Ian stood there in the common room, watching Heidi walk to the parking lot in front of the community building between the residence halls. Then he looked at the pieces of paper on the floor. Without thinking about it, he squatted down and picked up the pieces. Carefully, he cradled them in his hands and made his way up to his room on the second floor.

Once in his room, he sat at his desk and stuffed the pieces into his old journal and bound it up with the rubber bands. Finished, he lay on his bed and looked out his only window. Outside, the setting sun crushed the sky to crimson and pink. To the right of his bed, his mother had arranged a variety of Penelope's artwork from his room back home: both sparring atop Hagshead Peak in the Islas Encantadas, creeping around the abandoned space station in the Taluride cluster, fighting alongside the wood elves of Fharendale, hunting vampires in eerie forests of the Schwarzwald, riding down the Blackhats in Cactusback Flats, and fighting back-to-back as the masked wonders Shadowstrike and Deathpriest in Atlantis City.

All the worlds they created in their heads. The adventures they had. The stories they crafted together. Ian wondered how things would have turned out if they had kept their minds grounded in this reality and focused on each other. Somewhere, in another far-off reality, it was happening. Penelope and Ian together forever. He tried to focus on their happiness, glad that at least someone was getting what they wanted.

Ian turned his head and stared out to the stars emerging from the indigo night outside his widow. Instinctively, his mind connected the constellations—their paths arching together like a blue bolt of cosmic lightning, stretching out to infinity. His mind finally drowsy and his eyelids heavy, he drifted off to sleep. Only, before his mind shut down, he felt a familiar, whiny whisper in his ear, brief and warm with breath.

Inhaling deeply, Ian rolled over and ignored it.

IAN WILDER'S ADVENTURE CONTINUES IN . . .

ESCAPE
- FROM -
ATLANTIS CITY

SCOTT R. WELVAERT

After the pirates on Islas Encantadas, Ian Wilder whiles away his days in Oakhaven Treatment Residence, trying to forget that Penelope left him behind for the Infiniuum. Luckily his therapy is working. Ian is happy to move on and get back home in a week.

But that's just it, the Infiniuum won't let him. Days before his release, Ian mysteriously wakes in Atlantis City in a far-off reality. Worse, he's accidentally brought two residents with him, and they've been kidnapped by a freakish ring of meta-human criminals. When he finds his way back to Oakhaven and Steve, Ian learns he too has become a traveler of infinite realities.

But Ian can't leave his friends behind in the Infiniuum. That's what Penelope did to him. Can he take what he learned on the high seas and help his friends escape from Atlantis City? Or will he fail and end up in Oakhaven, spending the rest of his life in therapy?

About Scott R. Welvaert

Scott lives in Minnesota with his wife, two daughters and a deaf husky named Rocket. He has authored numerous books, including *The Curse of the Wendigo, The Mosquito King, The Alabaster Ring, Grotesque,* and *The 13th Floor.* An avid outdoorsman and comic book nerd, he enjoys writing stories that bend the fabric of reality and offer something more than this world can conjure.

Acknowledgments

I couldn't have gotten this far without a great many people. So foremost, thanks to my wife and my three kiddos. Would also like to thank the Blue Skunk Society alumni, past and present. Special thanks to James Anderson, Tim Schindler, and Connie Odenthal, who were the test subjects for this book and its sequels. I promise, I'll write something normal when this is done. Deep thanks to Blake Hoena for getting my first fiction publishing gigs and putting up with my less-than-eloquent nature. Also need to thank all the profs back in grad school: Terry Davis, Rick Robbins, Roger Sheffer, Dick Terrill, Cathy Day, and Donna Casella. And special thanks to the readers.

To learn more about
Skywater Publishing Cooperative
and our upcoming releases,
visit us at *skywaterpub.com*
or scan the QR code below.

Milton Keynes UK
Ingram Content Group UK Ltd.
UKHW031042120324
439302UK00001B/63